HOLLY FOX lives in Dorset with her daughter. She is the author of *This Way Up*.

UP AND RUNNING

RUNNING

HOLLY FOX

POCKET
BOOKS

LONDON • SYDNEY • NEW YORK • TOKYO • SINGAPORE • TORONTO

First published in Great Britain by Pocket Books, 2002
An imprint of Simon & Schuster UK Ltd
A Viacom Company

Copyright © Holly Fox, 2002

1 3 5 7 9 10 8 6 4 2

Simon & Schuster UK Ltd
Africa House
64-78 Kingsway
London WC2B 6AH

www.simonsays.co.uk

Simon & Schuster Australia
Sydney

A CIP catalogue record for this book is available from
the British Library

ISBN 0-671-77387-9

Typeset by SX Composing DTP, Rayleigh, Essex
Printed and bound in Great Britain by Bookmarque Ltd, Croydon, Surrey

For every Adele who knows a Jack.

UP AND RUNNING

1

Meg lay on the floor of the flat, naked, waiting for the man with the ladder.

She even had time to consider what fun it would be.

What headlines.

Just too bloody marvellous.

Churchill-Twines partner DEAD! the tabloids would say. But ten to one, they wouldn't even know her name. *His* name, oh yes. National hero and all that. They'd get *him* right. But not her. She could almost see the opening paragraphs now.

Churchill-Twines woman, Moggy Somebody, not nice body apparently, surprising really, definite PAUNCH, slain by central heating, SLUMPED on low-cost Berber twist.

And what would Will say, when they finally located him?

Churchill-Twines bereft on Arctic ice floe.

Brave patriot weeps on windswept tundra.

Tears freeze solid on beard.

Meg sighed deeply.

Well, sooner or later she would have to move. She could hear the media pack mumbling below the window. They were no doubt plotting their full-frontal assault on her privacy.

All she had done was come out of the shower five minutes before. Deeply preoccupied with Will's disappearance, she'd neglected to wrap a towel around her. That, combined with the open bedroom curtains, had been all that the press pack needed. Such carelessness was stupid, of course – she might have known that they would be circulating by now, like a pack of overweight grizzlies sniffing around dustbins. Yet she hadn't even realised that they had been there until lights started flashing in the street below, and curses filled the quiet road as photographers fell over each other to gain purchase on the garden wall.

She had dropped to the carpet, heart pounding.

She had glanced at the bedside clock.

Six thirty. Six thirty in the morning, just four hours since Michael – Will's agent and manager – had phoned her to say that Will was missing on his solo trek to the North Pole. Meg had had four short hours of broken sleep and then had lain staring at the ceiling, she had finally got up and gone for a shower. Five blissful minutes standing under hot water, mind blank, before she'd finally drifted out into the bedroom.

To the flash of a dozen cameras.

'Oh no,' she'd groaned, realising her mistake at once. One whiff of tragedy, and she might have expected the press to be at her door. She would have kicked herself had it been anatomically possible on all fours.

It had been vital to get across the room to draw the curtains, so she had crawled on her hands and knees to the window. But, just as she reached up, she had seen one resourceful sod climbing a tree in the garden of the house directly opposite. She had ducked back down, and, in doing so, caught her chin hard on the top of the radiator under the window.

Now, she lay on her back, stunned for a while. The man with the ladder was surely only seconds away.

Seconds would be all it would take for one of the obese grizzlies to climb up and take Shock Candid Pics of Ice Man's Bird.

She propped herself up on one elbow, her jaw throbbing. Her mouth was bleeding. She had bitten her tongue.

Then, she heard a sudden slamming of car doors outside, and a flurry of voices.

'Any news, mate?'

'What's he done, fallen down a crack?'

'Now, really, lads . . .' Michael's apologetic tone.

'Disappeared up a crevice?'

She heard the garden gate squeak as Michael pushed through it, and his footsteps on the path. 'Now, now . . . come on, lads.'

'Give us a grieving photo, Mike.'

'No need for grief.'

'You heard from him?'

'We will.'

The doorbell rang.

Meg crouched on the carpet.

Then the phone rang.

She lifted it to her ear suspiciously, and heard Michael's voice.

'Meg? Open the door,' he said. 'It's me. I'm downstairs. For Chrissakes open up.'

She scrabbled back from the window, into the bathroom, where she grabbed the dressing gown that she should have been wearing all along. She ran down the stairs. Taking a deep breath, she slipped the latch of the door and then scuttled back into the kitchen. The door slammed back on its hinges. There were one or two thumping noises, an *ooooff* as if someone had been elbowed, and the door slammed again.

'Bloody press,' Michael muttered.

He walked after Meg into the kitchen. She was opening the fridge, and retrieving ice cubes from the freezer compartment.

'What's up?' he said.

'Don't ask,' she muttered, pressing an ice cube to her lip.

Obligingly, Michael busied himself putting the kettle on, whipping bread from the bin and stacking it in the toaster. He glanced around himself at the mess in the kitchen – he was well used to Meg's appalling untidiness – and, without a word, rescued two plates and mugs from the sink, and washed them. By the time that tea was in mugs and the toast on plates, they had settled down opposite each other at the kitchen table.

Michael smiled grimly. 'Meg, I'm sorry about all this.'

She shook her head wearily.

'It's only twenty-four hours,' he said. 'Radio's down. Bloody terrible white-out.'

'He's been missing for longer before,' Meg murmured. 'Why is there all this fuss now?'

'Up-Line Cable are going berserk,' Michael said.

They gazed at each other wordlessly.

Will's assault on the North Pole was being covered by a cable TV company, Up-Line. It was the first time that they had landed such a contract and both Meg and Michael were convinced, by now, that no-one in the station was cut out for the job, to judge by the constant gibbering and twittering from them. In two days, they were due to fly out to film Will at his last equipment drop, on the roof of the world. Will was only six days away from the Pole, at his current rate. And the Up-Line producer was hysterical that after all their investment, they would miss out. They had been that way since day one, constantly ringing up to make sure that Will was not dead, and their money was not about to be flushed down the drain.

Once Will had actually started on his trek six weeks ago, the Head of Adventure Broadcasting had been convinced that their investment would be drowned, frozen, or eaten. If Will so much as sneezed on the radio transmissions, a squawking went round Up-Line like a farmyard at Christmas-time.

Michael stared morosely at his mug of tea. 'They're manic,' he said, resignedly. 'Somebody rang me at four thirty, weeping.'

Both of them looked up at the huge wall map pinned up in Meg's kitchen. Red flags marked Will's daily progress. Here, in her leafy London suburb, Meg could look out – when she was *able* to look out, like a normal person – on a street where the cherry blossom was just showing pink. The sky lightened at seven. The worst weather was rain. The days were becoming balmy. But Will was experiencing a slightly different spring.

Where Will was, the temperature was about minus thirty. Celsius. Give or take twenty degrees. Where Will was, the sun was shining for twenty-four hours a day. The day before yesterday, Meg had spent an hour in the garden, wandering about weeding. Will, on the other hand, had walked twelve nautical miles over rubble ice, dragging a sledge, while the wind howled at him and the cold tried to remove his face from the front of his head.

Probably, of the two of them, Will had enjoyed his day more.

But then, William Churchill-Twines was no ordinary man.

Meg had met him eighteen months ago, at a party.

He was easy to spot. For a start, Will was six foot five. And the first thing you noticed about him – apart from the expression on his face, which was of a man condemned to hell, because he was in a situation where he was being forced to talk to people and try to smile at them – was the colour of his hair. And beard.

Will had sandy hair with a lot of grey in it, so that it seemed he had had a very expensive root highlight job to make himself look like Richard Branson. The white streaks were so startling that you were sure they had to be fake. There was one particular one, right at the front, that ran from his parting across the top of his wiry-fleece head. He was a walking male version of Cruella DeVille.

Then, of course, there was the beard.

Will had a beard as a kind of badge. For Polar explorers, they were mandatory equipment; there was no option. It was part of the job. You couldn't go hiking across a thousand miles of ice with a shaved head or face. Hair was insulation. Hair was protection. But, more than that – oh, so much more important – it was a *man* thing. Square-jawed heroes wore Beards. Apparently. Naval officers wore beards. Climbers of Everest wore beards. And a man like William Churchill-Twines could not, would not ever, be shorn of his face hair, even if it did make him look like he was hiding behind a hedge of Shredded Wheat.

The beard wasn't too long on the night that Meg first saw him, hovering as it did about collar length. William Churchill-Twines was a bloody arresting sight, like Santa Claus dropped in the middle of NW4. Six foot five, seventeen stone, broad of shoulder, narrow of hip, Branson hair plus some, and gripping his glass like an electric shock had just passed through him.

Meg – bless her – had thought that the sight of her had sent tremors up the man's spine. She had given a little flirtatious smirk, put her head on one side, and looked at him from under her lashes in a way that, at twelve, she had copied from *The Lady and the Tramp*. Not that Meg flirted often. If ever, in fact. But the vision of Will staring down at her as though he had been struck by lightning exerted a temporary insanity. She went all coy. Afterwards, of course, she learned that the look on his face had nothing to do with the sight of her. He had not been struck dumb with desire. It was just that he loathed parties, and was desperate to leave.

He had put down his glass on the table next to him, and made for the door, swatting guests aside. Meg had seen him, apparently making a beeline for her, and she had smiled broadly. As he got closer to her, she had held out her hand.

'Meg Randall.'

He had stared at the hand, then, tentatively, held out his. He had a grip like a heavyweight boxer. 'Churchill-Twines,' he said.

'That rings a bell,' she said. 'Why would it ring a bell?'

He had blushed. Interesting sight. Red face, white hair.

'Pole,' he had muttered.

'A Pole?' she said. 'You're Polish?'

Redder still. 'No . . . Poles. North. South.'

She had frowned. 'The South Pole?'

'Last year.'

Light had dawned. 'Oh,' she said. 'You're that ice bloke.'

And so began a relationship that was rather more off than on.

That same year, the year that Will had ended up in her bed, she hadn't seen a great deal of him. In the spring, he had gone to the Himalayas for fourteen weeks. And in the next autumn he had gone to Nepal, and, in December, he had trekked up and down the Scottish peaks dragging a sledge, to ready himself for the assault on the Pole this spring.

In short, ever since Meg had met Will he had been either preparing to go somewhere, been somewhere, was coming back from somewhere, or recovering from going somewhere. And the time had passed like that – itching to go, gone, returning knackered, and itching to go again.

Will had wanderlust. In fact, he had wandercraving, wanderyearning, and wanderwantonness. Everything he did in life was about moving. Every damned thing was a challenge. It was really beginning to get on her nerves.

When he was home, Will couldn't just go to the shops and get a pint of milk. Not him. He had to run to the shops the long way round, with an eighty-pound pack on his back. William Churchill-Twines couldn't just amble round the park on his way to a pizza. He had to powerwalk there with weighted boots.

Will was incapable of meandering, loafing or idling. The idea of lying in the sun, for instance – a dream of Meg's for the last year – was, to Will, the equivalent of sticking his head in a mincing machine. A swimming pool meant nothing to him unless he could churn a hundred lengths through it in record time. A sun lounger was like living death. A beach was purposeless unless you had several large cliffs to climb arranged alongside it. A palm tree would be just a thing to clamber up carrying a two-man tent. Seas, rocks, hills and even the gentle slope up to Sainsbury's were forces of nature to be beaten, bashed into submission.

Will had moved in with her a month after they met.

All right, it was stupid. It was asking for trouble. You don't let a man move into the flat that you have agonised to buy and keep, your little pristine patch of private heaven, your place where you have placed a white sofa – fool that she was – unless you can manage to get a written agreement out of him not to cause any kind of stain that can't be wiped up. You do not, more to the point in Meg's case, let a Polar explorer into your kitchen or bathroom. Because before long your kitchen will have bits of primus stove scattered about it, and your loo will be knee-deep in sealskin socks. And, all the time, the phone will be ringing, because the man was A National Treasure, and constantly in demand.

'Can Mr Twine do GMTV with Lorraine?' a stranger's voice would ask.

'No,' she would learn to say, almost parrot-fashion. 'He's in training. And it's Churchill-Twines.'

'Lorraine's doing thermal vests. Could he model one?'

'No, I doubt it,' she was ordered to reply. 'Not unless you made a donation to the Pole trek.'

'Oh . . .' the answer would be. A long pause. 'We could put his picture on the weather map?'

'And sponsor him?'

Silence.

'With money?'

'We'll plug his book.'

'Thanks. He hasn't written one.'

Another ring. Another week.

'Would Mr Churchound suck our lozenges?'

'Churchill-Twines. No. He's up Kinder Scout.'

'Not even suck. Just put it in his mouth on camera.'

'No, I . . .'

'He could spit it out again right after.'

'And money?'

'If he put our logo on his head.'

'Sorry,' Meg would say. 'His whole head's spoken for. You could have his right knee.'

A tut-tutting on the other end of the line would follow. 'You see, your tongue's in your head, isn't it? Your sucking bits are all in the head. Your throat's attached to your mouth, you see. Mouth, nose, throat for lozenges. We couldn't have his neck?'

'I'm sorry. Bulldog Sausages have got his neck.'

Another ring. Another month.

'Would Willie take Vaseloo with him?'

'What the hell is Vaseloo?' Meg had demanded, astounded.

'It stops anal frostbite.'

She wished she hadn't asked.

In fact, Meg's life since William Churchill-Twines came into it, was one long phone call, radio transmission, or Internet picture.

Even when he was actually with her, he wasn't. He was always, mentally, up a Pole.

Meg dragged herself back to the present. Michael was frowning at her across the table.

'I think it's serious, Meg,' he said.

She looked at him over the rim of her cup. 'On a scale of one to ten?'

Michael paused before answering. 'Eight,' he said.

'Eight,' she repeated.

There was a short silence.
'Has it ever been eight before?' Meg asked.
'No,' Michael replied quietly. 'No, Meg, it hasn't.'

2

It was eight thirty in the morning, and a deathly hush had fallen upon the offices of Up-Line Cable.

Because Eric Cramm had decreed it.

The Managing Director of the UK's most ambitious cable network stood now on the eighteenth floor, at the floor-length window of his office that overlooked the River Thames. He was staring hard at St Paul's Cathedral, wearing a very pained expression, and curling his silk tie round his index finger.

He wasn't actually, actively, thinking of much. Not even of Adventure Broadcasting and the disappearance of William Churchill-Twines. He was Alpha Wave instead. He was Creating.

If you asked any of his staff, ten to one they would tell you that it was impossible to know what was going on in Eric Cramm's mind. He had a face like a wet weekend, and his expression never altered. If Eric Cramm was annoyed, his face looked grim. If Eric Cramm was thoughtful, his face looked grim. If Eric Cramm was deliriously happy, in the throes of ecstatic joy, his face looked . . . uh-huh, grim.

And so, if any one of those hallowed number of employees – and they were easy to spot, they all ground their teeth at night and had nervous rashes – had been put in front of Eric now, not a single one of them would have been able to guess that a vision of unearthly genius was unfolding in his head.

And, when Eric was deep in creative mode, as now, he began to fixate. He couldn't help it. It was simply the way he was. Sometimes it was a fixation on paper-weights, sometimes cricket umpires, or flowerpots, or Rawlplugs, or the FT Index. It could be anything. There was nothing personal in it: Eric could fixate for England, and become obsessive in seconds.

Today, it just happened to be St Paul's Cathedral.

It was a bloody nuisance, that cathedral, he was thinking, as he stared unblinkingly across the Thames. The building looked all wrong. For a start, it was a funny dome shape. Cramm frowned deeply, winding the end of his tie into a spiral. What business had it having a dome? He asked himself. Domes were so *last year*. You'd think the Church of England could get a grasp on this public relations thing. How long had they been at it? Two thousand years. Two thousand years, and they still didn't have the first idea about marketing, he thought.

The phone beside him rang.

Cramm nearly jumped out of his skin. He snatched the receiver up, furious. 'What?!'

'Mr Cramm, it's Giles Penriddock on line one . . .'

'Bloody hell!' Cramm yelled. 'Bloody bloody hell, woman! Don't you know what time it is? Look at your watch, you cretin! It's Silent Quarter!'

There was a sharp intake of breath from his new secretary. 'Oh. Mr Cramm, I forgot. I'm sorry . . .'

He slammed the phone back into its cradle. *Christ!* he thought savagely. *That's another one I'll have to fire.*

It made six that year.

Feeling the sudden pressure of the knotted tie on his

neck, Eric forced his fists to unclench, and smoothed the material against his linen shirt. Now, where was he? He considered. Ah . . . churches. They had always tried his patience to the limit, he told himself. For a start, churches and cathedrals took up so much space. All that prime freehold. Why did they need all that valuable land, right in the middle of London? To *sing* in? Pah! It was ludicrous! If he had his way he'd knock them all down and build some nice tower blocks, on half the land. You could fit fifty apartments into the space where one church had been, and all the bloody tenants could sing all day long if they wanted.

God! His head ached.

Eric put one fingertip against one temple, and pressed.

He glanced in the large mirror next to his desk, and admired, for a moment, his own square jaw, pointed nose and craggy forehead.

Lines . . . he thought admiringly. That's what his face had. Angles. No smooth-as-a-baby skin for him, no rounded cheeks, no snub nose, no full lips, no accommodating manner. No . . . look. *There* was a man, he decided, smirking at his own reflection. His image was chock-full of penetrating, uncomfortable protrusions. It had true character. It was full of challenge. It was an armed uprising of a face, a baton charge, a clash of forces. There was nothing cuddly in it – it wasn't a face you could lie down in with a cup of tea and a chocolate Hobnob. Ah, no, by George. *His* was a man's face. It was about as comfortable and approachable as a sharpened spike. Geniuses had these sorts of faces, he concluded. It was a birthright.

Still, Eric thought, tearing his gaze away from the mirror. He had to stop thinking about St Paul's and the way it irritated him every morning. He wondered if Einstein or Fleming or Marie Curie had ever become annoyed by a shape. Perhaps they had. Perhaps all creative people with An Idea were that way.

He picked a tiny piece of fluff from his collar. Fixation was obviously the price one paid for being a mastermind. Michelangelo probably had to look the other way when he came into work, he considered. Michelangelo had probably been forced, on a daily basis, to ignore the jobbing painters reading the fifteenth-century equivalent of the *Star*. The great maestro probably had to try not to see that the yellow ochre had gone all lumpy again. Or tear his attention away from a splinter in the scaffolding. Cramm flexed his fingers, and inspected his expensive manicure. After all, what was it that Oscar Wilde said when the poor benighted sod was dying? 'Either that wallpaper goes, or I do.' Something like that.

Cramm knew *exactly* how he felt.

Slowly, methodically, he turned his back on the offensive house of God, and glared downriver. Ah . . . there it was. Canary Wharf. The faintest of smiles lit up his profile. How comforting. The Wharf was a sublimely sharp, square thing. A lovely tall square thing. That was *much* better. Oh . . . so much better.

Sharp points soothed Eric's soul.

If he had his way, he would raze the whole city of London. For a start, he'd get rid of the winding streets. And slopes. He would put in all straight lines. That's what the city needed. A bit of tidying up. A few unnecessary fiddly bits knocking over. I mean, he thought, all those arches. Admiralty – that was one. What good was it? What was it *for*? Nothing at all. Just a bloody great lump of masonry. The Law Courts on the Strand – they looked like something out of a Hammer Horror film. St Pancras Station. What the hell was that? Whacking great slab of red stone with thousands of curly whatnots. The Natural History Museum. Christ in heaven! An *abomination*.

They should all be pulled down and replaced with things like the new British Library. Now – that was a masterpiece, he knew for a fact. A triumph. It had blank walls and open spaces where the wind howled on the mildest days. There wasn't a frill in sight. Most importantly of all, not a single book. The management of the place, and the architects, had it completely right. Books, paintings, people . . . all put underground in airtight vaults. Fantastic. Visionary.

Of course, he considered, staring at the long brown ribbon of the Thames below him, the big problem in London was really the river. It had curves in it. Loops. And while the river had loops and curves, its banks would have loops and curves, and while its banks had loops and curves, the streets would have them. What would be best of all, he thought, would be to enclose the river in concrete channels and then run the streets parallel. Cramm lost himself in this vision for a second, thinking of the endless smooth vista of promenades, and obedient lines of traffic. Paradise. Not so much Elysium Fields as Elysium City. Perfect. Elysium *Cramm* City, even. When he was Lord Mayor.

He nodded to himself, happy at last, and turned to gaze round his own office. He glanced at the wall clock.

Eight forty.

The eerie silence still reigned.

When Majolica – the owner's – son had been here,

this very office, Cramm had been horrified to discover, had been full of dust and toys. Strange, that someone as pointed and sharp as Majolica, a man that Cramm admired deeply, a man who had first thought of Up-Line Cable, and who had cornered almost every market he had cared to dabble in, should have had a son like Owen. The boy had been a flighty romantic who was even now cruising the Caribbean with his girlfriend instead of running this company. Cramm shook his head. What a disappointment that boy must be to the great man. What a disappointment indeed.

Mind you, Owen Majolica's departure had meant that he, Cramm, had been brought from Los Angeles to London by Majolica himself. *A safe pair of hands*, Majolica had called him. A compliment that even now could bring a faint flush of pleasure to Cramm's face.

Pity about Owen, of course. But what could you expect of a boy who occupied himself with pencil sharpeners that played 'Waltzing Matilda', and flowerpots that farted? Owen had even had a life-size plastic Jack Russell on the conference table, a supposed work of art that actually vomited on to a plate. And the rest of the building . . . Cramm shuddered involuntarily. Mindless disorganisation.

Little beeping trains running on every floor, carrying interdepartmental memos that no one ever read. And the *messages* . . . stickers on every available surface yelling *frolic!*. Christ, it had been bedlam. A nightmare.

The very first thing that Cramm had done on the day he flew in from America was to get forty cleaners in – that very same afternoon, armed with scrubbing brushes and polish. Every single *frolic!* sticker had been torn from its place – from stairs, toilets, doors, handles, telephones, VDUs, televisions. He had had the place scoured and cleansed. He had had the plants thrown out, the beeping trains, the giant cricket wicket in reception where visitors and staff alike had been invited to throw softballs at pasteboard celebrities. On the day he had arrived, a team of dispatch riders had actually been lobbing missiles at Ann Widdecombe. Widdecombe, the Divine One! Cramm had been incensed. He had admired her from across the Atlantic for months. The woman had such presence! And here she was – or at least, here her cardboard cut-out was – being ridiculed by the dregs of society. In *here*! In this building! *His* building! His *empire*!

Cramm had marched at once over to the placard, narrowly being missed by several fluorescent tennis balls, and he had torn the effigy down.

He had not shouted, of course. He had barely spoken a word. But he had gone to the Director's Suite and summoned the Board and told them in no uncertain terms what he expected in Up-Line Cable from now on.

And it was a different world to Owen Majolica's.

Oh yes, indeed. A different planet entirely.

Planet Straight.

Suddenly, the flow of memories was interrupted. From somewhere below him, he could hear the very faint ring of a phone. Somewhere in the bowels of the building, someone's mobile was playing 'I Should Be So Lucky'. Cramm clenched his fists.

Striding over to the door, he wrenched it open.

His two secretaries were seated at their desks, their hands folded in front of them, as instructed.

'What the hell is that noise?' he demanded.

They stared at him, each unwilling to speak. Silent

Quarter – the fifteen minutes that Cramm decreed must be absolutely silent each and every single morning – was in its dying seconds. Their eyes strayed to their watches.

Eight forty-four and fifty seconds.

Fifty-six, fifty-seven . . .

The Work Alarm rang.

As if the entire building had suddenly been plugged into the mains, it came to life. The lifts began to whirr. Feet began running along corridors. Computer keyboards began to be mercilessly hammered. Each employee had endured The Quarter, when they were required by Cramm law to sit in perfect peace and contemplate the good of the company. They sat for a full quarter of an hour and concentrated on the mighty expansion of Up-Line and how they could contribute to it. They reflected upon, probably most of all, how their balls would be on the line and their possessions in the street if they dared raise an eyebrow, let alone a voice.

Cramm slammed his fist down on the nearest flat surface, making the desk, and the girl behind it, quake.

'Go and find that phone!' he yelled. 'Bring the phone to me that rang at eight forty-four!!'

Then, easing a finger round his collar, he walked back into his sanctuary, crashing the door shut again behind him.

Alone again, he took several deep breaths.

And then he turned on Adele Buchanan.

Of all Eric Cramm's many rituals, this was the one of which he was most fond. Every day at the same time, he would ease himself into the mammoth black leather chair behind his desk, and press a small button discreetly hidden inside one of the desk drawers.

In the opposite expanse of black marble, a screen

would slide back to reveal a video wall. And every day, at precisely 8.45, Eric Cramm would unite here with Adele, a remote control in one hand. He would replay yesterday's *Hey! Today!* from start to finish, fast-forwarding every shot of the assorted cooks, fitness gurus, madeover housewives and sincere psychologists that made up the morning TV show on the opposition's channel. For the only thing that Eric Cramm was interested in at all was the presenter, the gorgeous Adele.

He admired her so.

And he so wished that she belonged to him, and not to his arch rival, Lawrence Bugle.

That was where The Idea had started.

Eric had tried to get in touch with Adele many times. He had a desperate desire to take her out to dinner, to sit opposite her and admire her at closer quarters. Never before in all his life had he experienced this deep fascination with a woman, and the pity of it was that she was never likely to know, because he could never get hold of her. The very phrase, *getting hold of her*, made his pulses race, and he had to take a few more deep breaths.

It just wasn't fair. Cramm stared at her image now, admiring her smile, and returning it like a flattered schoolboy, as if Adele Buchanan had been smiling just for him. God, she was marvellous! She was tall, and blonde, and she had very long legs, and she always wore sharp-heeled, pointed shoes, and neatly tailored jackets, and she always had beautifully manicured pointed nails. Not only that. She was bright. Spiky, almost. What an extraordinarily talented person she was, he thought. Running a show like that five days a week. Winning all those awards. Beating off the puny opposition with a stick. Feminine, and yet tough! A jewel in the television crown.

Five days ago, this very same thought was where The Idea began.

Cramm had been sitting right here, thinking of Adele, and thinking how great *Hey! Today!* was, when he was struck with his spark of genius.

If he couldn't have Adele, he would *make* an Adele.

He would re-make Adele in her own image. He would have another Adele, just like the real Adele, sitting in the studios of Up-Line Cable, running a morning show. And beside Adele . . . his mind began to thunder onwards, gathering pace . . . he would have a whole cast just like their cast.

He would have a nice understanding psychologist, and he would have a cuddly doctor who wasn't afraid to show how to inspect your testicles, and he would have a sensuous gardener, and a thin fitness freak, and . . . well, he would have them all. Except it wouldn't be them. It would be *His Team*.

The more he thought about it, the more it all made sense.

All the other TV channels had long ago given up trying to outclass Adele, and retired to a corner, whimpering, licking the wounds of their appalling ratings. In fear and frenzy, the other channels had thrown cooking programmes at the watching public, until every last soul in the United Kingdom knew how to dish up *andouillettes flambées aux abricots* in their sleep. Soon, it was likely that the other channels would lose their nerve completely, and just show a picture of a potter making a teapot for the whole four-hour morning schedule. It was game, set and match to Adele, and the nation knew it.

Until The Idea.

The trouble before was that, in trying to combat Adele, networks had tried to be different to her. But that was exactly where the trouble lay, Cramm had decided. The country didn't *want* a different programme to *Hey! Today!*. They *loved* it. They loved Adele. What the nation actually wanted was *more* of her. More of them all.

Lots, lots more.

Last night, the thrilling simplicity of The Idea had woken Cramm up at 3 am. It was audacious, it was cunning. It was the televisual equivalent of a city of straight streets, with not a dome in sight. It was direct, undiluted, unadulterated, undeviating. Why try to buck a trend? he had asked himself, in the pitch dark of his lonely bedroom. Why try to outdo perfection? All that Up-Line Cable had to do was to replicate *Hey! Today!*. All he had to do was find another bunch of people who looked and talked like Adele's bunch of people. Who would object?

He considered the thought, for a split second, that maybe Adele herself would slam him with a lawsuit. But how could she? How could she possibly object to something that was designed as a homage to her, an acceptance of her total domination of the morning television world? An objection would be trivial – beneath her. After all, if someone came up to you and told you how marvellous you were, and how they wanted to be just like you because you were so stunning, you wouldn't punch them in the face for their trouble, would you? You might be a bit surprised, granted. You might even be a bit unsure when you saw them every day wearing clothes like yours. But how could you be angry? It was a compliment. It was the result of admiration and respect.

Unconsciously, Cramm started to spiral his tie again.

He couldn't wait. He would start today.

This hour.

This very minute!

For he had to find The Team, and quick.

The sooner he found His Team, the sooner he would find his very own Adele.

3

The Blackmoor Vale lay very still in the first morning light, waiting for someone to admire it. Delicate sunshine picked out the colours of the spring woods, the neatly hedged fields, and rolling road. In the distance, Shaftesbury sat smugly on its picturesque hill, gathering its houses to its hem, like a woman in a crinoline arranging the fall of her frock.

And the houses were particularly lovely that morning.

They looked utterly English. Even too English. Their neatly cascading roofs, a touch of clean-air lichen here, a quaint little cobble and flint there, looked as if they had been picked from the airbrushed and over-coloured page of a calendar, or had been painted for a film set. A few elderly residents sat on the seats by Abbey Gardens and gazed out over the Vale with justifiably proprietorial expressions. Fiercely proud of its history, they would be prepared to defend it to the last cream tea, especially on a day like this, when it almost trembled with its own particular beauty.

Nothing – but *nothing* – could disturb the town. Nothing could ever alter the wobbly little iron gates in wobblier walls, the blowy yellow roses just in bud, the daffodils in the Council gardens, the awkward bend in the road by the traffic lights, the bow-fronted shops, or the narrow pavements. Kingdoms may come, empires might fall, meteors might hurtle towards the Earth at ten thousand miles an hour . . . but there would still be Earl Grey brewing on Shaftesbury's hill, and someone in the Oxfam shop knitting a tea cosy for Christ.

Penny Arthur lived in one of the villages at Shaftesbury's foot, deep in the green ocean of fields. And she was not far from home this morning, standing up to her knees in mud, with Euphorbia Amygdaloides in one hand and a bunch of Bergenia Silberlicht in the other.

She was waiting for Harry to come back.

Penny had been a garden designer for twenty-nine years, and had suffered many setbacks and frustrations – sprinkled liberally between her successes – but never in her life, *never in her life*, had she ever been so frustrated as she was now, after hiring Harry Randall.

She could see him now through the trees, standing just outside the knot garden by the long sweep of monastery lawn, chatting to one of the monks. You'd think he didn't have a care in the world, she thought grimly. Hands in pockets – when he wasn't pushing the long floppy hair back from his eyes – smiling and talking.

'Harry!' she shouted.

He'd probably forgotten all about her. Forgotten that she'd only asked him if he could nip over to the kitchen garden and ask Brother Brindle if he had any twine. It should have only taken two or three minutes. Max.

It had obviously totally slipped his mind that she was standing in the millstream waiting to be handed the shovel that even now was staring at her, winking

in the sunlight, on the far bank. She had the euphorbia
right where she wanted it now, and she didn't want to
trek back across those slippery stones in the middle of
the water just to catch hold of it.

'Harry!' she shouted.

He was worse than useless.

Of course, none of the clients saw it that way. Harry
Randall was one of those infuriating people that
everyone seemed to get on with. It wasn't just that the
women almost keeled over when they saw him.
Although that was bloody annoying enough. Many
was the time that, on opening the door to Harry and
Penny, the female client had fastened her eyes on
Harry's face, or bum, or both, and barely torn her gaze
away for the rest of the day.

And Harry wasn't above playing up to it. He would
just grin, push that hair back with one hand, and lean
on the nearest upright surface while returning their
smiles. Very good he was, at leaning. Very good at
chatting. 'Oh, *right* . . .' he would say, laughing. 'Yes,
right . . . absolutely . . .'

He even had the nerve to do it with her.

'Harry!' she called. And then, more plaintively,
almost to herself, 'Oh Harry, please . . .'

Luckily, Harry took that moment to look up. He
held up a hand and waved. She waved back with the
Amygdaloides. He trotted over, through the dappled
sunshine, through the carefully manicured beds, past
the modestly bowing grove of *davidia ungulata*, under
the laden boughs of fragrant lilac, and came to the
riverside, and smiled at her.

'What the flaming hell are you playing at?' she
demanded.

He looked shocked. 'Playing?' he echoed.

'At,' she repeated.

He waved a hand behind his back. 'Brother Benjamin used to be in a chapter,' he told her.

'What of?' she asked. '*The Book of the Dead*?'

'A biking chapter,' Harry replied. 'A Hell's Angel.'

'Is that why he's got those black circles under his eyes?'

Harry sighed. 'He was into stuff,' he said.

'What stuff?'

'I don't know,' Harry replied aimlessly. 'What stuff do you suppose he meant?'

She looked at him. 'Harry, would you please hand me that spade?' she asked.

'Oh, sure,' he said, obeying.

'And the twine?'

'Twine,' he repeated.

'The thing you went for.'

'Ah no,' he said. 'No twine, exactly.'

She gritted her teeth. 'Anything at all, exactly?'

'No, not exactly,' he told her.

She dug fiercely down into the streambed, and secured the planting with some difficulty. Harry started whistling.

'Shut up,' she said. 'Bloody whistling.'

When she looked up, he was wearing a comic pout, which he quickly converted into a grin. She got out of the stream and surveyed her work.

'Awfully pretty,' Harry said. 'Really awfully pretty.'

She eyed him, exasperated.

She asked herself for the thousandth time why on earth she had allowed herself to be persuaded to take him on.

He was what, twenty-six? She rapidly calculated the age of her old school friend, Abigail Randall. Abigail was Harry's mother. Sixty-eight. She had had Harry when she was forty-two, two years after her daughter Meg.

Penny was the same age as Abigail, and her own children, Mac and Robbie, were already at university when Abigail Randall decided to reproduce. Abigail, as a press photographer, had travelled the world, and declaimed all over it that she would never have children. She had remained single all the years that Penny herself was having babies, raising them, and trying to carve a small niche for herself as a designer, often trailing children with her as she measured, dug and planted.

She had so envied Abigail Randall back then. Oh, yes. Envied her so much that she could have cheerfully killed her. Abigail was always sending postcards from some devastatingly glamorous place, a place where Penny would have loved to be, and invariably the postcards were full of complaints.

Ouarzazate, Sahara, March 1968
I simply cannot believe that a film about camels and somebody who died falling off a motorbike will make any money at all even if David Lean is doing it.

Or –

San Gimignano, Italy, 1970
Everyone in Tuscany is an absolute bastard.

Or –

Hong Kong, April 1971
Filthy.

Abigail was not known to mince her words.

In fact, she was such a fearsome woman that Penny had been quite sure she would never marry, simply because no man would be either brave enough or stupid enough to take her on. Penny had often imagined Abigail's romantic encounters – of which there were many – in terms of a bullfight. Some poor man would get mesmerised by her – she could stand out in a crowd of ten thousand, could Abigail – and, like the poor Spanish bull, he would be tricked into cantering into Abigail's private arena. Whereupon, after taunting him for an hour or two, she probably lashed him with whips until she got what she wanted.

Not in her wildest dreams could Penny imagine Abigail as a romantic. Her friend's speciality was bawling and complaining at the top of her voice, and Penny couldn't imagine that any male would tolerate her for long, once the scales had dropped from his eyes.

And so it had been quite a surprise when Penny, late in 1971, had received an actual letter, as opposed to a postcard, from Abigail. It had been short and to the point:

Dear Pen,
I met rather a nice sort in Amman, and we're getting married in West Sussex in January. Here's the invite. Hope you can come.
Abigail.

Penny and her husband George had wondered feverishly about Abigail's husband. The happy couple only flew into the UK three days before the wedding, so sitting in church one snowy Saturday had been the first chance that Penny and George had had to clap eyes on the poor devil. There was a private bet between them that the new husband would either be eighty-six and about to kick the bucket, and certainly stone-deaf, or that he would be twenty-one and desperate for an English passport.

As it happened, Ernest Randall had been neither. He was handsome, tall, smiled rather shyly, was amazingly softly spoken, and was also exceedingly poor. Recently retired from the Civil Service, he was Abigail's senior by fifteen years.

The plain fact was – and it *was* utterly plain, from the moment that they arrived, hand-in-hand – that Abigail had fallen in love. She adored Ernest, and they rapidly had two children – Meg and Harry – and then, ten years later and very quietly one morning, poor Ernest had died of a heart attack. In that, Abigail and Penny were the same. They were both widows now.

Penny sighed to herself now as she put all her tools into the canvas bag. Harry was still standing, still smiling, and still admiring the stream. She straightened up, and looked at him.

Harry was so like his father.

Abigail had never been anything but brisk – even rude – to her daughter, Meg. But to Harry . . . well, Harry, the youngest, was a different story. Harry, from the second of his birth, had been petted and admired and indulged and adored. And, because he had his father's genes so acutely, Harry did not grow to be bad-tempered and spoiled, but rather flourished under Abigail's adoration, like a beautiful flower blooming in the sun.

And that's just what he was, really. Tall, languid, sweet. Harry was also handsome, and laid-back to the point of catatonic trance. Shielded from life's storms, he simply didn't see any bad in the world, or bad in anyone in it. It drove Penny crazy, not least because she herself was a confirmed cynic.

'Harry,' she said, almost to herself. 'What on earth am I going to do with you?'

He turned to her, lifted her mud-stained hand, and pressed it to his lips. 'You,' he said sweetly, 'are going to let me make you a nice cup of tea.'

It was lunchtime by the time that the tea had been drunk, and Brother Benjamin had been said goodbye to. Penny watched the monk's mournful face disappear in the wing mirror as she rounded the bend in the long gravel drive. She headed for the main road, putting her foot firmly down on the Land Rover's accelerator.

'What time is it?' Harry asked.

She glanced at her watch. 'Almost one.'

'Where are we going now?' he asked.

'Well,' she said, easing the car out on to the main road, 'I have to go and do an estimate at a place in Sherborne. I expect you'll want to go home for lunch meanwhile.'

To her surprise, she actually saw Harry's face blanch. 'Well,' he replied hurriedly. 'Actually, pro-bably not.'

'Not?' she said. 'Why not?'

'Can't I come with you?'

'It would mean holding a tape, Harry, and writing things down,' she told him. 'I couldn't possibly put you to the trouble.'

Her sarcasm, as usual, was lost on him. 'It's no trouble at all,' he assured her. She noticed that he had

begun to scratch his ear, a sign that he was preoccupied.

'Why don't you want to go home?' she asked.

He pulled a face. 'Mum is selling the house,' he said.
'And the estate agent's coming today.'

The news was shocking enough to make Penny slew
the Land Rover to one side of the road and pull on the
handbrake.

'Sell it?' she repeated. 'You're joking.'

'I'm not,' he said.

'But Halfpenny Acre!'

'I know,' Harry said glumly. 'She's set upon it.'

'But what the hell for?' Penny demanded. 'It's the
most beautiful house in the world.'

And Penny's stomach actually turned over at the
thought that Abigail was going to let go of that rosy-
walled fifteenth-century treasure, tucked into a
hillside in Somerset. She had suddenly had the most
awful premonition that a developer would get his
hands on it, and turn it into forty redbrick boxes
overnight. She had spent so much time in that garden,
not just to help Abigail, who was useless at gardening, but actually – more secretly and selfishly –
because she adored it. She had devoted three weeks
last summer – her holiday, supposedly – to turning
the lower terrace into a knot garden. She would have
quite happily lived there, she sometimes thought –
not in the house itself, but curled in one corner of the
vegetable plot, like a dormouse. Halfpenny Acre had
her own ex-Council house knocked into a cocked
hat.

It came to her all at once now, that she thought of
Halfpenny Acre as hers, really – her garden, at any
rate. She felt a lurch in her chest, like a Hollywood

actress must feel as she sees someone else walk away with the Oscar.

'Are you all right?' Harry asked.

Penny passed a hand over her forehead. 'I think I'm getting hot flushes eighteen years too late,' she muttered. She turned in her seat to look at him. 'Harry,' she said softly. 'Why on earth does she want to move?'

Harry shrugged. 'She's got a bit of a bee in her bonnet,' he said. 'She says she wants to be in London.'

'How ludicrous,' Penny retorted. 'Nobody wants to be in London.'

'She keeps on saying that she's getting old,' Harry said. 'She says that everyone's waiting for her to fall into the grave.'

'At sixty-eight?' Penny echoed. *She* was sixty-eight, and had never felt better. 'What's the matter, is she ill?'

'No,' Harry said. 'But she's got one of her funny moods on. She says that when the time comes and she's crippled with arthritis, and no-one cares about her, she'll fall into the millpond one morning, and have to wait three days for anyone to come and fish her out, and then sit for a week in Cramberely District Hospital on a trolley, and then be put behind curtains in a side ward while they let her catch pneumonia and die, and then no-one would come to her funeral.' He sighed heavily, after a pause to draw breath.

'Oh, for Christ's sake,' Penny said. 'Has she been taking St John's Wort again? You know how depressed it makes her.'

'I dunno,' Harry muttered. 'She throws things.'

Penny revved the accelerator, and signalled to pull out. 'As if I haven't got enough to do,' she muttered darkly.

4

Meg was going to be late getting to Halfpenny Acre.

She didn't know why she had given in to her mother's usual emotional blackmail and agreed to come, today of all days.

To cap it all, she was having the most horrific driving experience of her life. The moment she had come out of the house, the remaining tabloid fiends that were left in the road set off after her. It had been like re-living the Charge of the Light Brigade.

And her Peugeot was not a well car. In fact, if it had been human, it would have been receiving the Last Rites by now, and its relatives would have been leafing through floral arrangement catalogues. It really wasn't up to the challenge of actually going anywhere. For weeks now, it had been making an ominous grinding sound on bends. She couldn't afford to get it repaired – God knew, she could hardly afford to fill it with petrol – so she had tried to develop a driving deafness, and did not react if people in the street turned to stare at the noise. The Peugeot was moaning regularly now, as she scudded across central London, her heart in her mouth.

You would have thought that the press could have left her alone after the news this morning, and turning up on her doorstep at six o'clock. She and Michael had even done them the unwarranted favour of standing on that same doorstep at eight o'clock and actually handing out an interview. She had posed, trying to look fraught and worried, which wasn't difficult, and terribly brave and British, which was, and she thought, after that, that she would have seen the last of them. That they would have had the decency to let her alone.

As if.

No sooner had she got out of the house again at midday, than the journalists and the photographers had been on her like a pack of killer bees. In response, out of sheer fear, she had speeded up. The ancient Peugeot had responded with a coughing fit, and clouds of black smoke. It had been necessary to say a short prayer as she missed an opening taxi door on Talgarth Road, nipping in between slow-moving vehicles. Behind her, she could see that pedestrians were jumping out of the way of the pursuing paparazzi bikes like Olympic triple-jumpers. And they were still there now, as she turned into the Great West Road – looming in her wing mirror – four massive beast-like bikes with mad photographers on the back of them. She had a mental picture of the bit in *Jurassic Park*, as the tyrannosaurus rex surged after the Jeep, with Laura Dern screaming blue murder in the passenger seat.

Meg didn't scream, however. Even when a lorry with *Essential Pistons* emblazoned along its side swung out towards her. She just pulled hard on the wheel, saw the traffic lights rushing towards her, and bumped the kerb as she stamped on the accelerator. The poor little Peugeot wailed up the dual carriage-way, making a grinding, keening sound. Behind her, caught by a red light, the line of bikes slewed to a stop.

'Theirs not to make reply,' Meg muttered, triumphant. 'Stormed at with shot and shell, boldly they rode and well, but not quite well enough.'

The speedo miraculously crept over ninety as she hit the M4.

Meg had spent her life having eventful journeys.

It would be some sort of compensation, perhaps, if she could say that this meant she had spent most of her childhood up Kilimanjaro or down a diamond mine, or on board a Turkish yacht, or under a fur blanket on the Siberian Express. To be fair – if life was fair, which of course it wasn't – she could have looked forward to such journeys almost as a birthright. Her mother had travelled all over the world working as a photographer, and been a bystander-with-lens at some of the key events of history.

So Meg might have reasonably looked forward to at least a couple of rides on a camel and a forced overnight stay in some foreign jail, minimum. What she got, by way of contrast, was actually very different.

She got Drive-Out Sundays.

When Abigail had got married, it was as if Meg's mother had suddenly taken an oath never to be adventurous again. Someone, it seemed to Meg, had come briskly along on the morning of her mother's wedding, watched while the deed was done, and then stepped forward and given Abigail a sharp blow to the head with a mallet. Because nothing else could explain the almost complete change of character. Her mother apparently went from unwashed-in-a-camel-train to starched-in-West-Sussex in the time it took to say *I do*.

When Meg had once summoned up the courage to

ask her about it, Abigail had been at first evasive, and then angry.

'But we never go anywhere exciting,' Meg had complained bitterly, at the news that they were to spend another summer holiday in Littlehampton.

'Exciting is a state of mind,' her mother had promptly told her. 'If you had seen as many tent latrines as I have, you would know what you're talking about.'

Meg had slumped on the sofa, eight years old and sulking, twisting her plaits around her wrist. 'I would bloody love to have a latrine,' she retorted.

'No you bloody wouldn't,' Abigail said. 'And don't say bloody, you precocious child.'

'But I want to go to Egypt.'

'*Shit.*' Abigail had turned her back to her daughter and was doing things to a bowl of Victoria Sponge mixture. Not very successful things, to judge by the curses.

'And Sarawak,' Meg had added.

'You don't even know where Sarawak is.'

This was true. But it sounded fabulous nevertheless, like Tashkent and Kashmir. Why didn't England have names like that? she had wondered. How could you get all enthused by the sound of Funtington, for heaven's sake? They had passed through it in the car only the week before. Fittlesham, Lickfold, Codmore Hill. Codmore Hill! Who on earth had thought of that? It wouldn't win any competitions with the Côte d'Azur, would it?

Her small girlish heart had sunk into her shoes. 'I want to go to Murmansk.'

Abigail had merely snorted. 'I wish you *would* go to Murmansk.'

Meg, who was a bit more prone to crying than she would have wished, had felt her eyes fill with tears. Abigail had looked over her shoulder. 'Don't start that,' she'd said.

Meg knew only too well what that meant. For some reason, her mother hated her to cry, which made her propensity to cry all the worse.

'You are a mean pig,' she'd gulped.

'Get out.'

'And a bloody misery.' Meg had had the good sense to say this while scrambling out of the chair and heading for the door.

'I am a misery in the cause of bloody *Good Housekeeping*!' Abigail had yelled. Then, almost to herself, 'Thou shalt honour thy father and thy mother.'

Quoting the Bible was a real danger sign. Brought up by strict Methodists, Abigail reverted to biblical quotations whenever she was really mad.

As a family, the Randalls had never got much further than Littlehampton. Or possibly Bognor, if her father was feeling wild and reckless. Which was almost never.

Travelling with Abigail and Ernest, in their two-tone green Vauxhall with the tail fins, was an experience never to be forgotten. Harry had been too small to remember, tucked in his booster seat and stuffing Jelly Babies into his mouth. But Meg . . . oh yes. *She* was old enough to remember.

Abigail, chained to this new idea (for her) of being the perfect housewife, only ever allowed herself Sundays off. So Sunday was devoted to an afternoon ride out in the car. Meg always felt that, actually, the words ought to be in capital letters. THE CAR.

Because, in Meg's father's mind, this was royalty among cars. Somewhere in the first flush of married life, Abigail and Ernest had plumped for suburban bliss, in the shape of this unremarkable family saloon. But, to Ernest, the car was Nirvana, and it was surprising that he had restrained himself from putting a flag on the front. Not for the sake of the occupants, but just to designate that the car itself was sublime.

It was a shame, really. Her father couldn't help it. All his life had been spent carefully minding things for other people, and the car was his one personal extravagance. The one thing he owned for sheer pleasure. The one thing he had irreducible power over.

Until he got married, that is.

All his Civil Service career, Ernest Randall had been responsible for the costing of army movements – the back-up, and the logistics. He had fought Aden, for instance, at his own desk, wrestling the supply of uniforms, soap and munitions. Trying to find columns to put expenditure in. He had deserved a medal for it, but, of course, there was no pinning of gongs to civilian suits.

And his personal battle career was never-ending. It had lasted thirty-eight years. When one war ended, another one would begin somewhere else. Minor skirmishes with tribesmen. Vast punch-ups with mad dictators. Whatever the scale, whatever the war, Ernest Randall had dotted its 'I's and crossed its 'T's. He had been remarkably calm, actually, considering the vast acreage of form-filling he had endured. The flak from other departments. The hand-to-hand combat in Treasury committees. Yomping through airports in far distant countries, trying to find a taxi without a goat and a crate of chickens sitting in it. Not to mention the thankless bloody slog across London, back to a bachelor pad in Wimbledon.

Life had always, in fact, been so organised for Ernest that it was to be expected that he would get a little obsessive about *something*. Everyone was obsessive about the occasional detail, after all – turning loo rolls a particular way on the dispenser, perhaps. Or being a West Ham fan. Or only ever wearing green socks. Harmless little addictions like that. And, Meg supposed, her father's love of his car – well, his roaring great passion for his car – might well have passed unnoticed in Wimbledon, where there was no-one inside his little flat to notice. But once he was married . . . that was different. What might have been a lifelong unsuspected devotion to a green tail-finned Vauxhall suddenly became very visible indeed.

It ruined their Sundays.

The first two hours of every Sunday morning, Ernest would spend in the garage with the car. He would clean the Vauxhall, and then polish every inch. Every tiny bit of thick chrome bumper. Every fragment of glass. He would even lie on the floor and polish the underside of the wheel rims. You could see your face in this car, and Meg remembered standing next to it, possibly herself only as high as the door handle, gazing at the looped reflection of her own face in the driver's door. The paintwork looked so thick and so perfect, it was as if the car had been neatly covered in a layer of green fondant icing.

While he polished the Vauxhall, her father would talk to it, softly, in a mournful and apologetic voice. 'We won't be out long,' he would say to it. And if it were raining . . . oh, God forbid that it would be raining. A rainy Sunday morning was like a cloud from erupting Vesuvius hanging directly over their heads, because Abigail would still insist upon her ritual trip, and Ernest loathed getting the car wet.

Meg would get up, see the rain, and feel the tension, even before she got downstairs. Abigail would be in the kitchen, making porridge. This was another ritual that had been imposed upon them. Abigail hated porridge and so did everybody else. But it was good for you. So it appeared on their plates and they, each of them, mournfully shovelled it down.

Meg winced as she whipped along the outside lane of the motorway now. What used to make her angry, then, was the fact that Harry had always been allowed to have a huge dollop of maple syrup in his dish. More maple syrup than porridge, in fact. But she wasn't. And she smiled wryly to herself at the memory, and rubbed the frown from between her eyes with a free hand.

How very stupid, she thought, to let such a little thing annoy you, twenty years down the line. How petty, how trivial. But annoy her it did, and the closer she got to her mother's house, the more such petty little grievances would occur to her, until she would arrive at Abigail's in a state of suppressed indignant fury, which took all her powers of deceit to cover up.

Come eleven o'clock on a Sunday morning, back in the Randall family home, Meg's father would come back in the house wearing the expression of someone who has just been told that his faithful dog had been put through a sawmill by mistake. He would sit at the kitchen table, and Abigail would put a cup of milky coffee and two pink wafer biscuits in front of him. Then she would sit down next to him while he opened the Sunday paper with a sigh.

Abigail would remain sitting there, arms crossed, her Vesuvial face getting ever darker, watching Meg's father slowly turn the newspaper pages. Then, eventually, the suspense would get too much for her, and she would say, 'Well, are we going out or not?'

There would be two full minutes of silence. And then Meg's father would put down his paper and say, 'Where did you want to go?' as if this were a complete revelation to him.

Abigail would give him a glare. 'Oh,' she would say, 'don't bother, if it's going to be too much trouble.'

Meg's father would slowly, agonisingly slowly, raise the paper again. There would be another two minutes silence, while Abigail stared at the front page of the newspaper as if willing it to melt.

Then Ernest, sensing that Abigail was about to explode in a full rain of white-hot lava, would ask, 'Do you want to go anywhere or not?'

This time, it would be Abigail's turn not to reply. A look of incredible wounded hurt would pass over her face. Eventually, she would mutter, 'It's not worth it now. Look at the time.'

She would turn to the kitchen clock. Invariably – for this whole scenario was, Meg was convinced, timed to perfection, honed by repetition until it was exactly right – it would be exactly eighteen minutes past eleven.

At that very moment, Meg's father would get to his feet and say, 'We'll go out for an hour. I'll go and start the car.'

It was pronounced in tones of doom. Anyone eavesdropping, who didn't quite catch the words, might have guessed that he'd said, 'I shall just go and chain the car to a pylon and run a hundred thousand volts through it.'

He would go off into the garden, along the short drive to the garage doors, all the while slumped over the keys held reverently in the palm of his hand. His body language had always been grief-stricken. Because inside the garage was a lovely, lovely car and, reckless and thoughtless people that they were, they were about to get into this car and actually drive it out on to the road while exerting enormous pressure on the tyres by sitting in it. It amounted to nothing less than murder.

Poor Ernest. He had so adored that great lump of metal.

Not that he didn't have one or two other, more minor, passions. None of which Abigail shared, but Meg tried to. Like Ernest himself, his hobbies were modest.

As she considered him now, she thought how very typical of her father that was. Ernest would have been constitutionally incapable of some roaring great deceit, like running a mistress, or blowing his pension on the 4.30 at Doncaster. Meg tried, for a second, to imagine her father in a dinner jacket and a pencil moustache, slugging back vodka martinis at a roulette table. She tried to imagine him booking the Bridal Suite at a Brighton hotel, with a blonde on his arm. But the idea was preposterous. Ernest had no more been capable of having an affair or running himself into financial ruin than he had of running a two-minute mile.

She smiled to herself, unconsciously, at the memory of her father on holiday. Sitting in a deck chair, with his trouser legs rolled up modestly to mid-calf, patiently looking at the shells that she had brought back to him. His knowledge of them had seemed to be encyclopedic.

'Now, Margaret,' he would tell her, 'that is a very nice *pecten glaber*, of the *pectinidae* family.' He would be holding up a scallop shell. 'And the ones we saw for sale in the shop just now, those were *cymatium lotorium* of the *cymatiidae*; they eat each other, you know. And they all have hairs on their periostracum.'

'For heaven's sake,' Abigail would grumble, 'you'll put the child off her dinner.'

Ernest would merely smile. Meg became nearly as expert as he was, which was a skill she took incredible pride in until she was well into her teens. There weren't many eight-year-olds who could tell a siliquaridae from a strombus sinuatus.

Somewhere in a drawer at home now, she had a plastic bag full of pheasant shells, tiny little iridescent curls of terracotta and silver and ochre, which Ernest himself had collected from the coast of Sri Lanka. He hadn't told her much about that trip: only that he had been sent to find forty-five field kitchens missing from the Treasury accounts. But his eyes had misted over a little, and she had imagined him – a lonely, awkward beanpole of a man, sitting on a beach.

When she looked at the shells now, she wondered if she had known him at all, except through the pheasant shells and the tail-finned Vauxhall.

When Meg was ten years old, Ernest had been found in the car one Sunday morning, a Drive-Out Sunday that never materialised. For, while he had been polishing the dashboard clock, his own little allotted portion of time had run out.

He had died of a heart attack.

Suddenly, Meg saw the signs for Little Doubting. The huge blue motorway indicator board broke her reverie. She indicated left, swerved between the lanes, and managed to veer up the slip road just in time, while several cars behind her flashed their lights in reproof.

At the roundabout at the top, she had to come to a halt. As she sat there, flushed, heart racing, she shook her head at herself.

She stared at her hands on the steering wheel. She sighed deeply. These same hands had almost propelled her into The Great Car Park In The Sky today.

I never, never drive like this, she thought.

And then corrected herself.

The lights changed, and she put the still-clattering Peugeot into gear.

'I only drive like this on the way to my mother's,' she muttered.

5

Adele Buchanan was having trouble.

It was nothing that any woman, anywhere at all in the world, wasn't capable of having at any time of the day. Only in her case, it was magnified a thousand times.

Or four million times, she thought morosely, as she stared in the mirror. That was how many people would have seen her face today, on the nation's favourite morning TV show.

She sat in the loo and stared at her shoes in despair. She wasn't unusual, she told herself. She wasn't a freak. She was just like everyone else – every woman over twenty-one. She had spent the last ten minutes staring at a reflection that seemed to belong to a stranger, a woman who was at least twenty years older than herself.

She put her hands over her eyes, as if that would shut the image out. It wasn't as if she hadn't spent a fortune on looking perfect. She hated to think how much she had invested in this face and body. The manicures, pedicures, massages, facials. The personal trainer, the reflexologist, the naturopath, the osteopath, the nutritionist. God! She had seen them all in her time. She had had her hair dyed, her teeth fixed, her ears lowered, her lips enlarged, her chin smoothed, her eye bags nipped, her nose straightened, her thighs suctioned and her calves plumped. There wasn't a single part of her that she hadn't sacrificed to the great God of Looking Good. She had offered herself up to the process on a plate, willingly allowing all sorts of strangers to manipulate her. Even her bowels weren't her own. At least . . . they were her own, but they weren't private. Not after they had been colonically irrigated every fortnight. She had let people pummel and pound her; she had been under the surgeon's knife so often that she could have had a long-stay parking permit in his operating theatre. She had swallowed appetite suppressants, and mood enhancers, and seaweed, and her own urine, and the placentas of various animals unknown to the western world, all in the cause of eternal youth.

And she had been winning the battle . . . surely, she *had* been winning the battle, until last week.

A cold wave of horror washed over her.

Last week.

Last week.

If she didn't pull herself out of this, she told herself severely, then it certainly would be her last week. She would get fired, and plummet from the great heady heights of morning television into the abyss of No-one's Watching Broadcasting. She would end up doing something terrible. Something so nondescript that it didn't even make the *Radio Times* magazine. The thought was too terrible to contemplate. She would be posted to something bleak in the outer reaches of television, given the human-interest stories at the end of some local news somewhere. Or she would end up being the link woman in *Children In Need*, the one in an anorak on a windswept beach, trying to sound enthusiastic about six lifeboatmen dressed as Wonder

Woman. She would finish her life on the till in the BBC canteen, in a ginger fright wig and too much eyebrow pencil.

'Don't let it happen to me,' she whispered. 'Don't let it happen.'

She shook her head to herself, and dropped her hands into her lap.

She tried thinking positively.

After all, didn't everyone despair sometimes? Even if you didn't really give a damn about your looks, even if you were some earth-mother type who had never touched a cosmetic in your life, even if personal body image was nowhere on your list of priorities, even if you had gone into politics and taken an oath never to look human again, surely everyone, at some moment of their lives, occasionally stopped dead in front of a shop window, and wondered who the hell it was looking back at them.

But Adele Buchanan wasn't allowed to be like every other woman.

She wasn't allowed to have face trouble, because it didn't make good television. In fact, she wasn't allowed to have face, neck, upper-arm or thigh trouble. She wasn't allowed to bulge or wrinkle in perfectly normal places; she wasn't allowed to have flab, or bags.

Instead, she had to be cheese.

The thought brought an unrestrained sob to her lips.

That's exactly what she was. That was precisely it. She was *cheese*. And not even a decent cheese, either. She was that bloody awful kind of cheese that didn't taste of anything once you had wrestled the layers of packaging off. She was a piece of shrink-wrapped cheese on a supermarket shelf, the kind that was entirely free of normal cheese-like properties, and so didn't have dents or dimples or streaks. She was absolutely bland and even, unnaturally preserved beneath layers of Cellophane.

A tear crept out of one eye.

Oh God, it was hopeless.

'Holy Gorgonzola,' she whispered, to nobody at all.

Even the shoes stared back at her accusingly.

Taking a deep, deep breath, Adele Buchanan took stock.

Here she was, at thirty-two. Well, thirty-two, that is, if you didn't do anything so crass as look at her birth certificate, which quite plainly said that Adele had been born Janet Tebbs in Bootle in . . . don't even think about it. Her birth date was just moments after the dinosaurs ruled the earth. Certainly before the wheel was invented, and thousands of aeons before TV cracked open its shell.

The crumpled publicity shot lay on the floor next to her, next to the shoes. The Head of Light Entertainment, Lawrence Bugle, had sent it to her that morning in a plain brown envelope.

No note, no message.

Just the horrible, unflattering picture that she had had done last week.

She eased one sandal off now, stared venomously at both it and the photo, and then threw the shoe at the door. It landed with only the faintest clatter of heel, since it was made of nothing more than a piece of leather with some hideously expensive silk stretched over it. Silk shoes! *Christ.* She'd practically had to have her last three toes surgically removed to get into them. Just look at that shape, for heaven's sake! she told herself. What normal woman, with five ordinary-sized toes, could possibly get her foot into *that*?

The whole process of buying and wearing shoes seemed to have undergone some kind of change in the last two years, she thought. It was like going back to nineteenth-century China. Why didn't women, she considered grimly, just bind their feet at birth, and be done with it? In fact, why bother to walk at all? Why not just ask every midwife to slice off the toes of newborn girls, and accept that every woman would just stuff her stumps into an eggcup for the rest of her life?

'Oh God,' Adele sighed. She grabbed her handbag and opened it, fumbling about for the blessed pale green packet. Finding the sedatives, she swallowed one dry. *My life is over*, she thought.

Over.

It wasn't just the publicity shot, but that was bad enough.

She ought to have known that something was up last Friday, when she had caught the make-up girls sniggering as she came into the studio. Oh, they didn't know that she had seen them, of course. And their attitude was just the same as she sat down in the make-up chair. They still wittered on about Kate Winslet and doing the faces on *Titanic*, and they still asked her how Jack was.

The bitches!

If she could fire them all now, she would.

If only someone – anyone, anyone – in her life would tell her the truth for once.

Unconsciously she began chewing on her thumbnail.

Once, when she had started this morning show

eleven years ago, she had just been one of the girls. She had been just like them – twenty-something, out for a laugh, pretending to be hard-bitten, and yet a sucker for a chat-up line. She had been a young journalist then, catapulted into the limelight when the original *Hey! Today!* presenter – that hoary old lecher Marcus Binnerman – had got a raging flu.

She'd sailed into that morning, the whole morning's presentation, without an ounce of nerves. She didn't really think that anyone would be watching. But she'd reckoned without the great British public, who – though they denied it to their families – all switched on the TV the second that they had the house to themselves. To ward off the evils of ironing, they gratefully submerged themselves into the screen, and, when they found Adele looking back at them instead of the supercilious Marcus with his out-of-control sideburns and visible-waistband Y-fronts – the nation had almost whooped for joy. She was just a girl . . . the girl next door. Not the one with an impossible bum and neon-white teeth, but a real girl – a girl who handled the interview with the Education Minister so badly that he swore at a cameraman, and stormed off the set. A girl who didn't have the first notion how to help make shortcrust pastry, said she could think of better things to do with half an hour and a warmed bowl of oil, and whose taste in clothes was obviously more Oxfam than Issey Miyake.

Oh, they loved her.

They *adored* her.

She just said what anyone else would say. That was the knack of it. Of course it drove the legal department mad, and of course she was carpeted a dozen times in that first week. But once the letters started pouring in, the carpetings changed. Instead of being roundly slagged off standing up, they offered her a chair. Then they offered her coffee. And, by the end of the second week, the Producer was sitting by her side, telling her about his affair and asking her if he should leave his wife, and never trying it on with her once, because those were the days when no-one even suggested that she have a nip-and-tuck. Not like they did once she turned thirty.

And, even then, after thirty, she had just accepted it. Started changing herself to please them, because she liked to get on with everybody, and didn't think that it mattered, because she just liked people. She liked everybody.

And that was the whole bloody trouble.

Liking, and pleasing. Like a lapdog.

She had liked Jack all right, four months ago. Liked him enough to get him promoted to her personal assistant. She had liked him enough to ignore the sidelong glances from the rest of the crew, the whispered conversations that abruptly stopped when she got close.

All right . . . he was twenty-three. What did it matter? Who on earth cared? She was thirty-two – in a dim light with the wind in the right direction – and he was twenty-three. What was it? Only nine years difference. Nine years was absolutely nothing. Women could have what they wanted, couldn't they? Just like men, who wanted girls of eighteen when they themselves were sixty. Well, she was just the same. Nine piffling inconsequential years. If it had been twenty-nine years, maybe. Maybe then she would have deserved the sneaky looks and the whispers.

She had shrugged it all off. She had put it down to

jealousy. After all, she knew for a fact that Anna in make-up was married to the most obese Lebanese on the face of the earth. And it wasn't even as if he were rich. He had a fifteen-year-old Mercedes and a pizza habit to support. And look at Fran . . . bony little Fran, who couldn't say boo to a goose, let alone that hulking great barn door of a husband of hers, a man who always smelled strangely of paint stripper, and who was, reputedly, something in building. He ought to be something in building, too, Adele considered. Part of a box girder, preferably.

They had just been envious of Jack, she had told herself. Jack, on the production team. Jack with his lazy, sexy voice, his long blond hair that ought to have been naff, but didn't look naff on him, because, while you were just beginning to think it *did* look naff, you suddenly noticed his eyes, and all other thoughts were wiped from your hard disk.

They had got on so well, from the very first moment. He had been a breath of fresh air – Liverpudlian, rude, and relentlessly cheerful. His first comment to Adele had been to insult her hands – 'What have you done with them, have you been mixing concrete?' and the second thing he had said to her was to declare that he had adored her from afar for years.

Classic hunting technique, of course.

Reel them in with a hook, let them go on a promise. Hook, reel, relent. Hook, reel, relent. Knock the chair from under you, then help you to your feet. She never quite knew where she was with him. She began thinking about him when she was on set, and then she began thinking about him when she was in the car going home, and then she began thinking about him when she was at home, and then she began thinking about him when she was at home in bed.

And, once she had got that far, there was no hope for her.

She thought that he felt the same. He had certainly given her all the signals.

She had gone out with him for a drink one night – just casually. Just very very casually asking him if he wanted a drink with the rest of the crew, one Friday. Just dropping it into the conversation and casually saying, 'Fine, then,' when he said he would come. 'Fine then, maybe see you,' she'd told him.

And then she'd casually run out to Harrods and rifled through four hundred frocks, and lost her temper with a half dozen assistants, and then she'd casually sprinted to the hairdressers, and had a dozen fantasies between there and home, and then she'd casually thrown herself into a bath and lathered herself with a gallon of exfoliant and scraped her body with a cutthroat razor in an effort to rid herself of even a millimetre of hair anywhere at all, and then she'd casually had a screaming fit of self-doubt when she put the casual three-hundred-pound jeans and slash-neck top on, before running out into the road to hail a taxi.

He had walked up to her the very second she walked into the wine bar.

Oh, he was lovely. Not clever, or sardonic, or cutting, or rude at her expense. Not any of the things that men usually were when she dated them. He didn't look her over and calculate how much her jewellery had cost. He didn't bore her with stories about his failed relationships. He didn't try to score points. He wasn't overly charming – the kind of charm that stuck in your throat – and he wasn't overly complimentary, and he wasn't snide or abusive or jealous about her job. He was just sweet, and human, and he could talk.

He talked about the things that men never talk about.

He talked about his family. He had three sisters. He talked about his mother in a perfectly affectionate way – and God, she had lost count of how many men she knew who hated their mothers, or, alternatively, loved them in a very creepy fashion. And he had laughed about summer holidays they'd all had when he was a child, these four resolute Liverpudlian women with the much younger baby brother in tow – the holidays in Morecambe, where they all struggled into swimming costumes behind collapsing windbreaks – and he talked about their house in Skelmersdale, and about helping his mum play bingo . . . all the kind of things you just *never* admitted to if you wanted to be cool . . .

And he talked about the colours he liked, and the kinds of houses, and he talked about films and books, and he liked the kind of films that men never liked, the comedies and the romances . . .

And he talked about being afraid to be old, and about friends he had had at school, and what his weaknesses were, and the things he had failed at, and . . .

And he never once, never once all night, talked about a single sport. Or car. Or gadget.

Or his job.

She ought to have known then.

She ought to have guessed that he was just too good to be true.

They went for other drinks, with other people, and they progressed to meals with other people, and then, last week, she had taken the plunge and invited Jack over to her house, for supper.

She asked him because she was used to asking. People were usually intimidated by her, and she had got the message long ago that if she wanted something, she had to ask, because, more often than not, they were too frightened to ask her.

And he said he would be there. He smiled. He seemed pleased.

She started to cry now, real tears, just like last Tuesday. And Wednesday, and Thursday, and Friday. In fact, she had been crying – on and off – since supper with Jack.

She had told him to come at seven.

He had arrived with a big bunch of white lilies, and had at once started to arrange them while she nervously poured the wine, and watched him walking around her home with the vase extended in one arm, occasionally closing one eye to see where it would look best. He had finally decided on a table by the window, after first removing the books she had piled on it. Then, he'd walked over to her, and, without asking, started to help her make the pasta sauce – just easy, easy like that, picking up the herbs, moving round her as she worked, telling her that the colour she had on suited her – 'Where'd you get this? Looks great. In Bath? When were you in Bath? I love that city. You know the gallery on the square?' One sentence running into another, a constant flow.

And, when he looked at her, he really looked. With affection. With interest. Her heart had fluttered. So stupid. So schoolgirly. She had to turn away, while she stirred the pasta, so that he wouldn't see her blush.

They drank a lot with the meal. He seemed to be able to drink gallons without once slurring his words or losing the thread of the conversation. She, on the other hand, knew that she was drunk, and laughing too much. But it didn't matter. They strayed to the couch and stared out at the expensive view of the river, and she leaned her head on his shoulder, and he put his arm around her, and he asked her why she had never married.

'I never saw the point of marriage unless you wanted children,' she said. She looked up at him, and smiled. Such warmth invaded her, the complete knowledge that she had met someone on her wavelength at last, with whom she didn't have to try, someone with whom she just gelled. She would never have to sit with her back to the light; she would never again wear a polo neck; she wouldn't cover herself up when she came out of the shower, or be afraid that he would wander. She just knew, in that instant, that they had been born for each other.

'And will you ever want children?' he asked.

'I do now,' she said.

Oh, my God.

How stupid.

He drew back from her, and a look passed over his face. If she had ever wanted to see an illustration of the expression *and the scales fell from his eyes* – which she hadn't, not now, not anytime, not anywhere, and particularly not with him – well, she saw it now.

Jack dropped his arm from her shoulder.

'What?' he said.

She felt a little confused, and muddled. 'Children,' she repeated.

'I don't get you,' he said.

She ought to have taken that as enough of a hint. But she didn't. Maybe because she was drunk. Maybe because she wanted to rekindle the looking-at-the-river moment.

'Married,' she said. 'Children.'

'Adele,' he said, putting down his glass.

'I don't mean now,' she had told him hurriedly. Then laughed. He didn't laugh with her. 'Of course I don't mean this minute,' she said. 'But the right man . . . you see, with the right man . . .'

'Adele,' he repeated.

'Don't tell anyone, will you?' she said. She had meant to sound coquettish, but it came out all wrong. Suddenly it didn't sound flirtatious at all. It didn't even sound attractive. It sounded terminally, embarrassingly, *excruciatingly embarrassingly* stupid. She had just told him her darkest secret – that she wanted children, and she wanted them soon, and was looking for the man, and – *Lord help her!* – she had just more or less told him that he was that man – and now here he was, looking at her as if she'd just confessed to being a mass murderer.

She had fought hard against the rising tide of horror.

'I mean, it isn't a secret,' she lied, 'but with the right man, you know, and I thought . . .'

'Don't even say it,' he said.

There was a moment of absolute silence. It was rapidly followed by at least ten more moments of absolute silence.

Then Jack shook his head. 'Oh, Adele,' he said. 'I'm sorry.'

'Don't be,' she said. 'I don't know why I said all that. Forget it.'

He was staring at the floor.

'There's been a misunderstanding here,' he said.

'No, no . . .' she began.

'Yes. Listen . . .'

'Forget it,' she said. 'Please.'

'Adele,' he interrupted. 'I'm seeing somebody already.'

God, will you please, WILL YOU PLEASE, just obliterate this evening? Can you turn the world back a couple of hours? Even a couple of minutes? Please . . .

'Oh,' she said. 'Right.'

'I'm sorry.'

'No, no . . . of course . . .'

'I shouldn't have come here,' he said, getting up.

Of course you shouldn't. Where does this someone think you are tonight? You mean you're sleeping with her? You mean sleeping with her, don't you? Of course you do. Of course you do, you . . . You brought me flowers. What was that all about, the flowers?

'Of course you should,' she heard herself say. 'Just dinner.'

'No. I didn't think. You see . . .'

'It doesn't matter,' she said. 'Look, have another glass.'

An insane babble of confusion raged through her head.

Flowers?

Why come at all!

To dinner!

What someone?

Who?

Who is she? What's her name? Do I know her? WHO?

He was picking up his coat. 'I'm well known for getting signals fucked up,' he said. 'I really . . .'

'It's fine,' she said. 'Fine.'

Fucked up! I should think you did, yes.

'Goodbye,' he said, at the door. He fixed her with that look again, the attentive, sexy, lingering look, the look that she had thought she understood, and now didn't understand at all, and she said, 'Goodbye.'

He paused on the stairs on the way down, and looked back at her.

She could have killed herself there and then for still being at the door, watching. Probably with a vacant, sad, poodle expression.

God!

'I'm sorry,' he said. 'I'm sorry, Adele.'

There was a soft, but insistent, knocking at the toilet door.

With a wrench, Adele brought herself back to the present.

'What is it?' she asked.

'Miss Buchanan?' came a whisper.

It was Carly, one of the researchers.

'Yes,' she said. She stood up, and picked her shoe from the floor.

'Are you all right?'

'Yes,' Adele said, through gritted teeth.

'Can you come out?'

'Look,' Adele replied angrily. 'I will come out when I want to come out, so leave me alone.'

'Yes,' Carly said, on the other side of the door. Under the gap, Adele could see Carly's feet, encased sensibly in trainers.

For a split second, Adele longed to be in those trainers. To be unknown, and twenty-one.

'Please go away,' Adele whispered, almost to herself.

'I can't,' Carly replied plaintively. 'It's Lawrence Bugle. He sent me to look for you. I've been looking for half an hour, and . . .'

'And what?' Adele demanded.

'He wants to see you right away.'

6

Meg didn't have to wait long to see her mother when she got to Halfpenny Acre. Abigail was already standing on the doorstep, wringing her hands.

There was no greeting at all when Meg got out of the car – or rather, none of the more normal greetings.

'Hurry up!' Abigail shouted. 'He'll be here any minute.'

'Who will?' Meg asked, locking the car door.

'The man,' Abigail replied, hurrying back into the hallway.

'Horrendous,' Meg said.

'Is he?' Abigail asked. 'But I got him from the Yellow Pages.'

'The journey,' Meg said. 'In case you asked, which you didn't.'

'But he's only to come from Sherborne,' Abigail retorted. 'How can a journey from Sherborne be horrendous?'

'*My* journey,' Meg said. 'From London. And thanks for the cup of tea.'

'It's on its back legs.' Abigail's eyes strayed to the couch, wedged half in and half out of the sitting room.

'Just milk,' Meg said. She put her bag down wearily and opened the flap, checking her mobile phone to make absolutely sure that it was still switched on.

Abigail turned round to stare at her. 'What on earth

are you talking about?' she demanded.

Meg sighed. 'Me,' she said. 'Would it be too much to ask for a cup of tea? I'm absolutely shattered.'

'I'll put the kettle on in a minute,' Abigail said. 'This is an emergency.'

Meg stared at the couch. 'What are you doing?'

'I am trying,' Abigail retorted, 'if you would listen to me for half a minute, to move it into the sitting room.'

'But that's where it usually is.'

'Well, *I want it back there*,' Abigail cried, as if this comment had just broken the last reserves of her patience. 'It's been in the hall and it's been in the kitchen! For heaven's sake, Margaret! Why are you always so *awkward*!'

Meg paled. She edged round the couch and heaved on the back legs, stuck under a ruck of carpet.

'Why didn't Harry help you?' she asked, as they manhandled the enormous bulk back to its original position.

'He's very busy,' Abigail said. 'He's working.'

Meg pulled the couch straight.

She wasn't working. She didn't have a job. She hadn't had a job since she had been made redundant from the patent attorney's where she had used to work, just off Chancery Lane. And she hadn't applied for another job because the run-up to Will's departure had been so fraught. None of which was worth explaining to Abigail.

As far as Abigail was concerned, Meg had lost her job and hadn't bothered to find another. Whereas Harry was slaving night and day – actually occupied in hard physical labour.

Poor Harry.

'Nothing looks right anywhere,' Abigail said. She pulled off her rubber gloves.

Meg tried to damp down the rising red tide in her head. To be more accurate, this was a rising red tide in her left eye. This peculiar phenomenon – she really did see red, and it really was in just one eye, which she had had checked out by her GP, who saw nothing wrong and plainly thought she was off her trolley – only ever occurred in conversation with Abigail.

She had once mentioned it to Will.

'Red?' he had asked, amazed. 'You actually see red?'

'In one eye.'

'When Abigail talks?'

'Yes.'

Will started to laugh. 'How long has this been going on?' he had asked.

'Since my back molars stopped aching.'

'Your back molars?'

She had started to laugh with him. 'I used to grind my teeth whenever my mother spoke,' she admitted. 'I used to get headaches. As soon as I realised what I was doing, I made an effort to stop it. But . . .'

'But then you started to see red,' Will said.

'Quite.'

Will had come over to her, and given her a bear hug that almost cracked her spine. 'Just stop talking to her then,' he said. 'Before she gives you a stroke.'

'I can't just stop talking to my mother,' Meg had told him.

'Then sort her out,' he'd replied.

'How?' she had asked.

They had both thought about this for almost a minute.

'Left uppercut,' Will finally decided.

A rattling sound wrenched Meg back to the present.

Abigail was rearranging the ornaments in the dresser.

'What man will be here?' Meg asked her.

'Man?' Abigail said.

'When I turned up,' Meg replied, with overstated patience, 'you said that a man was going to be here any minute.'

'The man from the estate agent. And someone to view.'

'You mean a buyer?'

'No,' Abigail said. 'I mean a viewer. It's an appointment *to view*. I told you on the phone, Meg.'

She disappeared into the kitchen.

Indeed, Abigail had told Meg on the phone. She had rung last night to tell Meg, in a series of twittering squawks, that someone was coming to look at the house, and that it was a *perfect tip*, and that all the furniture was in *the wrong place*, and that no-one had helped her clean the windows *in years*, and that there was cow slurry *up to the roof*.

There was cow slurry, of course. Or, more accurately, a few cowpats. In the field next to the house. Which had cows in it. As usual.

Meg looked around the room. It was immaculate. As usual.

And the windows gleamed. As usual.

She followed Abigail to the kitchen.

Her mother was laying a tray with her best cups.

'A mug will be fine,' Meg said.

'I can't give strangers mugs,' Abigail replied.

Meg sat down.

What the hell am I doing here, she thought.

I shouldn't be here at all.

I should be sitting in my own kitchen, waiting to hear about Will.

'I'm waiting to hear about Will,' she said.

Abigail stopped filling the kettle. 'Oh, of course,' she murmured. 'Oh, yes. Poor Will.'

'His radio is down.'

'Yes,' Abigail said. 'Snow. Poor Will.'

'A storm.'

'Look,' Abigail said. 'I listen to Radio Four. I know about Will.'

Her mother's rudeness was, as usual, a symptom of her embarrassment. Embarrassment because what was happening to Will was undeniably serious, and because Abigail had just realised that she had been tactless and unsympathetic. But, since Abigail had perhaps only once or twice in her life expressed any kind of sympathy for Meg, and certainly had never apologised to her, she was at a complete loss what to say.

Various words seemed to be struggling to emerge from Abigail's mouth. An almighty battle went on, evidently between *oh darling, I'm so sorry, you must be out of your mind with worry, please forgive me for making you drive all the way down here*, and the final version.

Which was, 'Harry.'

A car was blowing its horn on the drive. Abigail sprinted from the kitchen like Linford Christie, to meet Harry and Penny as they got to the front door.

'Thank God you're here, darling,' Abigail said, hugging her son to her bosom.

'Hello, Ma,' Harry said. 'You shifted it back, then.'

Meg walked out into the hall.

'Oh Meg,' Penny Arthur cried, brushing past Harry and Abigail, and holding out her arms. 'You poor kid. I heard the news about Will.'

Meg smiled as she returned the hug. 'Hello, Penny.'

'Any developments?' Penny asked. 'Have they found him yet?'

'None,' Meg said. 'No.'

'Oh, darling. You must be worried sick.'

Meg couldn't say a word.

It had always been like this. Penny was one of Meg's earliest memories – a much younger Penny of course, a Penny with auburn hair that always spilled from two tortoiseshell combs, a Penny in a shirtwaist dress with a checked green shirt – and, in Meg's memory, she was rushing down the lawn of the house.

It had been summer. She must have been about six. The two ancient apple trees at the end of the garden had been heavy with fruit. Meg had built herself a tree house in the oldest and biggest – a scanty affair with a couple of planks from the potting shed, and a bit of rope to pull herself up with. The tree house, in all its two-plank glory, had crashed to the ground. Meg had fallen about eight feet on to the lawn.

And it was Penny who had come running. Abigail behind. But much further behind, Harry on one hip.

'Are you hurt, darling? Are you hurt?' Penny had asked.

Meg remembered the perfume. A very old-fashioned lilies-of-the-valley. Flowers. Penny always smelled of flowers.

The same memory came hurtling back now, and promptly filled Meg's eyes with tears.

'Don't cry,' Penny whispered. 'He'll come back.'

She took a handkerchief from her pocket and pressed it into Meg's hands.

'Oh Penny,' Meg said.

'He's here!' Abigail cried.

Both Penny and Meg turned to look down the drive, both women half-expecting, given their conversation, to see Will Churchill-Twines mushing a dog team towards them. But it wasn't Will, of course. It was a green Range Rover.

'The man, the man,' Abigail said. Her hands fluttered at her side like two frantic birds.

'What on earth are you getting yourself so worked up for?' Penny demanded.

'They might not take it,' Abigail said.

'Good,' Penny retorted.

Abigail glared at her. 'If you're going to be like that,' she said, 'you can go away.'

A man got out of the Range Rover. They all looked expectantly for the buyer who was supposed to be with him, but the estate agent was alone. Meg's heart sank a little as she watched the man stride towards them, resplendent in yellow flannel trousers, striped shirt, and checked tweed jacket. He had his hand out while he was still ten feet away, and a huge grin plastered to his face.

'Mrs Randall,' he said. 'How lovely, how lovely.'

Abigail shook his hand.

'House and garden looking wonderful. Wonderful,' he said.

Abigail looked behind him, to the car. 'The viewer?' she asked.

But Land Agent Man wasn't listening. He was busy shaking everyone else's hand and saying every last word of every sentence twice. 'Super, super,' he responded, as they all introduced themselves. 'Whole family. Family.'

'The viewer,' Abigail repeated.

'Ah yes, viewer, viewer,' he replied. 'Can't come. No. No.'

'But we had an appointment,' Abigail protested.

'Absolutely. Oh quite, quite,' he said. 'But I have something better than a viewer, rather. Rather!'

Meg sighed. 'Would you like some tea?' she asked. 'I know I would.'

They trooped through to the sitting room, where Land Agent Man refused to sit until all the ladies were sitting, which was a tad awkward as Penny was standing on principle, because she didn't like the look of him, and couldn't bear any man in yellow trousers who called her a lady with that patronising tone. Eventually, she sat on the window seat, with her arms crossed.

'Marvellously proportioned room,' the agent smarmed. 'South-facing leaded windows, lovely aspect. Lovely aspect indeed.'

'The windows leak in winter,' Penny said. 'The septic tank smells in the summer.'

'Why did the buyer drop out?' Harry asked.

The agent glanced at Penny, then back at Harry. 'Oh, he didn't drop out. Not at all,' he said.

'Well, where is he, then?' Abigail asked.

'Just let me just show you the details we drew up for you,' the agent said. He passed out a small, glossy folder, with a colour photograph of Halfpenny Acre on the front, looking sublime in late afternoon sunlight.

'Wisteria came out well, I thought,' the agent said.

'It has a very short flowering period,' Penny

muttered. She only glanced at the details before flinging them to one side. 'And you won't get anyone buying it for that price,' she added.

'It's a bit steep, Ma,' Harry said.

'It's nothing of the sort,' Abigail said. 'It's what Mr Hargreaves here recommended.'

'Terribly reasonable,' the agent agreed. 'Buyers from London, snap it up. Snap it right up!'

'Oh, come on,' Penny chided.

The agent smiled broadly. 'In point of fact, that is precisely what has happened,' he said smugly. 'Snapped up this very day at the asking price.'

'What!' Abigail said.

'Oh no,' Penny groaned.

'A client in the media,' Hargreaves insisted cheerily. 'Fell in love with it. Fell in love with the knot garden.' He turned the details to the back page and showed the picture of the knot garden on the reverse.

Penny stared at him, aghast at the news that she had lost her garden by her own design, literally.

Meg came back into the room with the tea tray.

'It's gone,' Abigail said.

'What has?' Meg asked.

'The house,' Harry said.

'The garden,' Penny murmured.

Meg set the tray down slowly on the table.

'For a fortune,' Harry said.

'To a man from the newspapers,' Penny said. 'It'll have a triple garage and a satellite dish in no time.'

'Not the newspapers, actually,' Hargreaves said. 'The TV.'

'Is it an actor?' Abigail asked.

'Is it Carol Smillie?' Harry asked.

'It'll be bloody Charlie Dimmock,' Penny moaned.

'Hey,' Harry grinned. 'Wicked-oh.'

'There'll be water everywhere,' Penny said.

'Is it Sadie Frost?' Harry said.

'Is it David Frost?' Meg asked.

'No, no,' Hargreaves said. 'It's a lady.'

Penny put her head in her hands. 'Satellite dish,' she whispered. 'Right up on the thatch. I knew it.'

'She's very keen,' Hargreaves told them triumphantly, 'very keen indeed.'

'Who is it?' Meg said. 'Anyone we know?'

Hargreaves smiled enigmatically. 'That,' he said, 'I am not allowed to reveal.'

7

Adele closed her eyes momentarily while she waited for Lawrence Bugle's secretary to open the door.

She was standing in the upper reaches of the building – in a thickly carpeted recess at the farthest end of a thickly carpeted corridor. As you came out of the lifts on the eighth floor, you immediately got the message that you were about to be admitted to A Presence.

There was no laminated flooring here; no framed prints of bygone hit gameshows; no silk flowers in painted jampots, masquerading as floral displays. Everything was hushed and discreet, and designed to obliterate completely the idea that the occupant was engaged in anything so tawdry as trade.

On the wall facing you as you came out of the lift was an enormous shield, painted with Lawrence Bugle's motto – 'I Hear The Call'. Just to underline the point, the shield was decorated with eighteen bugles, representing, so Adele had been told by The Presence himself, the eighteen years he had spent working his way to the top. There were no severed heads on the shield, however – which would have also represented Bugle's rise to power. Or perhaps knives in the back, Adele had thought to herself, as she turned left, towards Bugle's offices.

The rest of the corridor underlined the great man's

sense of his own importance. A sixteenth-century tapestry depicted various knights bowing with offerings before a knight. Two huge paintings showed a muscle-bound warrior first saving, and then ravaging, a damsel who evidently wasn't too fussed about where she had left her clothes. At the very door of Bugle's room stood a suit of armour designed to fit a giant; and the axe that accompanied it hung halfway out across the threshold.

Everything in the corridor was designed to give the same message: that Lawrence Bugle was a desperate beast of a man.

Suddenly, Adele heard his voice from beyond the mahogany door.

'Annie,' he squeaked. 'Don't let go.'

'I'm not letting go, Lawrence,' came his sixty-year-old secretary's retort. 'Just hurry up.'

'Careful!' Lawrence cried. 'It's no good at all if the leash is slack.'

'This leash is as tight as it'll go,' Annie was heard to protest. 'For God's sake, Lawrence, you're cutting off the blood supply to my wrist.'

'I have to get it over with!' Bugle cried, almost plaintively. 'Oh – sod it and double sod it, Annie. Poor Dido! Now look what you've done.'

There was a yelp, and a sound as if something very heavy had fallen to the floor.

Adele knocked again.

The door opened.

Annie looked out – dishevelled, her grey rinse in need of a swift shampoo-and-set. Annie wore her spectacles on a chain around her neck, but, just at the moment, they looked as if they were wearing her. The chain had knotted itself twice around her neck and the glasses were hanging down her back. She seemed as though she had just been strung up in them, like a noose. Irritatedly, the older woman started pulling them free. 'Thank God you're here,' she told Adele, and opened the door wider. 'I'm telling you, and I'm telling him. If that dog doesn't go, then I will. It's nearly strangled me!' She leaned forward, grabbed Adele's arm, and whispered, 'It hates me, you know. It *hates* me.'

Adele stepped aside to let Annie pass. She peered around the door and into the room.

Lawrence Bugle was sitting in the middle of the floor, weeping.

'Lawrence?' Adele asked.

He looked up. 'Oh . . . come in, Adele,' he said. He took a large handkerchief out of his pocket, and blew his nose.

Adele eyed him unappreciatively. It couldn't be said, by the wildest stretch of the imagination, that Lawrence was an attractive man.

Perhaps he used to be, back in the sixties. She could just imagine him in a paisley shirt with a scarf, and cerise pink trousers. Now, however, age – together with thousands upon thousands of dinners and bottles of wine – had taken its toll. Lawrence was about five feet ten inches tall, but he was almost as wide; a huge, treble-chinned whale of a man, with hardly any hair, an extremely red face, and rampaging high blood pressure.

He also loved the sound of his own voice, and wouldn't use one word where a whole paragraph would do. He was particularly fond of using archaic words, because he prided himself on being a guardian of the English language. Which was ironic, as he imported a vast number of American sitcoms.

He gazed at her now, shaking his head and his associated companies of neck flesh. Somewhere off to the right, Adele could hear another snuffling sound.

'I don't know what else to do for her,' Lawrence mumbled. 'Poor Dido. My poor little *canis familiaris*, my doggy, my hound.'

Slowly, Adele turned her head.

Dido, the white Highland Terrier, was sitting right in the centre of the overstuffed English-country-house couch.

Last year, Lawrence – at the Christmas party – had told Adele all about this couch. It was a Pompadour sofa, he said, with a lyre-shaped front, and dated from the late Regency period. Or possibly William IV. Privately, Adele thought this was very appropriate. Way back in time – the Janet Tebbs time – she had taken a history module at college, when her brain was still required, and had been more important than the size of her buttocks or her ability to squeak appreciatively at flower arrangements. She remembered William IV, the Sailor King, who had distinguished himself by living with an actress for twenty-one years, who gave him ten children, before dumping her to marry the eldest daughter of the Duke of Saxe-Meiningen. He had seven years on the throne before dying to make way for Victoria, a prime example of a chauvinist being eclipsed by a successful female.

Like the style of the sofa, Lawrence Bugle had also had a mistress for twenty years, whom he had cruelly dropped so that he could marry a halfwit called Elspeth Webberley-Synge, whose father owned Scotland and a merchant bank. Elspeth had been thirty-one years younger than Lawrence, and had a father fixation. There was no other earthly reason, Adele thought, why a girl that age should hitch herself to the gibbering buffoon before her. The marriage had lasted precisely ten months, and extinguished itself in a thermonuclear cloud of recriminations. Lawrence only just kept Dido's name out of the courts.

He had been single now, aged sixty-one, for a year.

Adele looked at him sourly, from the top of his shining bald head, down through the pale blue ghostlike eyes, and on to the pale pink bow tie, powder-blue suit and lilac-coloured socks that made up this morning's ensemble.

'It's anal glands,' Lawrence whispered, wiping his eyes. 'Such a vet! What a doctrinaire practitioner! What a pedantic theorist! I shall never go there again.'

Adele looked at Dido, who glared back before burying herself in her bottom and chewing savagely.

'She had her glands evacuated last night,' Lawrence sighed. 'And now she won't let me put cream on them.'

Dido emerged from her toilette and stared menacingly at her master, as if blaming him for the indignities that had been heaped upon her and, more disturbingly – as if she were plotting the way she could get her own back on him.

'Lawrence,' Adele ventured, 'do you think you ought to . . . you know, assert your authority with her?'

'What on earth do you mean?'

'Well, don't they say that about dogs?' Adele asked. 'Don't you have to be pack leader with them?' She glanced back at Dido. 'Not let them sit on the furniture, that sort of thing.'

A look of horror crossed Lawrence's face. 'But Dido *loves* that couch,' he said. 'And after all she's been

through, after –' he dropped his voice – 'after *Aeneas*
– and now this!' he shuddered. 'How could I refuse
her a bit of comfort, when she's positively con-
dylomatous? Discoidal prominences! Poor love!'

The Dido and Aeneas tragedy had been played out
in full colour on Adele's very programme. She thought
that it had quite possibly shortened her resident
animal expert's life.

They had a regular slot on *Hey! Today!* for a vet.
He was a nice man, but a rather anxious, rather fidgety
person, who mysteriously didn't like sheep, but was
perfectly OK with every other animal. He had had an
event with a sheep once, he told Adele in the green
room one morning – but he was very happy with farm
livestock generally, as long as he didn't turn his back
to them.

Adele had explained that she doubted they would
ever be asking his advice on sheep, as the programme
would be concentrating on problems with domestic
pets. The vet's face had lit up at this information.

'Schnauzers,' he said, happily. 'Will you have any
Schnauzers? I love Schnauzers.' He had gripped
Adele's arm suddenly. 'But not poodles,' he added
hastily. 'Not . . . anything woolly . . .'

The first programme with him had been a
resounding success. He discovered some warts on a
guinea pig, and was filmed giving a cat an enema, and
he went off whistling at the news that, the following
week, they would bring some rescued puppies into the
studio so that he could comment on behavioural
problems. 'Impose pack leadership on them,' he had
said, airily, as he went out of the door. 'That's all it
takes.'

It had worked pretty well with the first two dogs,

two adorable Labradors who did nothing more troublesome than chase a couple of cameramen. Adele thought it was all going fine.

And then came Dido and Aeneas.

They weren't called that then, of course; the rescue kennels had nicknamed them Widdle and Puke, and they arrived in a basket that had been chewed, apparently, by something very large indeed.

Dido was lifted out. Adele took her on her knee. The vet ruffled her hair and, as he pulled the fluffy fringe out of the dog's eyes, Adele saw him pause for a moment.

'Now . . . now here,' he said, 'here we have quite a . . . boisterous pup, by all accounts, and . . .' He stopped. He was staring into Dido's eyes. 'And what you have to do,' he continued, 'what you have to do, is to establish dominance with eye contact, and . . . and . . .'

Adele felt the puppy in her lap stiffen. Its claws dug down into her thighs. 'Ouch,' she murmured.

'And you have to stare at the dog,' the vet was continuing, 'stare at the dog and make them break eye contact, and whoever breaks eye contact . . .'

Adele could see that the man's eyes were watering.

'Whoever blinks,' he said, 'is . . . not the dominant . . . not the dominant . . .'

Tears crept out from under one eyelid.

'Whoever . . . what you have to . . .'

He picked Dido out of Adele's lap and stared into her eyes, holding the puppy level with his face.

'Eye contact,' he breathed. 'You mustn't . . . break . . .'

Dido fastened her teeth on his nose.

There was a flurry of activity while the basket was

retrieved, and the dog was unhinged from the vet, and stuffed back into it. By way of distraction, Adele lifted Aeneas out.

'Are you all right?' she asked the man.

'Yed,' he replied.

'This is Puke,' she said.

Puke sat shivering in Adele's grasp. If Dido – alias Widdle's – glance had been stone, Puke's was tissue paper. His little eyes flitted in terror about the studio, and, when the vet looked at him, he lowered his head between his paws and whimpered.

As it happened, Lawrence Bugle saw that programme. He had rung Adele up as soon as it had finished.

'I want a nice little dog like that,' he told her. 'Get me that nice little dog. And her sibling.'

And so Widdle and Puke had been transformed to Dido and Aeneas, and had, like Cinderella, found themselves taken out of their life of total rejection and into a life of total pampering. Nothing had been too good for them. They rode with Lawrence in his Mercedes, and they sat with Lawrence at his desk. They accompanied Lawrence on his royal progresses through the studios, and they sat next to him while he hired and fired. And, just to show that she had not forgotten her humble beginnings, Dido both widdled and puked wherever and whenever the fancy took her.

Dido was always in front, trotting along with her head held high like a circus pony. She was a born leader, a true Alexandra the Great of a dog, a Julia Caesar, an Anita the Hun. If Dido had been a human female, she would have had Margaret Thatcher locked up in a cupboard in a straitjacket in ten minutes flat. She would have had Russell Crowe

whimpering inside the gladiator tunnel, afraid to
come out. She was a very short dog who thought she
was seven feet three, and a very light dog who thought
she weighed twenty stone and could win the World
Wrestling Championships. This was a dog who had
no idea at all that she was a dog. She was, quite
simply, mistress of all she surveyed, unimpressed by
anything on two legs, particularly – and sadly – things
that walked on two legs, had ginger hair, wore bow
ties, and called her *Dido Diddle-dums*.

If Dido was Margaret Thatcher's fiercer sister in a
terrier suit, then Aeneas, unfortunately, was a very
junior minister indeed. Aeneas walked three steps
behind Dido, trying to keep out of her line of sight. If
Dido turned, Aeneas would whip off to one side and
flatten himself to the wall, hoping to mould himself to
the plaster. Dido had only to draw back her lips in the
faintest semblance of a snarl, and Aeneas would try to
burrow to Australia.

God only knew what terrors Aeneas had endured in
the puppy-carrying basket, or what horrors had lain in
wait for him when the kennel doors had closed and the
lights went out. Whatever had happened, it had left a
scar – for Aeneas was a shivering, mixed-up, walked-
over dog of the first order, a dog so far down the
pecking order that even an aged hen would have got
the better of him.

And Aeneas might still have been cowering in
Dido's shadow, had it not been for the laurel bushes in
the car park.

Every morning when Lawrence arrived at work, he
would walk Dido and Aeneas round the parking lot so
that they could – Lawrence simpered – *see to their little
bits and pieces*. The fact that Dido only ever saw to her

little bits and pieces in full view of visitors in reception didn't seem to deter him. Aeneas, by contrast, seemed anxious to obliged. Dido's brother would rush from the Mercedes and hurl himself into the flowerbeds, where he pebbledashed everything that grew there. It wasn't the poor dog's fault: he had been psyched out by Dido in the back of the car since West Chertsey, and his bowels had turned to water.

Everyone parking their cars turned away, holding their noses, from Aeneas while he redecorated the geraniums, but Dido saw the whole thing as light entertainment. Every morning, while Aeneas squatted down, Dido would creep around behind him and hide herself in the laurel bushes. Just as Aeneas would finish, tottering weakly from the soil and staggering up the drive, Dido would hurtle from the laurels at forty miles an hour, fasten her teeth on Aeneas's shoulder, and bring him, in a flurry of fur, down to the ground. It was a dazzling feat of doggy warfare, and one that Aeneas knew very well was coming, but was too preoccupied to avoid.

As the weeks went on, Aeneas seemed to get thinner and thinner, hovering over his task, all the while keeping one petrified eye on the laurels. Adele had to admit – having seen this spectacle dozens of times – that Dido had the attack off to a T. The dog would cleverly vary the timing, so that some mornings she would emerge like a white rocket just as Aeneas was still settling down, and, at other times, she would leave it for a whole agonising minute, the laurels waving unthreateningly in the morning breeze, and then launch herself just as Aeneas had become convinced that, for once, he had been spared.

It must have been hell.

In fact, hell began to be written in Aeneas's face. The look of fear degenerated into something else – something darker, something more desperate. The shivering stopped and rigidity took over; until Aeneas's daily walk looked more like he had substituted stilts for legs, and was having trouble getting his knees to bend at all. He seemed to have gone into a premature state of rigor mortis. Perhaps because he thought that every day would be his last.

And yet, because there is a God in heaven sometimes – when He hasn't left the answerphone on – Aeneas did get his revenge.

One day in January, when the ground was frosted over, and Aeneas had spent a very painful few seconds picking his way over the frozen soil, Dido emerged from the laurels too early. Impossible to say why she timed it badly that day: maybe her bloodlust just got the better of her.

She ran at full throttle out of the bushes, missed Aeneas's shoulder, and sank her teeth into Aeneas's head.

There was a moment of silence, a moment during which Aeneas was supposed to run yelping into the TV Centre. But Aeneas did nothing at all. Dido eventually unfastened her teeth and looked about her embarrassedly. She looking inquiringly into Aeneas's face, and then at his bottom, and then turned away.

Aeneas took a single step, and grabbed Dido's rump. Without even pausing to see the effect, he planted his feet hard in the flowerbed and shook his head. Dido was lifted an inch or two off the ground, enough to have her front feet barely scraping the soil. She tried to curl herself around to get Aeneas's nose, but it was no good. With a single effort, her brother hauled her up in the air, and threw her over the wall.

Several witnesses – including Lawrence – stood nearby in shock. They had seen a West Highland Terrier fly over a six-foot wall, but they didn't believe that they had seen a West Highland Terrier fly over a six-foot wall. From the invisible other side, they could hear Dido whining, having landed head first in a builder's skip.

They looked at Aeneas, and Aeneas looked back at them.

Then, with a bark of manic triumph, Dido's little brother was gone.

Lawrence had found it very hard to get over this traitorous villainy.

Both he and Adele stared at the dog now, the dog on the Pompadour couch, who had half of it in her mouth, chewing for all she was worth.

'Poor Dido,' Lawrence said. 'She's utterly traumatised.'

Adele tore her gaze away.

'Lawrence,' she said. 'You wanted to see me.'

'Did I?' he said, distractedly. 'Oh yes.' He straightened up to his full height. And width. 'Come and sit down.'

They adjourned to the other furnishing delight in the room. It was a love seat, or what Lawrence preferred to call a conversation piece, the most awkward contraption ever designed, and hopeless either for loving or talking on. Four seats, their triangular backs harnessed together in the centre, faced the four points of the compass. Lawrence liked to sit on the seat that faced into the room, and where he put you depended on how much he liked you. Favoured stars sat on his right-hand side; fading ones on the left. If you had really pissed him off, you got the seat facing the window.

To her dismay, Lawrence showed Adele the left-hand seat.

'Now, darling,' he began, 'I've got a surprise for you.'

Oh God, she thought. *That's a bad sign.* Lawrence's surprises usually took the form of a P45 and five minutes to get your stuff out of the building.

'Is there anything wrong?' she ventured, her heart in her mouth.

'Wrong?' he echoed. 'Nooooooo, no, no, no. Nothing awry. Amiss. Nothing.'

I'm in the anorak already, she thought. I'm making my way down the beach on *Children In Need* night.

'You are,' Lawrence continued, 'one of the brightest little twinklers in my heaven. We enjoy a tremendous coalescent comprehension.'

She was undoubtedly marching across the shingle to find the lifeboatmen.

'Except . . .'

And talking to the men dressed as Wonder Woman.

'Except?' she echoed.

Lawrence leaned back in the seat, and patted his lap. 'Come, Dido Diddle,' he called, 'come to Daddy.'

'Is it the show?' Adele asked.

'The show? No, no.'

'I can let the chef go,' she offered. 'He's just got a thing about entrails. I can let him go.'

'I adore sweetbreads,' Lawrence said, watching Dido trot across. 'And Dido has an extraordinary relish for liver.'

'Oh, right.' She shrugged, smiling. 'He stays, then. Fine.'

'It's not the chef, darling,' Lawrence murmured. 'It's you.'

She wanted to say, *Me?* Brightly, conversationally. As if she didn't feel threatened. As if she couldn't see the figures of her mortgage repayments racing across the room towards her. But she didn't say anything. The words were stuck in her throat.

Lawrence half-turned towards her. Dido fixed her with a venomous stare. 'We're very worried about you, Dido and I,' Lawrence said. 'You're looking a teeny bit disjasket.'

'I am?' she said. 'Is that bad?'

He smiled patronisingly. 'Tired, darling. Weary. Jaded.'

Tired!

'I'm fine,' she trilled. 'I'm not the least bit disjasket, Lawrence, honestly.' Even to her own ears, she sounded like a budgie being strangled.

'I think you should have Fridays off.'

'Off?' she repeated. 'Fridays?'

Friday was the best day of the week. It had the highest viewing figures.

'I've had an idea,' Lawrence said.

'What sort of an idea?' she said.

'A couple.'

'A couple of ideas?'

'No, darling,' he retorted, and he tut-tutted.

Never before had she heard Lawrence Bugle tut-tut in reference to something she said. The nearest he had ever come was to fix her for a few long seconds with what he liked to think was his penetrating, searching stare. But this noise . . . 'Tsssk, tsssk, tsssk, hmmph,' was just like a death warrant. It implied foolishness on her part, impatience on his. She felt the hairs on the back of her neck bristle, not with fear, but with outrage. How dare he *tsssk* her! How dare he *tut* her!

'Lawrence,' she said, 'I want Fridays. There's nothing wrong with Fridays.'

'It's the weekend, you see,' he replied smoothly.

'But we do makeovers on Fridays!'

'I know.'

'And *What's For The Weekend*,' she said. 'We *do* the weekends, Lawrence.'

She noticed Dido flexing her front paws.

'Well, darling, actually you don't,' Lawrence retorted. 'I mean, you don't get anyone inspired. There's a definite lack of stimulation, of illumination. A quite visible deficiency of afflatus. You don't do, "Let's All Get Moving For The Weekend." You do, "Let's All Give Up For The Weekend."'

'I do not!' she cried. And she thought, digging her nails into her palms, *I'll give you afflatus, you hairless megalomaniac. Whatever it is.*

'I fell asleep last Friday,' he told her.

She stared at him. Dido stared back. The dog's top lip was twitching.

'You fell asleep,' she repeated. 'Were you sick?'

'During *What's For The Weekend*,' he said. 'I mean, honestly, Adele. A day at a Steam Fair. For God's sake!'

'It was irony,' Adele said. 'The man with the hand-cranking . . . And the pig wrestle . . .'

'You see?' Lawrence demanded. 'There you have it! A hand-cranked pig. That's what Fridays are. I'd have more fun watching Prime Minister's Questions.'

'But the makeovers!'

'Frumps in new frocks.'

'Lawrence, these are our audience.'

He shook his head. So did Dido.

'Our audience are not frumps in new frocks at all,' he said. 'They are ladettes taking a sickie. To use common parlance.'

She tried to clamp her mouth shut, because it had just dropped open. With her lips compressed together, she counted to ten, watching while Lawrence stroked Dido's neck.

'Have you been reading market research again?' she asked, when she felt less choked.

'I have indeed,' he said. 'Most certainly.'

'And market research says . . .'

'That four per cent of the population take Mondays off because they hate work. And six per cent take Fridays off, because they hate work.'

'So take Mondays from me,' Adele retorted.

'Aha,' Lawrence said, holding up one hand. 'But. Of the four per cent who take Mondays off, sixty-seven per cent are men with a hangover. And. Of the six per cent who take Fridays off, eighty-two per cent are girls under twenty-five.'

'What a load of crap,' Adele said.

'It is not crap,' Lawrence said. 'I commissioned it myself.'

'All right,' Adele replied. 'I'll do man things on Mondays and teen tart things on Fridays. We'll makeover everyone to look like Britney Spears. Charlotte Church. Jamie Bell. In fact, we'll makeover Charlotte Church to look like Jamie Bell.'

'Don't be silly,' Lawrence said. 'And don't do that with your mouth.'

She stopped in her tracks. 'What thing?'

'This thing,' he said, and drew the sides of his mouth down in a clown's arc of mock despair.

It shut her up. She sat back in the chair as if she had been slapped.

First the *tsssk*. Now the piss-take.

Lawrence gave her a pat on the knee. 'You see what you're doing,' he told her. 'You're working round the same concepts. Even when you're making fun of my research. For which,' he added, 'I thank you, incidentally.' He shook his head, as if to rid himself of the insult. 'But I don't *want* the same concepts,' he continued, in a slightly louder and more petulant voice. 'I don't just want someone different making-over someone different, or something younger walking round a different kind of garden doing a different kind of flower arrangement. And when I talk about weekends, I don't want people even thinking about garden fêtes.'

Adele looked past him, at the torn sofa on the other side of the room.

The last little speech of Lawrence's had contained sixty-eight words.

But she had only heard one.

Younger.

There was a moment of silence.

Then, Dido farted.

Lawrence smiled indulgently. 'Dear me,' he said. 'Manners, Dido.'

Adele brought her gaze back to man and dog.

'Who have you got in mind?' she asked.

'Dido shot a bunny,' he said.

'I didn't mean, who have you got in mind for farting,' Adele sighed. 'Who is going to do Fridays?'

'Belinda and Jack,' he told her.

The word *Jack* really threw her for a second. She felt herself blush, and cursed inwardly at this giveaway. 'Jack,' she repeated.

Lawrence started to laugh. 'Oh, don't pretend you don't know who Jack is.'

If she felt mortified before, it was nothing to what she felt now. The walls seemed to crowd in on her for a second; the air was sucked out of her throat. How did Lawrence know about her and Jack? *Did* he know about her and Jack? The *details*?

'Jack is my personal assistant,' she replied. 'He's never been in front of a camera in his life, except when the weather girl fainted.'

'Quite,' Lawrence said. 'Exactly. Freshness.'

She bit her lip, thinking, *oh, fine. Oh great, fine, lovely.*

Lawrence smiled hugely. 'Dido and I had a brainwave,' he said. 'And as soon as we'd had it, I thought, Dido, you are a very, very, very clever dog. Because we thought, Jack and Belinda. Belinda and Jack. Fun.'

'Fun,' Adele echoed.

'Big Breakfasty. Big Brotherish. Lots of games.'

'Screaming,' Adele said. 'Shots of the crew. Researchers dressed as nuns.'

'Davina McCall jaunts.'

'Tightropes and wheelbarrows.'

'Fast stuff, shouldercams.'

'Uplift bras,' Adele murmured.

'Belinda,' Lawrence breathed.

And Adele knew exactly, without having to ask, which Belinda he was talking about.

Because there was only one Belinda.

It had to be Blanket Belinda from Up-Line Cable. Belinda had been nobody until she bought a body, having had her breasts inflated to a gigantic size. On Up-Line, they used her as a weather girl on the early

morning show – hence the nickname – and she was
well known for getting all the weather appallingly
wrong, pointing at bits of France and calling it Wales,
and giggling through every autocue. Belinda was so
incredibly un-PC, so devastatingly stupid, that she had
gone beyond the bounds of witlessness and almost
come round the other side again, so that her brainless
drivel almost seemed clever, almost Zenlike in its
simplicity. There were some, Adele knew, who
actually thought that Belinda was an Oxford graduate
with a PhD, and that all her fumbling was an act,
devised to hide her enormous IQ.

The truth was less interesting, of course.

Because Belinda was just a twit with a large
chest.

'Belinda,' Adele murmured. 'Jack.'

Lawrence leaned forward and grinned.

'You see?' he said. 'You see? You have an image of
my concept?'

Adele got up. She saw, certainly. She understood.

She understood that Jack, who was a bloody
coward, and a deceiver, a commitment-phobe, and a
bastard, and a person who was not at all handsome, or
sweet-natured, or kind, or good to talk to, not that she
was interested, because he was still a bastard – and
Belinda, who couldn't add two and two – yes, she
understood that these two people, virgins in the art of
broadcasting, hopeless amateurs, *bastards bastards
bastards* . . .

Well, whatever they were, and however low down
they were in television's hall of fame, and however
lacking they were in even the elementary qualities
needed to entertain the nation . . .

One thing was still perfectly obvious.

Whatever they were and whoever they were, they were better equipped to host Fridays than *she* was.

Adele took one last despairing look at Dido, and turned for the door.

8

It was evening when Meg got back to London.

When she had called in at Fleet services, and glanced at her mobile, she had got a text message to meet Michael at Up-Cable at seven. She at once tried Michael's direct line, but he didn't answer. She had got back in the car, wondering if he had heard anything. Wondering if Will was all right.

Deliberately, all the way to the South Bank studios, she kept the radio and her mobile turned off in the car. If something *had* happened to Will, she didn't want Brian Perkins telling her through Radio 4. And she didn't want to be behind the wheel of a car, either, while her mobile screamed at her.

The Up-Line building was a blaze of light as she pulled into the car park.

'Meg Randall,' she said to the security man on the gate.

'Go straight through,' he told her.

She looked in her driving mirror at him, suspiciously, as she manoeuvred the Peugeot into a gap. Only a week before the very same man had taken one look at the broken wing mirror of the car, the rusted headlights, and the thin green line of lichen growing along the rubber window seals, and he had told her to park in the street.

She was trying to lock the door, when Michael came running over.

'You're late,' he said.

'I've been late all day,' she acknowledged.

'Hurry up,' he said and yanked her, by the arm, into the building.

She and Will had first visited Up-Line last year, when the deal for TV coverage had been set up. Will – who got very hot inside any building – had sighed heavily at the tropical temperature inside the offices. Meg vaguely remembered seeing Up-Line's opening a couple of years ago, when the décor of the studios had been orange, yellow and red. She was sure that there had been a little beeping train running round all the upper floors, carrying parcels and messages; now, however, the prospect ahead of her was much bleaker.

Everything had been painted grey. There was a giant picture hanging over Reception of Eric Cramm, Up-Line's Managing Director. On his right shoulder perched the logos of Up-Line's top shows. Not the faces of the presenters, Meg noticed. Just a black-and-white rendering of *Stuff Money* and *Jelly Poo*. *Stuff Money* was an adult gameshow where the contestants had to see how much money they could stuff down their partners' shirts. *Jelly Poo* was a child's game-show where the contestants had to see how much jelly they could stuff down their team's trousers. Between them, the picture of Eric Cramm's face wore all the hallmarks of deep disapproval.

A girl was waiting nervously by the lifts, holding a clipboard to her chest. To Meg's eyes, she looked like a terrified rabbit, and not more than fifteen, with her hair scraped into six ponytails that bounced all over her head as she moved. When she saw them, she seemed to crumple with relief. 'Ooooh, you're here,' she whimpered. 'Oooooh, good.' She jabbed the lift button.

'Traffic,' Meg explained. 'Mothers, brothers, estate agents.'

'Eric Cramm is waiting for us,' Michael said, in Meg's ear. 'Pawing the ground.'

She turned to look at him. 'Is he?' She had met the great man only once, and didn't like him. 'What for?'

'Bit of a crisis,' Michael said.

They got in the lift.

'Top floor, ooooh,' said the girl, hopping from foot to foot. 'Late, late, Mr Cramm, uh-oh.'

'Is he dead?' Meg asked Michael.

He stared at her, astonished.

'Will,' Meg said. 'Is he dead? Just tell me, Michael. Quickly.'

'Will isn't dead,' Michael said.

Relief rushed through her. 'Thank God,' she said. 'Is he injured?'

'Not critically.'

Meg gripped his arm. 'Not critically?' she repeated. 'But seriously? Slightly? What?'

'He hasn't broken anything big,' Michael said. He smiled at her.

The lift doors opened.

'Here, aaaah,' the girl said. 'Oooh-uh, aaaah-ha, hello, hello, hello.' And she moved forward, shooing a path like a collie with a flock of sheep.

To Meg's surprise, the sheep were made up of quite a large group. There must have been fifty or more, and Meg recognised some of the faces as she glanced among them, wishing now that she had managed to get back to her flat before coming here, so that she wouldn't be standing in front of all these designer-suited media types in her muddy shoes and creased, eight-year-old jeans. She had the unpleasant feeling that she smelled a bit, because the last thing she had done before leaving Halfpenny Acre was to help Penny turn the compost heap.

Yes, she saw plenty of faces she knew. Here were men who had patted Will on the back, and said – being liars – that they wished they were going with him to the Pole. Here were women who had blushed when Will talked to them, and said – being liars – that they would hate to go with him. There was, Meg noticed, the series producer, Dan, who always sounded as if he were about to have a nervous breakdown, and there was Amy, the woman who was going to ghostwrite Will's account of the trek. There was Stephen, who was going to doctor the video footage to make it look professional, and to edit Will's curses from it; and there were the sponsors, who all wanted Stephen and Amy to paste in mentions and shots of their logos.

It was the sponsors, Meg noticed, who looked particularly glum. In fact, everyone had the same air: as if they had come to a funeral wake. Nobody met their eyes.

Just at that moment, the door behind them all opened. Eric Cramm walked out, dressed in a black Christian Dior suit, with a black shirt and a black tie.

He walked over to Meg, and shook her hand.

'What is it?' she asked. 'What's he done? What's happened?'

The crowd parted as Cramm walked her over to a long conference table. It was empty, except for a single tiny, high-tech tape deck. Without another word of explanation, Eric Cramm depressed the *Play* button.

There was a lot of crackling for a moment.

Then, Meg heard a stranger's voice.

'British Bulldog, British Bulldog. This is Bulldog Base. Over.'

Meg looked over at the Managing Director of Bulldog Sausages. He had sat down, crossed his arms, and was staring at the floor.

The voice – the radio operator at Resolute Bay, trying to contact Will, came on again. 'British Bulldog, do you read me? Over.'

'Yes,' said a voice.

It was Will. And yet it was not Will. Will had never sounded this defeated in his life. Meg frowned, and took a step closer to the deck, leaning down to listen. Will was only a hundred nautical miles from the Pole. Why did he sound so miserable? He had already covered three hundred miles. By his standards, he was almost there. They had heard his radio transmissions daily – or, almost daily, if the storms didn't white him out. And she knew that, normally, having managed to get through on the radio at last, Will would be buoyant, confident, optimistic. Because he always was. Because that was him.

But this was not him. He didn't even bother to sign over.

The puzzlement could be heard in the operator's reply.

'British Bulldog, this is Resolute, Bulldog Base. Good to hear you, mate. What is your position, over?'

'Fucking prone,' Will replied.

More crackling.

Eric Cramm shook his head.

'Say again, Bulldog,' said the operator.

'Lying on my bloody arse,' Will replied.

Meg gasped, and then winced.

But the radio operator was laughing. 'Bulldog, you got trouble, mate? Over.'

'Bloody well say so,' they heard Will mutter. 'Over.'

'What's your weather, Bulldog? Over.'

'Fucking sunny,' Will replied.

'What's your temperature, Bulldog? Over.'

'Minus fifteen. Over.'

'Fifty? Over.'

'Fucking deck chairs out here, mate,' Will responded dully. 'Selling Walls ice-creams. Just going out to make a sandcastle. Punch and Judy on in a minute. I said *fifteen*. Over.'

'What's the ice doing? Over.'

'Melting,' Will said. 'Walked four miles west on a lead, no way across the water. Not the worst thing. Over.'

Meg's heart started pounding softly.

Not the worst thing.

'What's the problem? Over.'

There was a considerable silence. Meg thought she could hear the wind blowing wherever Will was – a warm, deck-chair breeze of fifteen degrees below freezing, instead of the usual thirty or forty below he might have expected, with a wind chill of another twenty degrees.

Then, Will's voice came back on.

'Coccyx,' he muttered. 'Over.'

'Cock what, mate? Over.'

'COCCYX,' Will yelled. 'I broke my coccyx. Over, over, fucking over.'

'You broke your spine? Over.'

'I broke my arse,' Will retorted.

Eric Cramm suddenly leaned forward, and switched off the tape.

'Hey,' Meg objected.

Cramm turned to the room. 'Well, ladies and gentlemen,' he said. 'There you have it. I'm afraid that the Churchill-Twines attempt on the Pole is over, and so is Up-Line's coverage.'

'You can't do that,' Meg objected.

'What Miss Randall means,' Michael interjected, 'is that there's still plenty of drama left in this situation. There's still plenty of programme material.'

'That isn't what I meant at all,' Meg said. 'I meant you can't just leave him. When are you going to get him out of there? He's injured.'

'A plane's already gone,' Michael said to her. 'And a cameraman, and a journalist from Up-Line News.'

She looked at him, then at the rest of the room. 'You might have told me sooner,' she said. 'How long have you had this?'

'It came in at lunchtime,' Michael said. 'We've all heard bits of it. Mr Cramm wanted us all to hear it together.'

Cramm had walked towards the sponsors. 'We shall film the pick-up, naturally,' he said. 'And the homecoming.'

'It isn't the same,' Bulldog Sausages said. 'How can you make a cracked arse look heroic?'

Meg felt herself flush.

'We expected to see our product at the top of the world,' someone else moaned.

That did it.

'You bunch of hypocrites,' Meg said.

'Meg,' warned Michael.

She shrugged off his restraining arm, and advanced on the sausage man.

'I expect you'd rather he died,' she said to him. He

looked just like a bulldog himself, with his four chins
overlapping his collar. 'That would have been much
better, wouldn't it?' she demanded. 'You'd have liked
him to do a Scott, wouldn't you, and write a diary, and
say the last thing that crossed his lips was your
horrible processed rubbish.'

'Meg,' Michael warned.

She wheeled on the room. 'That's it, isn't it?' she
said. 'Either get to the Pole, or die on the way. Doesn't
matter which. Either way is dramatic. Stopping before
the end for a daft thing like excruciating pain – that's
not quite dramatic enough, is it?'

She looked around at every one of them. 'What do
you want him to do?' she demanded. 'Hasn't he
delivered enough for you? Maybe you'd like it if he got
duffed up by a gang of murderous seals. Great! Great
TV. Or maybe he could fall through the ice a couple of
times? Lovely shot of him chipping his toes off with an
ice pick, that would be. Maybe you'd like a polar bear
to bite off his head?' She put her hand to her mouth in
mock horror. 'Oh no, can't do that, that wouldn't do
– Bulldog Sausages on hat! Can't have the hat
swallowed. But hey . . .' She pretended to think about
it. 'Tell you what he could do . . . he could whip off the
hat and leave it lying pathetically on the ice, and *then*
the polar bear could bite off his head. Fantastic! Six
o'clock news! Sad hat all that remains of British hero.
Fabulous.'

To his credit, Bulldog Sausages wouldn't look at
her.

'You nag us all year after you've backed him,' she
went on. 'You think you own him, and you ring us up
at all hours of the day and night, and you ask him to
do ridiculous things, like standing in a sealskin suit on

the Albert Memorial with your bloody sausages and throat sweets and thermal pants, and there isn't one of you, there isn't *one* of you, who would go out in the dark to walk the dog, never mind walk four hundred miles dragging a sledge.'

'Meg,' Michael repeated.

At last, Meg took a deep breath. Thermal Vests Incorporated stood up.

'We think Mr Churchill-Twines might have carried on,' he said.

There was a little frisson of agreement.

'Carry on?' Meg said. She looked at Michael. 'Could he?'

Michael shook his head. 'A very large lead has opened up,' he said. 'A stretch of open water. So large that it can't be crossed. It can't be walked around. There is no bridging ice. This is what global warming means.'

Thermal Vests wasn't satisfied. 'It's not as if he's broken his arms and legs,' he said. 'Why can't you just 'copter him over the water, and put him down on the other side?'

'Because that would totally defeat the idea of walking unaided to the Pole,' Meg retorted. 'It would be cheating.'

'A broken coccyx is painful,' Michael added. 'He did it five days ago, while dragging the sledge over rubble ice. The sledge fell after him down a ridge, and hit him in the back.'

'But he can walk,' Vests said.

Meg strode over to him, so that she was staring him in the face. 'How'd you like to walk with an injury like that?' she demanded.

'I would if a fortune were riding on my back,' he replied.

'Look,' Meg said. And she caught a dangerous warning flicker, an Abigail sort of red flicker, in the corner of her eye. 'Will isn't there to make a fortune. He's there because *it's* there, the Pole and all that, it's a dream, and it's a challenge. The only fortune on his back is the potential fortune you can make out of him. Do you think he cares about money?'

Thermal Vests smirked. 'Evidently not,' he said. 'My point precisely. And –' he turned to the others behind him – 'if we may speak about badgering in the context of such a selfless, non-publicity-seeking venture, may I remind you, Miss Randall, that you were not above badgering any one of us for sponsorship.'

Meg felt her blood pressure rising. She could almost hear the blips on a pressure monitor, rapidly rising off the scale.

'And it shouldn't happen,' she said. 'I agree with that. I shouldn't have to badger you! You should fund this stuff, just fund it. You should give it to him, because he's prepared to do something amazing, something that no-one else will do, or dare to do, and you should give it without him having to trek there labelled up like a Christmas parcel. For God's sake, his logos weigh more than his tent!'

'Meg, Meg,' Michael said. He really pulled on her arm now, and managed to get her off balance sufficiently for her to remove her wagging index finger from Thermal Vests' nostrils.

She walked away, and sat down heavily on a sofa.

Vests looked at Sausages.

'Well, gentlemen,' he said. 'Our business is over, wouldn't you say? Miss Randall has made the position quite clear.'

There was a murmur of agreement. The whole

group filed out, even Cramm and the production team. At the door, Cramm looked back at Meg with a strange, lingering expression. Then, he shut the door behind him.

'Congratulations,' Michael said. 'Well done.'

'I don't give a damn,' Meg said. 'Couch potatoes, the lot of them. Vegetables. Pigs. Amoebas.'

'Make up your mind,' Michael said, going over to the tape deck.

'Pigs are nicer,' Meg muttered. 'Pigs are sociable.'

Michael shook his head. 'Sometimes you are just like your mother,' he said.

'Oh gee, thanks,' she retorted. 'That's made my year. I shall go home happy now.'

Michael was looking out at the river, one hand on his hip. 'Well, it'll take a miracle to finance the next trip,' he said.

'Good,' Meg said. 'Maybe Will can stay home for a change.'

'Is that what you want?' he asked.

'Yes,' she said. 'No.'

'Which?'

Meg put her hands over her face, and was silent for a second or two. When she lowered them, she stared at Michael, and shook her head. 'I don't know,' she said, quietly.

'We've had crises before,' Michael replied.

She continued to shake her head. 'I don't mean sponsors, or trips or . . . I don't mean that,' she murmured.

Michael walked over to her, and sat down. 'What do you mean, exactly?' he asked.

She took a deep breath. 'It's Will,' she said.

'What about Will?'

'I don't know him,' she said. 'And don't smile.'

'I'm not smiling,' he replied. 'Go on.'

'I'm serious, Michael,' she said. 'We got together in a rush, and all the time we've had together – what time there's been – has been in a rush, and I don't know any more.'

'But about what, precisely?'

She looked away, out over the view of London. 'About Will and me.'

Michael started to laugh. 'Now I know you're joking.'

She closed her eyes. 'But that's exactly it,' she said softly. 'I'm not joking. I got swept along – my choice, I know – but suddenly I wake up, and I'm Will's right-hand woman, involved in all this, and . . . I just don't know what I feel.'

'But you've been Will's biggest supporter!'

'I know,' she said. 'And I admire him, I really do. I've never met anyone like him. But . . .' She looked back at Michael now. 'I'll *never* get to know him, do you realise that?' she asked. 'Because when it comes right down to it, Will is a solitary person. He doesn't like noise, and people. That's what all this exploration and adventure is about. This dislocation from life. That's what he wants, you see? Whatever he might say or not say. That's his driving force, the reason he's alive. To be out there. Somewhere. Anywhere. But not home.'

Michael reached over, to put his hand on hers. 'I'm sure he feels a lot for you,' he said. 'He loves you.'

She frowned. 'But I don't know if I love him,' she said, at last.

Michael sat back, astonished. 'I can't believe you said that,' he muttered.

She shot him a glance. 'You want to know the

truth?' she asked, with the faintest of smiles. 'Neither can I.' She bit her lip, and her voice fell to almost a whisper. 'And, even if he did want to stay home,' she murmured, 'I'm not at all sure that I'd want to stay with him.'

Michael watched her for a few seconds more, trying to read her closed expression. Then, he switched on the tape. 'The last bit of the radio transmission was for you,' he said. 'Just you, nobody else.'

She looked up, surprised.

There was a fizz of static, and then Will's depressed and defeated voice came back on.

'Base,' he said. 'Relay a message. Over.'

'Fire away, Bulldog. Over.'

She imagined Will, hunched over the transmitter, the GPS that he would be holding showing quite plainly that he was stranded far away from where he wanted to be. He had told her before he left, that he dreamed for so long of standing at the top of the world, where all directions were south, and that there would be nothing to beat that feeling, and nowhere else that he would want to be.

'Will you tell Meg,' Will said, 'thanks for all she's done, with the back-up, and the sponsors, and everything. She's been great, the way she's handled them. Tell her that I'll soon be home.'

There was a crackle, a silence.

Then, 'Over and out.'

For a moment, Meg stared at the table.

Michael gently switched off the tape.

Then, Meg put her head in her hands, and cried.

9

Adele paused for a moment after she had closed the door in her flat.

There was silence, complete silence; a silence that ought to have been pleasant after the day she'd had. She stood on the perfect beechwood floor and stared at the perfect view of the river. Between her and the view was a perfectly designed room, with perfectly placed sofas in perfect complimentary colours, with a perfect galley kitchen to one side and a perfect bathroom beyond.

She knew it was perfect because the designer had told her so. It had been Elenna Angler from *Hey! Today!*. She ought to admire Elenna, she knew: Elenna was bright, and determined, and she had spent her life pleasing a whole load of awkward customers that most sane people would kick into touch after the first five minutes. And she had two kids and no partner, and she didn't give a damn what other people said about her, and she seemed to spend most of her days laughing and telling dirty jokes, and making a great deal of money. And, what's more, Elenna was at least seventeen stone, and had frizzy hair, and thick ankles, and a very loud voice, and she smoked.

All things that Adele would never dare to be, or do.

Adele just couldn't admire Elenna, because she envied her too much.

She kicked off the torturous shoes and put down her bag, and looked at them both. All day she'd worn those shoes. All day she'd carried that horrible ponyskin bag. All day she'd eased the waistband of this too-tight skirt with the wrapover front, the kind that you were permanently trying to pull together so that you didn't show your pants. All day she'd had this lipstick on, this Day-Glo shade. All day her hair had felt like it had been sprayed on with quick-dry cement. All day she'd sweated inside these bodyshaper Lycra tights. All day she'd been hungry.

And why? She asked herself, still staring at her living space. *Why?*

Because someone else – some expert – told her to.

God! She was so sick and tired of doing what was expected of her. She wasn't a person, she was a commodity. A piece of merchandise that had been built by morning TV. She wasn't herself any longer. She was an image, a manufactured thing that was bullied into a TV-Personality Shape every morning. What did that make her? Less than human.

If she'd been human, she told herself – if she had an ounce of her old spark – she'd have told Lawrence what he could do with Jack and Belinda today. She'd have stood up for herself. She'd have thrown a Celebrity Tantrum. Celebrities did that all the time, didn't they? That was one of the things that made you a celebrity in the first place – squawking and stamping your feet until you got what you wanted. Turning up at restaurants and expecting the best table. Turning up at theatres and expecting the best seat. It wasn't just a case of *asking* for the table or the seat. Or even demanding it. Stars like Madonna didn't ask or demand, did they? Adele told herself. They just walked straight through. And this morning – well, if she'd had an ounce of gumption, she'd have screamed blue murder – *walked straight through* – instead of accepting Lawrence's mad ideas.

That was it. That was hitting the nail square on the head.

She was too bloody accepting.

She walked to the kitchen, tore off a piece of kitchen paper and angrily rubbed off her lipstick. Then, she stared down at the paper, balled it in her fist and threw it across the room.

She'd never put lipstick on again, ever, if she had her way, she thought, taking another piece of kitchen roll and rubbing it across her mouth. Especially not this sticky stuff that took paint stripper to remove. All Day Colour! Immovable Kissability! It made her feel as if she had two pieces of sticking tape over her lips. She would give her eye teeth – perhaps even all her teeth – never to wear make-up again. Never to have to spend twenty minutes putting it on and never again to have to spend twenty minutes taking it off. Forty minutes a day, that was. She could write a novel in two years, at that rate.

Suppose – just suppose, for the sake of argument – that she'd spent that time walking somewhere. If she walked at six miles an hour for forty minutes a day, not only would she be thin, but she'd also be one thousand, four hundred and sixty miles from here in a year's time. In ten years, she'd have travelled the world. She'd have crossed deserts and Poles and jungles and continents, seen Kazakhstan and the Great Barrier Reef and camels and turtles and the Grand Canyon and Niagara Falls, and eaten yak's cheese and fried cockroaches and a huge amount of key lime pie, and ridden white water and wild horses, *and all because* . . . and all because the lady hadn't caked herself in cack.

Forty minutes a day. What a towering waste. And maybe she spent another hour dressing and undressing. Maybe, on average, twenty minutes a day thinking about, or buying clothes to wear in public, clothes expensive and flattering and fashionable enough for people not to point at you and say, 'My God, didn't you use to be Adele Buchanan?'

If she lived in a remote cottage somewhere, she wouldn't have to bother with clothes like that, or make-up. The thought was breathtakingly blissful. Not only would nobody ever look at her – or, worse still, sigh in a critical well-I-daren't-tell-her-about-that sort of way – but she would get an hour-and-a-half back in every day. A whole, huge hour-and-a-half. What else could she do with an hour-and-a-half?

She could paint something. She could make something. Hell, with an hour-and-a-half every day, she could make cakes, or macramé potholders, or work a loom, or throw pots. She could learn another language in an hour-and-a-half a day. A really complicated one. Russian. Polish. Chinese.

And if she didn't have to research the subjects for the show, and go over scripts and running orders, she'd have another hour-and-a-half. Three hours! And if she didn't do the show . . .

She frowned suddenly.

If she didn't do the show, she'd be the poorest marathon-walking Russian-speaking macramé-maker in the world.

Welcome to the circular fantasy, here's where you came in.

She walked over to the kitchen and opened the fridge.

When Elenna had first decorated and equipped the place, Adele had had the devil's own job trying to find anything. After listening to Adele moaning about the clutter in her life, Elenna had taken it upon herself to de-clutter Adele's living space. 'It'll be real soothing for you,' she'd told Adele, smiling.

Soothing! It had driven her bonkers.

Not only was the fridge hidden away – disaster! – but so was the cooker and the toaster and the wine rack. She ought to have confessed to Elenna, she supposed, that she had to lay her hands on a toasted teacake and a glass of Merlot as soon as she came in from work. But she didn't. She was too embarrassed. So, for the whole of the first week that she was in her new soothing space, she spent half the time crashing about, flinging open what she thought were cupboards, only to find that they were the screened boiler, or the air vents. She had been reduced to a near screaming fit on the first night when she couldn't, for the life of her, find the corkscrew in the secret cutlery drawer.

And then, she'd found that she couldn't sit down.

Well, she *could* sit down, if she wanted to sit on a sofa where the cushions were huge and couldn't be plumped, and kept sliding off when she slumped against them. Or she could have sat down at the dining table, forced upright on a black plastic retro chair with a steel back.

Eventually, she'd taken her glass and her bag of crisps (Elenna hadn't found those, because she'd hidden them herself in the laundry basket before she went out) and she'd lain on her bed. Thankfully,

Elenna's brief to re-design hadn't extended as far as
the bedroom, so Adele could lie in peace on the blue
bed in a lilac and yellow and red room, which was blue
and lilac and yellow and red because the walls were all
dotted with samples from paint pots from B&Q, and,
months later, Adele still couldn't decide which was
best, and was too shattered to have painted anything
even if she could decide.

She looked at the contents of the fridge.

Peppers, sun-dried tomato paste, organic pasta,
organic quail's eggs, organic goat's cheese, celery,
carrots, grapefruit, guavas, mangoes, Tabasco, low-fat
mayonnaise, non-fat milk, dried apricots, and smoked
mackerel.

Not one single decent thing to eat.

And that was another thing. Shopping. She had all
this stuff in the fridge because, whenever she did go
out, she couldn't buy what she wanted. The minute she
hovered near the cakes, or the chocolates, or the cans
of non-Diet Coke, some fool would come up and say,
'It's you, isn't it?' She had tried denying it, and it
hadn't worked – not unless you wanted to get into a
row – so she could have to own up and admit that, yes,
it was her, and yes, it was a marvellous show, and yes,
she did love meeting all those people, and yes, wasn't
it a shame about the wife whose husband had the
affair and then rang in and gave her name and said she
was useless in bed for the whole nation to hear, and
yes, wasn't the chef handsome, he was lovely, and all
the time, she'd be trying to stuff a dozen Mars bars
into the trolley without being seen.

Even if she did manage to get round the shop
without being accosted, the till was another nightmare. Inevitably she would join the queue that took

the longest, and then there would be someone behind her eyeing up what she had put on the conveyor belt. And there was a limit to how many biscuits you could hide under a lettuce. So she would come out of the supermarket with healthy, low-fat meals, and have to load them into her car and take them home, when all she really wanted to do was lob them straight out of the car window.

She lay on the bed and stared at the ceiling. She knew what was wrong, of course. What had always been wrong, all her life.

In her private life, she was a pleaser.

She wasn't like Elenna. She might be rattled if the show went wrong, or something like that, but she wouldn't work herself up to a true, scalding temper. She was too frightened to think what might happen if she did. She didn't want people to say she was a bitch. She wanted them to like her, basically. Whenever she did voice her opinion she heard herself apologising first. 'Sorry, but . . .'

Put like that, of course, it sounded terminally stupid. But it was simply that it was easier, if a thing wasn't right, to shut up and do it yourself. How could she possibly tell Elenna, for instance, that she hated minimalism? When Elenna had described it, it had sounded great, and she had persuaded herself that it would be great. If it wasn't great . . . well, she could buy some other sofa. And kitchen. And table. And chairs.

It was exactly the same with every relationship she had ever had.

Alone with her crisps, her mind ranged back over the last twenty years.

Number One had been Alan.

Alan had been older than her, and she wouldn't have gone out with him at all if a girl in her class hadn't asked her to make up a foursome. She was fifteen. He was twenty-two. The girl said that he was very nice and a bit lonely. And when Adele saw him, she knew straight away, within the first two seconds, why he was lonely. It was because he was very very thin and very very bald and very very ugly.

Nevertheless, she had felt sorry for him, and she had gone out to the pictures with him for a month, every Friday for four interminable weeks. And she had let him try to find her bra fastening in the back of an Austin Allegro, because she didn't know how to tell him that he made her flesh crawl.

When she did finally summon up the courage to dump him, he had phoned her at home the next day to say that he was going to commit suicide. In the end he made her cry, and she promised to meet him the following Friday. When she didn't go, she felt incredibly guilty, and she had kept looking in the papers for ages afterwards, expecting to see that a very thin and very bald and very ugly person had thrown themselves off Beachy Head.

Number Two was David.

David was a very shy eighteen-year-old at the Tech. He was doing an engineering course, and Adele was doing Media Studies. Dave was a sad person who didn't want to be an engineer, even though his dad, an engineer, had insisted. Because Dave was an artist. A musician. Instead of a tongue, he had a soul. Dave would play her his songs on his portable keyboard, and they would sit in bus shelters while he serenaded her with titles like 'Blackness My Friend' and 'Steppin' In The Styx'. Being with Dave was a totally mournful, funereal experience, as it turned out, in more ways than one. The highlight came when he finally took her to his flat, which happened to be above a mortuary. Adele had lost her virginity while listening to coffins being nailed down.

Not exactly the happiest experience of her life.

Number Three was love.

Danny had loved her, and she had loved him. It was the last year at college. Adele was writing a column in the local paper as well as doing her course, and Danny was the only professional on the town football team. Danny was big and broad, and blue-eyed, and made her laugh, and they would spend weekend nights on the pebbly beach ten miles away from the town, a secluded bit that was a good long walk from the car park. And they would scoop out a shelf in the pebbles, and light a fire, and plan what holidays they were going to take, and where their house would be when Danny got snapped up by one of the big clubs. And he would smile at her indulgently when she said she was going to work on a London newspaper, because he probably didn't ever quite believe that she meant it. But she did mean it. It was part of the master plan. Danny at Spurs or West Ham or Arsenal, and her at the *Guardian* or *The Times* or the *Telegraph*.

Then Danny broke his knee. It was a difficult injury, and, to match it, Danny became difficult too – morose and moody. He didn't want to go down to the beach any more, or have Adele drive him anywhere.

She went with him to the hospital on the day – six weeks later – that they told him that he wouldn't play professionally again. He wouldn't speak to her, but, as she opened the car door, talking ten to the dozen in an effort to cheer him up, he paused as he came alongside her, eyed her for a second, and then punched her in the face.

She still had a little scar right in the corner of her mouth.

She didn't date anyone at all after that, for two years.

And no one had ever again lit the fire for her, on beaches or anywhere else.

Not that she hadn't, eventually, tried. There was the first psychologist they had employed in the first ten-week series of *Hey! Today!*. He was Tibetan, very spiritual, very calm, very sweet and rather sexy. It had been a wonderful time, she thought. Back when everything was still a laugh, still fun. He had been the first man to take her to Paris, and, when she thought of him now, she would think of him under a sort of neon-lit title, *My Days In Paris*. The memories were sweetly sentimentalised inside her head, like a still from a hazy-focus film, arm-in-arm along the banks of the Seine, kissing under the clock in the Musée d'Orsay.

She could have married Antoine; she had already picked out the wedding invitations and the colour scheme for the bridesmaids. And then she had realised that he had analysed her at every turn, and the veils fell from her eyes rather quickly, and she had understood – thank God, not too late – that he was a martyr to compulsions. Antoine had Obsessive Compulsive Disorder, which meant, in his case, that he had a slight problem with going in and out of doors, and going around roundabouts. It was, he had explained off-handedly and rather superciliously to her one day, a case of checking that the door was, in fact, open, and that the roundabout was, in fact, round, or oval. In short, that the door was a door and the roundabout was . . . quite.

Adele had at once felt terribly sorry for Antoine's fixations – which he hid fairly well, unless you knew him intimately. But the pity was soon drummed out of her. Antoine, instead of admitting his problem, had a way of making her feel that it was *her* who had difficulty because she *didn't* check doors and roundabouts. She started to have a sneaking feeling that he was right, and she was wrong, because he – well, he more or less said so. In fact, he told her that it was a deep philosophical question – after all, how did she really know that a door was there unless she checked it? – and she almost believed him. *Almost*.

He said other things, too. He said that her non-checking was the sign of a simplistic mind. Not simple. Not quite such an insult. But, in Antoine's charming, soothing voice, '*Simplistic*, darling.' And he had stroked her hand as he said it.

The next afternoon, she had found herself driving twice around a roundabout, to check that it was, in fact, round.

And she had had the good simplistic sense to finish with him that very evening.

He was probably the best, she told herself now, crumpling the empty crisp bag. She seemed to have lost the shine after Antoine. Nothing was soft focus any more. No wedding stationery at all.

Who else came close to qualifying? Nobody.

A one-night stand with an actor. Folded after one show.

A week with a golf fanatic. Big driver, small putter.

A fortnight with a plumber. Blocked pipes.

She had even answered a small ad once. It was when

she first connected to the Internet at home, and she had drunk almost a bottle of wine by herself one Friday night, sufficient to make answering a small ad seem perfectly reasonable. She had found herself scrolling down the names going, 'Aaaah, cyclist. Nice. Aaaaah, cats. Nice. Aaaah, Gemini. Nice.'

She replied to *Happily single adventurer, 40, no ties, OHAC, told I am handsome, seeks happily single lady with warm heart, interested in travel.*

'You don't want to answer those,' her cleaning lady told her. 'They're all perverts. Don't go anywhere alone with them. They all have knives.'

'I'll be fine,' she had said, laughing, despite the fact that, when sober, she had been horrified to see the response in her emails. Still, she had told herself, it was worth a try. Nothing ventured, nothing gained. Her reflexologist told her a story of a friend who had been suicidal after her divorce, had answered one of these ads, met a millionaire, and was deliriously happy. If it could happen to her reflexologist's friend, *55, miserable as sin, can't stop crying, feel like taking a hacksaw to men generally, call me if you want to end your life in a hail of bullets*, then why couldn't it happen to her?

She met him at eight one Saturday night.

By nine, she was home, alone.

Mr Happily Single had been very overweight, and, when Adele walked into the pub and he recognised her, he kept bunching his jumper in one fist. Happily Single turned out to be Quite Unhappily Single because he had a severe personal odour problem. It turned out to be his mother who told him that he was handsome; and his interest in travel extended to a train set that occupied the whole of his loft. So, he told her, grinning at his own joke, *OHAC* did not mean Own House And Car, but Own Hornby And Carriages.

And that, five months ago, had been her last romantic fling.

If you didn't count Jack.

She sat up, swung her legs off the side of the bed and rubbed her eyes. With an effort, she pushed the thought of Jack away, because it brought an ache to her heart. She sighed deeply, and wondered how she would phrase her own small ad in the personal columns.

TV personality, suspects age creeping up on career and bathroom scales. Would like to have family before bits finally fall off. Has it all and doesn't really want it any more. In deepest fantasies not told anyone about, would like to run small B&B in rural location. Wouldn't care if mud up to armpits. Anyone considered, providing not gay, married, bald, thin, ugly, musician, depressed, lives over mortuary, footballer, psychologist, actor, plumber, golfer, toy train collector. Must have own teeth, no warts, decent height, not live with mother, not call me by wrong name in middle of night, not have tattoos, not wear football shirts at weekend, not whistle Chirpy Chirpy Cheep Cheep in shower, not possess early 1970s Genesis LPs, not eye up flat like an insurance assessor, nurture no fantasies of threesomes, not expect tea on table, oral sex, or oral sex on tea table.

She shook her head, slowly, at herself.

She ought to get up, she thought, and have a shower, and settle down with a nice salad and a good book.

She considered the idea for a minute.

'Sick,' she muttered. 'Sick, sick, sick.'

Then she got a second bag of crisps from under the bed and lay back down.

10

No one knew where Eric Cramm lived.

Or who he lived with.

He liked it that way.

It was two days later; and he was very tired. He walked along Long Acre, with his coat collar turned up and his hands dug deep in his pockets. At the junction with Drury Lane, he looked down towards the river and saw the theatre crowds beginning to come out. *The Lion King* was just finishing, and families were walking towards him, half of them pretending to be giraffes on stilts, or zebras, or Scar with a limp, and the other half clutching Simba toys. Good feeling was washing up Drury Lane and flowing down High Holborn, and Eric winced, as if he had inadvertently stepped in something, as if the feel-good factor had stuck to his shoes.

He increased his pace, turning up into Great Queen Street.

He so hated the theatre.

For a start, you couldn't rewind theatre and cut out the bad bits. Unlike TV. The thought of being involved in a nightly show like that – being a producer, say, or a stage manager – made his blood run cold. You had to get involved with people, doing a job like that. You would have to go round making sure that all the giraffes had their heads on straight, and that all the musicians had turned up, and that all the men who did the bird things had the birds, and the wobbly lines to put the birds on. God, it must be terrible, Eric considered.

Every night another drama. And that was just backstage. Every night another case of nerves, or laryngitis, or PMT. How did any theatre manager cope with any show, he wondered. The off-stage affairs and the bar staff not showing up, and the sound system failing, and the plumbing going AWOL in the Royal Circle toilets. There were so many variables in the cast alone; and then, at seven every night, two thousand more variables turned up in the shape of the audience. Horrible! All that clapping. All that dancing. All those curtains going up and down, up and down. All the sweet wrappers to pick up when it was all finished.

Nightmare.

Eric did his best to have as few live audiences as possible on Up-Line Cable. Canned laughter, in his opinion, was a wonderful thing. Whoever had thought of it ought to be given a medal. You didn't have to find a seat for canned laughter. You didn't have to make sure there were fire exits, and toilets, and refreshments. You didn't have to worry about offending it. You just clicked it on, and on, and on. And every time was the same, predictably the same. It was neat. Mechanical. Your scriptwriter told a joke, and the canned laughter laughed at the joke. Joke, laughter, joke, laughter. It had the remorseless rhythm of a train running over points, and, what's more, it didn't go silent at crucial moments, and then ask for its money back.

There were some shows, of course, that needed a live audience, much to Eric's regret. If he could have got rid of such laborious and boring events, he would have done, but the confessions shows were the ones that made the most money. You had to have live people, unfortunately, in order to yell at the ones on the stage, and, occasionally, to get up on stage and hit someone, so that the bouncers could rush in and, not too quickly, mind you, haul them off stage again.

The bouncers were artists, in their own way. They took their work deadly seriously, and they had a union – COCOP (Chuck Off, Chuck Out Performers). COCOP members had a stringent rule of practice for confessions shows, which they stuck to religiously. Rule One was never to get up on stage too quickly. If you saw someone running down the aisle towards the stage with, say, a hammer, or a heavy handbag (equally dangerous) you had *on no account* to intercept them. You had to let them stagger up the steps and swear a bit before you made your move. Rule Two was *never* to pinion the attacker's arms so tightly that they couldn't get at least one smack in. Rule Three was that, on removing said attacker from the stage, you must *never* remove them too quickly, without allowing them to swear a bit more (see Rule One) and try to land another hopeless blow. Rule Four – and this was possibly the most important – was that you must *never* remove the attacker entirely from the auditorium. This was to enable the attacker to go through the whole thing again (see Rules One, Two, Three and Four), the next time that the people on stage claimed their brother was gay, or had two wives, or made out with gardening implements, or whatever it was, and this final Rule thus ensured that the show's ratings went stratospheric within the week.

If Eric admired anyone – and, let's face it, he

admired very few people, if you didn't count Adele Buchanan – then he admired the COCOPs. They knew what they were doing, and they did it calmly, and always the same. They were like robots, unmoved by anything that anyone said, ever.

If only everyone, Eric thought, as he crossed Kingsway, could be like them.

He crossed Lincoln's Inn Fields. In one of the little lanes that ran off it was a dark building. It hid in the centre of a terrace, trying to look like all the other office buildings around it, with tinted windows and a security grille over the entrance on the ground floor. Eric got his key out of his pocket, looked up and down the deserted street, and opened a heavy iron door in the grille. He stepped through, locked it behind him, and opened another door – a sheath of inch-thick steel – ahead of him. He pushed it open a crack and inched in, trying not to let any light spill out on to the street beyond the grille. The door closed behind him with a vault-like clang.

Badger was waiting for him.

If you were making your first visit to Eric's home, and weren't expecting a woman of Badger's size to spring from the woodwork as soon as you stepped over the threshold, she would have been a terrifying sight. Even if you *were* expecting her, she could make you take an extra deep breath. Standing five feet eleven, dressed entirely in grey, she approached with a towel draped over one arm.

'You shouldn't stay out in the cold,' she said, wrestling his coat from him.

'People have been shouting at me,' he told her.

'What people?'

'Just people,' he said. 'Men. And women. Woman.'

'A woman's been shouting at you?' Badger asked. 'Is she mad?'

'Furious,' Eric said, putting his shoes in the rack and following her in his pom-pom slippers.

The house was stiflingly hot, and the warm air vents were making a heavy-breathing sound with the effort of satisfying the thermostat. On the linoleum-floored landing on the first floor Eric began to undress, while the house groaned softly to itself, *uuuurgh, uuuumph, uuuurgh, uuuumph*.

Badger picked up each item of clothing and dropped it into the laundry basket. When he had finished, she turned.

'I'm thirsty,' Eric said.

'Cocoa later, bath now,' Badger chided.

Eric, now naked, walked into the bathroom, where the water was already drawn for him. He slid down into it and gripped his rubber duck.

'What did you do today?' Badger asked, from the corridor.

'Stuff,' Eric said.

'I moved your stakeholder to a five-year fixed bond,' Badger said. 'The interest rate was six three.'

'I'm starting a new show,' he told her. 'I interviewed six applicants.'

'Amalgamated Perpetual was down five pence,' she added.

'Six women and six agents,' Eric said. 'One was from Euro Bag.'

Badger put her head round the door. 'The Euro Bag issued a sales memorandum,' she reminded him. 'The sales process has been instigated through Landfinger.com.'

'I know,' he said, squeezing out his sponge. 'They're

desperate to offload staff, and you should see what they tried to offload on me.'

Badger laid a folded towel on the edge of the bath.

He looked up at her.

It was hard to say how old Clementine Badger was; she could have been almost any age over thirty-five. He had first seen Badger one afternoon in Los Angeles; she was the nanny at the house next door. Eric didn't like children because children had an annoying habit of laughing and running up and down for no obvious reason. The kids next door to him had been infuriating him for some time, particularly at weekends, when their nurse allowed them in the pool all day and they insisted upon squealing and pretending to be sharks. To add insult to injury, the oldest boy, about six going on forty-six, had cottoned on that Eric was alone in the vast mock-Tudor mansion, and had started calling him George Michael, and waving gladioli at him through the fence.

One weekend, however, he had noticed that next door was unusually quiet, and when he had sneaked a look over the fence, he'd seen that the children – all four of them – were sitting on chairs, reading. Next to them sat Badger.

He wondered if she had modelled herself on Julie Andrews in *The Sound of Music*. Badger had a pudding-bowl haircut and wore a pinafore dress with a white blouse underneath. The children, while not dressed in cut-down curtains, were certainly dressed. Their hair was combed off their faces, and they looked bemused. They were looking at Badger with a complicated expression, somewhere between fear and fascination. Eric later learned that, for the first time in their lives, they had been put to bed at seven, had ten hours sleep, been given a wholesome breakfast, and were currently engaged on a programme of pre-school learning. By the time that Badger left that house, each child could speak French, calculate compound interest, and play Telemann's *Presto in E Minor No:5 from Fugues légères et petits jeux* on the piano.

The oldest boy never called him George Michael again.

He called him *sir*.

But Badger had even more alluring assets than just being able to change been-there-seen-that LA brats into human beings. And the most alluring asset of all was her Understanding Ability.

In their very first conversation, Eric found no need to explain his love of order. Because Badger Understood. He had no need to describe his job, and the intricacies of keeping a financial rein on Jefferson Bluehorn Majolica's worldwide holdings, because Badger Understood. He had no need to detail his compunction to have his kitchen bleached daily, or his clothes arranged in alphabetical order, or his shoes polished, or the need to retain every single receipt he had ever been given, or the uselessness of flowers, or his love of military band music, or his collection of Swiss railway timetables, because Badger Understood. In a deranged world, Badger was calm. In a loud world, Badger was quiet. In a world devoted to sensation, Badger was a creature of pragmatism. She ironed, she baked, she sewed, she followed the stock market, she listened to the BBC World Service. She never wore make-up, or raised her voice, or went off at tangents. In short, she was the human equivalent of a straight street.

He would have fallen in love with her, if he had not

already given his heart, via satellite even then, to Adele Buchanan.

Instead, he hired her.

He had just been told that he was being moved to London, and he wanted someone to organise it for him – to buy the house, furnish it, handle the finances, so that all he would have to do was get on a plane and consider how he was going to turn Up-Line Cable around. As he had sat on his patio staring into space, considering this problem, Clementine Badger had walked into next door's garden and started cutting the hedge with a pair of nail scissors. And in that moment, he knew it. He knew that Badger – as she preferred to be called – would attack his private affairs with the same military precision, and leave them neat and tidy. He would simply be able to walk out of one house and into another, and, what's more, there would be no fuss, no tantrums, and no hand-wringing.

And he had been right.

Badger had accepted his generous pay rise, and left for London the following week.

Mind you, Eric had still had to deal with fuss, tantrums and hand-wringing, because, the day after Badger left, the woman next door had come around doing exactly that.

'How could you take her away from me?' she'd wailed. 'How could you do that?'

He'd shrugged. 'It was business.'

'Business?' she'd screeched. '*Business?* This isn't business. This is guerilla warfare! Sabotage! This is life, my life, my children's lives!'

'She was your employee,' Eric had said. 'Now she's mine.'

'She wasn't an employee!' the woman wept. 'She

was my sanity!' She'd advanced on him with a dangerous look in her eye. 'Do you have any idea at all,' she'd told him, 'what you've done? I used to be on Prozac. I used to drink. I used to mainline mud pie. I had to mainline mud pie! I had to drink! I had to take Prozac! I've got four kids under six! I've got corporate dinners to arrange for my husband! I have a Filipino maid who can't speak English!' She'd clutched her head dramatically. 'I can't think!' she'd said. 'I can't think what to do. The kids don't know what to do! They're sitting in there right now asking me what square roots are! Jesus!'

He'd got her out of the house somehow. Late that night he'd seen a caterers' van pull up, and two men carry in two boxes labelled *Big Mama's Lip-Smacking Deep Deep Triple-Chocolate Double-Cream Pie* and two boxes labelled *Southern Comfort*.

When he had arrived in England, all was just as he had envisaged. Badger had chosen a house that looked and felt like a tomb, she had had it painted grey, she had installed a grey kitchen of clinical sterility, and she had bought herself a grey uniform. She never betrayed, by word or gesture, that she had any feelings in the matter, or that she was interested in his feelings.

She Understood.

He knew she would.

He got out of the bath now, towelled himself off, and dressed himself in his Peter Rabbit pyjamas and dressing gown. He walked to the sitting room, where Badger had already laid a tray with two digestive biscuits and a mug of cocoa, and he turned on the television.

Eric liked to watch the opposition before he went to bed. His favourite night was Thursday, when

Question Time was on. He loved listening to politicians, and modelled himself on their prevarication and obliqueness. To his mind, they were perfect examples of words without emotion attached; claims without involvement. He admired their two-facedness immensely, their ability to bluster as if they cared about the subject in hand. Because you could see it in their eyes that they didn't care – if you looked closely, the eyes were flat, like staring into the soul of a haddock. The mouths worked overtime, but they were all dead below the waterline. There was nothing going on under there, except, perhaps, self-interest. And he thought it a great joke – well, it amused him more than anything else – to see the acting skills.

But it wasn't *Question Time* tonight. He flicked through the channels, and, as a last resort, turned to Up-Line's late-night news.

A Royal Navy helicopter was coming in to land.

On the tarmac stood a small knot of people, and the camera was concentrating on a woman with shoulder-length brown hair. She turned to the lens, and he saw that it was Meg Randall.

'Miss Randall,' a voice was saying. 'How is Will?'

'He's fine,' she said, a reflex of irritation showing in her expression. 'If you could just let me go.'

'How is his injury?'

'Painful, I should think. Let go of my arm, please.'

'Has he lost any toes?'

'Toes?' she repeated. 'I've no idea.'

'Extremities of any kind?'

'What?'

'Could be important, considering.'

'Considering what?' she asked.

'How many kiddies will there be, exactly?'

'Kiddies?' she repeated. 'What kiddies?'

'After his announcement, and everything?'

The rotor blades were clattering to a stop. A door in the helicopter was thrown open. William Churchill-Twines, national treasure and all-round decent bloke, macho man of distinction, medals, three ticks and a gold star, hero of the frozen North, appeared in the doorway, holding on to his left buttock with one hand, and waving with the other.

'What bloody announcement?' Meg asked.

'Meg!' Will called. 'Meg!'

She hesitated one more second, then turned. And, with a puzzled frown on her face, she started running towards Will.

Eric Cramm leaned forward, the remote still clutched in his hand.

Badger appeared in the doorway of the room.

'Eleven o'clock,' she told him. 'Bedfordshire.'

'That woman,' he murmured. 'That Randall person. Why didn't I see it before?'

'See what?' Badger asked. She walked to the table and picked up the tray.

'She's very photogenic,' he murmured.

'She's very argumentative,' Badger observed. She glanced at him, and then glanced again.

'It's her,' he said. 'It's her.'

'Who, precisely?' Badger asked.

'Her,' he said, nodding to himself in satisfaction. 'Her, The One.'

11

'Will,' said Meg, 'Will.'

He was dead to the world.

They had been in the hotel precisely twenty minutes, just enough time to register, get upstairs, and open the door of the room. Will had fallen over the threshold, fallen on to the bed, and fallen into a snoring, twitching sleep.

Meg had left him for a while, but now it was midnight, and not only did she fancy opening the bottle of champagne on the bedside table, but she would have liked a word or two, from him, should the strain on his coccyx not be too much.

'Will,' she repeated, nudging him, and then lifting one arm. He was spread-eagled, as if he'd fallen on to the bed from a great height. '*Will.*'

He opened one eye.

'Are you OK?' she asked.

'Hot,' he said.

'Roll over,' she urged him. 'Take off your coat.'

'Tired,' he said.

'OK,' she replied. 'Take off your coat and shoes and get into bed.'

He raised himself on one elbow. She looked at his face, what could be seen of it above the beard. His forehead and cheeks were red; his eyes were panda-like white circles where the snow goggles had been.

'How do you feel?' she asked.

'Shit,' he replied.

She started to help him off with his shoes. 'I never heard you swear so much,' she observed. 'It's not like you.'

And it was true; it wasn't. In some things, Will was a throwback to an earlier age. Swearing was one of them. When it came to bad language, Will lived in the 1940s, where women were all Celia Johnson in bad hats, and men were all Trevor Howard and never said anything worse than 'golly'. That he was awkward with women, and blushed when they talked to him, was one of the traits that Meg found appealing. He belonged somewhere else, she knew; some other time. Perhaps another century.

As she stared at him now, fumbling slowly with his trousers, she thought that maybe he was farther back even than Trevor Howard. He was Lawrence of Arabia in a snowsuit. He was Mallory. He was Livingstone. He had been born far too late, too late to have tea every day at four, too late to have a native bearer. Too late to shoot tigers and hang them on the wall.

'There's something I want to tell you,' he said suddenly.

She looked up at him. She had just pulled off his shoes, and he had just pulled down his trousers, and was standing there with them rolled round his ankles.

'Trousers,' she said.

He gazed down at them, confused.

'Socks,' she said.

He didn't move. 'I've been thinking,' he said.

'Let me do it,' she replied.

He caught hold of her arm. 'Thinking,' he repeated.

'Talk about it in the morning,' she said. 'You're too tired, Will.'

'Told Canadian TV,' he said. 'Better tell you.'

'Tomorrow. Trousers.'

'I want to marry you,' he said. And, quite suddenly, he kneeled down.

'What's the matter?' she said, mistaking him. 'Did you drop something?'

He caught hold of her hand. 'Marry,' he repeated. 'As in church, bells, confetti, pageboys picking their noses, etcetera.'

'I don't know anyone who could be a pageboy,' she said. 'Except Harry.' She smiled. 'It'd be worth it, to see Harry in knickerbockers.'

Will was frowning. 'I'm not joking,' he said.

'Neither am I,' she told him. 'In fact, I'd pay to see Harry in knickerbockers.'

'Shut up,' he said.

'No,' she retorted. 'You shut up. Get into bed. You won't remember any of this in the morning. You're just glad to get home, Will.'

'I am not glad to get home,' he snapped. 'That is, of course I'm glad to get home.'

'You aren't usually.'

'I bloody am!'

'No you're not,' she said, calmly. 'If you go according to form, you'll be hiking to the Cairngorms this time tomorrow.'

'I will not.'

'I'm not arguing, Will.'

'Look,' he told her, clearly annoyed. 'All you have to do is say yes.'

'Why?' she demanded.

He stared at her. 'Why?' he repeated. '*Why?*

Because I've asked for your hand in marriage, you stupid woman.'

'Oh,' she said. 'Charmed.'

He rubbed his hand across his face, wincing at the sunburn. 'No, no, no,' he mumbled. 'Marry. I want to get married. I want you to get married to me. I want me to get married to you. Please.'

She sat down suddenly on the edge of the bed. She was still holding one of his thick-knit oiled walking socks. He was still showing his hairy knees and thighs below a pair of underpants with *Bulldog Sausage* written across them.

'I mean it,' he told her.

She shook her head. 'Will,' she said. 'You don't. And I don't want you to.'

'What?' he said. 'Why don't I? And why don't you?'

She waved the sock at him. 'Because in the blink of an eye you'll have this back on, and somebody else's logo on your pants, and you'll be just a blur,' she said.

'No, I won't,' he said.

'Yes, you will.'

'No, I won't.'

'Why won't you?' she said. 'There are at least two more continents you haven't crossed, and at least twenty mountains you haven't hung from by your fingernails.'

'I don't want to do it any more,' he said.

There was a very long silence.

Then, the sense of Meg's words seemed to come back to him. 'Wait a minute,' he said. 'What do you mean, you don't want me to want to marry you? What is it you've got against marriage, anyway?'

'I haven't got anything against marriage as such,' she said.

He laughed. 'Oh, just against marrying *me*,' he said. As he looked at her, a light dawned in his face. 'That's it, isn't it?' he asked. 'It's me.'

'It isn't you,' she told him hastily. 'Look, you're exhausted. This isn't the time to discuss anything. Get into bed. Go to sleep.'

'Why don't you want to marry me?' he persisted. 'Is there somebody else?'

'No.'

'There is!'

'There isn't!'

'Who is he?'

'For God's sake, there isn't anyone. No-one at all.'

She put the sock down, and he, at last, sat back on the bed. He took her hand in his giant paw. 'Meg,' he said. He squirmed a bit. 'Bloody bum,' he muttered.

'This talk of giving up is a mistake,' she told him softly.

'No it isn't,' he said. 'I'm finished.'

'It's only a coccyx,' she said.

'It's not just that,' he said. 'I really am finished with it all, I tell you.' He scratched his beard abstractedly. 'My body's giving in,' he added. 'My elbows hurt. My knees hurt. I'm getting stress-induced alopecia. Every time I ate out there, there were more bloody hairs in my food.' He showed her his scalp. 'I'll be a billiard ball in two years,' he said. 'And then there's pork scratchings. I've eaten my last bag.'

Meg frowned. Will's rations were always full of things like scratchings because they were packed with calories. He used to love them.

'And I'm sick of crapping in tents,' he continued morosely. 'Or crapping outside and getting frostbitten. I want to crap indoors like everyone else.'

Meg smiled at him. But he didn't smile back.

'I want a house in the country,' he said. 'And I want Labradors and a garden and I want to walk about without advertising slogans sewn to my head.'

'You'd be bored out of your skull in forty-eight hours.'

'No, I wouldn't,' he retorted. 'I want to do crosswords and dandle my children on my knee.'

'Dandle?' she said.

'Dangle,' he corrected.

'Dangle?' she said. 'You mean, upside-down by their necks?'

'I'm serious,' he said.

'So am I,' she replied. 'Children would drive you stark staring mad.'

'They would not,' he said. 'Not my own children.'

'You *loathe* children.'

'I do not loathe children per se,' he said. 'Besides, my children wouldn't have snot.'

'They wouldn't be sick, or have tantrums,' she added.

'Whip into shape, that's the secret,' he said.

'Like huskies.'

'Precisely. Matter of tactics. Training.'

She had a swift flash of Will going down to a village shop, and six children pulling a sledge loaded with provisions.

'And who,' she asked, 'is going to have all these children?'

'You are,' he said. 'We are.'

She bit her lip. 'Right the first time,' she murmured. 'Unless you're thinking of making medical history. And how many children would that be?'

'Half a dozen,' he said. 'Eight, nine.'

'Oh God,' she murmured. 'No, no, no.'

'Five, then.'

'Five!' she repeated, aghast. 'Will, have we ever discussed this? *Ever?*'

'No,' he said. 'No need before.'

'I see.'

'Sons,' he said. 'A man needs sons.'

She bit back a retort, which was something along the lines that a man needed daughters to wash his clothes, cook his meals, look after him in his old age, and lie on the floor so he could wipe his feet on them. *My God*, she thought suddenly. *That was bitter. When did I get bitter? I'm not bitter.*

She gazed at the man in front of her. Well, maybe a little bitter. Maybe when he was away for so long. Maybe when people elbowed her out of the way to get to him. Maybe when she was supposed to stand in the background looking adoring, which she was, but . . .

A sick feeling started in the pit of her stomach. This was serious; marriage was serious. It wasn't a jaunt, or a laugh – not if her own parents' marriage was anything to go by. Although Will would probably do his damnedest to make it fun, even if he had to take an icepick to her.

He deserved a nice wife, she thought, almost objectively. He was a nice man. And he was right. He needed a nice wife and a nice house and a nice family. Just like in the old Oxo adverts.

Or worse.

Suddenly she could see it all. Endless numbers of real towelling nappies blowing in the sunshine on a washing line, and five pairs of Wellington boots in a muddy hall, and seven platters to be filled with wholesome, unburned, unpackaged food that she had cooked. Potatoes that she had torn from the earth with her own cracked, wizened hands. Meat she had slaughtered and de-gutted herself. Eggs she had found in warm, sweet-smelling hay. Served on a wood table that she had scrubbed herself, on a snow-white cloth that she had bleached herself, on plates that she had made herself in her own little unpretentious and yet terribly creative studio, probably while breastfeeding twins, and they would eat the meal washed down with wine she had trod herself in a spare moment, possibly before a roaring log fire of wood that she had hewn down herself, and using knives and forks that she had knitted herself on her own loom.

She closed her eyes momentarily. She felt very dizzy.

She'd be barking mad in a fortnight.

Less.

She opened her eyes. 'What were you thinking of living on?' she asked.

'How do you mean?'

'Income,' she said.

'We'd have to work,' he said. 'I thought, a farm.'

'A *farm*!'

'Pigs.'

'*Pigs*!'

'Organic.'

'*An organic pig farm*!'

He raised his eyebrows. 'Why are you shouting?' he asked.

She stood up. 'You've got this worked out.'

'I've had a lot of time to think.'

'Well, I haven't,' she said. 'This is all news to me.'

'But it's what you want,' he said.

'Eh?' she breathed. 'Uh?'

'Family. Women want families.'

'What do I want a family for?' she said. 'I've got a mother who behaves like a four-year-old already. I've got enough on my plate.'

'But you want children,' he said.

She slammed her hand to her forehead. 'When did I ever say that? Or even hint it?'

'But women do,' he objected.

'God!' she exclaimed. 'Women want George Clooney on a plate with a side salad, but we don't get him.'

'Who?' Will said.

'Look,' she told him. She had moved to the other side of the room, and had her back to the wall. In every sense. 'Will, this is crazy. We've never talked about marrying, or children, or anything. I'm twenty-eight, Will. I don't want to get married and I don't want children. Not yet.'

He strode over to her. Or he tried to, until the trousers wound themselves into a knot and he pitched forward on to the carpet. 'Bollocks!' he cried.

She reached out to help him, and then the funny side of it struck her. *If only I had a camera*, she thought.

'Well, don't help me,' he blustered, wrestling with the knot, flailing his feet. 'Shit, shit. Christ, my arse!' He finally kicked them free and looked up at her. She had pressed a fist to her mouth to try to stop laughing out loud.

He gazed at her, and she at him.

'I'm sorry,' she said.

'I'll do it right,' he told her. 'I'll wear a morning suit. There'll be hymns. A honeymoon by a swimming pool. In a hotel. And room service.'

She suddenly felt so sorry for him. She was acutely aware, sure to the roots of her soul, that she was never going to marry him, and that the children and the Labradors were never going to be theirs. Her heart squeezed with regret, so much so that it was hard to speak.

At last, she kissed him, very gently, on the forehead.

'Go to sleep,' she told him softly. 'Go to sleep, and let's talk in the morning.'

It was nine o'clock the next morning when Meg woke up.

At first she thought that the noise was another variation on Will's snoring, which had been like an Arctic storm next to her all night. The sound of it had penetrated her dreams, which had already been lurid, to say the least.

She was just at the part where she was dragging a huge bin of pig swill towards a barn, where a hundred-and-forty children were waiting to be fed, and glancing back at the farmhouse, where five piglets were staring out of the windows, when a vicious kick from the unconscious Will – no doubt thinking that he was scaling another patch of rubble ice – jettisoned her into the day.

The noise was coming from the door.

Someone was trying to batter it down.

'Who is it?' she called, sliding out of bed and pulling on her dressing gown.

'Who is it?' Will muttered from the depths of the bed. 'Shoot them.'

Meg opened the door.

Her mother fell in, quickly followed by Harry.

'Where is he?' Abigail demanded.

'Hi,' Meg said. 'Hi, Harry.'

'Been pursued all the way down the Strand, all the

way through the lobby, all the way up the stairs,'
Harry gasped.

'There he is!' Abigail cried. She descended on Will,
throwing her arms around him as he surfaced from
under the covers.

Harry kissed Meg on the cheek. 'Sorry,' he
whispered. 'But Ma wanted to see Will, and she
wanted to come up to town to look at houses anyway,
and we did try ringing.'

Vaguely, Meg remembered a ringing sound in her
dreams, which must have been the bedside phone.

'Mother heard you were on the TV today,' Harry
said.

'Who is?' Meg asked.

'You are. On *Hey! Today!*.'

'Oh no,' Meg muttered. 'No, no, no, no, no, no.'

Abigail had got Will in a half Nelson of adoration.
'Isn't he lovely,' she cooed. 'Isn't he marvellous.'

Meg looked at her mother sourly.

For someone who had been a feminist long before
Germaine Greer had thought of a book with a female
torso on a coat hanger on the front, Abigail had an
enormous blind spot. By example, she had
championed the right of a woman to go anywhere and
do anything, providing it was legal and didn't make
you come out in hives, and yet, in her private life, she
was the ultimate chauvinist. Her son counted over her
daughter, and her daughter's boyfriends counted over
her daughter. Long before Will, Abigail had favoured
all Meg's male friends, plumping up cushions for
them, and declaring that Meg didn't know how to
look after them, and showing them photographs of
Meg as a child, invariably with her woolly swimming
costume in folds around her middle.

It wasn't so much allowing for male superiority, Meg thought angrily. It was more that her mother never lost an opportunity to make her feel small.

She stared at Abigail now, and saw that her mother had a scarlet tinge.

Bring down the red curtain, here's your ma.

'Meg,' Will groaned. 'Save me.'

Abigail released her grip and pushed Will playfully on the shoulder. 'You silly boy,' she said. She got up and dusted herself down.

Meg walked to the phone.

'What are you doing?' Will asked.

'Phoning Michael,' Meg said. 'To fire him.'

'He's downstairs,' Harry said.

Meg put the phone back. 'Right,' she told him. 'I'll go down there and do it in person. Bloody TV!'

'What's the matter?' Abigail asked. 'They sent a car for you. It's like a bus, you should see it.'

'I don't want a car,' Meg said pointedly. 'I want to be here alone with Will.'

'Nonsense,' Abigail said. 'Get up, Will. You're on TV in two hours.'

'He's not,' Meg said. 'He's going to the hospital for a check-up.'

'You're booked for the sofa with Adele Buchanan,' Harry told them.

'I don't care if I'm booked for the sauna with Tony Blair,' Meg retorted.

Abigail shook her head. 'I simply cannot fathom you,' she said. 'This is Will's finest hour, and you want to put the mockers on it.'

'I am not putting the mockers on it,' Meg retorted. 'But if they want to interview Will, they have to give us some notice.'

Abigail made a harrumphing sound. 'This is *news*,' she told her daughter. 'It's news today, not tomorrow.'

'I don't need you to give me lectures about what's best for Will,' Meg said.

'And part of the news,' Abigail went on, 'is that apparently my daughter is getting married, a fact which she had omitted to mention to me.'

'Married?' Harry said, having had his receiver switched off while Abigail had been talking all the way to London.

'It's not true,' Meg said to Harry. 'Go back to sleep.'

'What isn't true?' Abigail said.

'Marriage,' Meg told her. 'We're not getting married.'

'But Will said it on *North Horizon News*.'

'He lied,' Meg said.

'Oh, Meg,' Will murmured.

They all turned to look at him.

He was lying cross-wise across the bed, trying to protect his bottom from sitting upright. One arm was hanging down the side of the bed, the other was flailed over the covers. His head was twisted side on, so that he could stare back at them, and the sheets were coiled round his body.

'How could you refuse him?' Abigail demanded. 'Look at him, the poor love.'

'He is not a poor love,' Meg said. 'Will, get up.'

'I've got nothing on,' he said.

'All hurting,' Abigail said.

'Get out,' Meg told her. 'And stop coming round here sticking your oar in, as usual.'

'Ma wants to come with you,' Harry said. 'To the TV.'

'Oh, I wouldn't dream of it,' Abigail snipped. 'That would be sticking my oar in.'

'For God's sake,' Meg said.

'Everyone so excited, and your mother relegated outside, looking in through the windows.'

'Christ!'

'Can I go for a pee please,' Will said. 'Just a small one, before my bladder bursts.'

'I suppose you won't even tell me where the wedding is, I'll read about it in the papers after it's over,' Abigail said.

'That's right,' Meg told her. 'That's a good idea.'

'So you are getting married?' Harry asked.

'We're buying a farm,' Will said. 'Meg is pregnant already with twins.'

'Jolly dee,' Harry said. 'Good going.'

'I'll need a hat,' Abigail said.

'Don't bloody mind me, will you?' Meg asked Will. The phone began to ring.

12

A different woman walked into the *Hey! Today!* studio that morning.

She looked like Adele Buchanan. She walked like Adele Buchanan. When she opened her mouth, she sounded like Adele Buchanan.

But she wasn't Adele Buchanan at all.

Instead of taking the car that had been routinely sent for her at seven each morning for the last umpteen years, Adele had sent the driver away. Instead, she had walked to the nearest road junction and hailed a cab.

The cabbie hadn't been able to believe his luck.

'All right, Delly?' he had asked as she got in.

'Hello,' she murmured. '*Hey! Today!* studios, please.'

'What's up?' he asked. 'Chauffeur done a bunk?'

'No,' she replied. She had got her dark glasses out of her bag, looked at them hard for a moment, and then replaced them.

'Abscond-de-monte,' the cabbie said. 'I feel like that, I do.'

She glanced at him in his mirror. 'Do you?'

'I tell you, no lie, for a couple of pound I'd smash this bleedin' cab to a pulp,' he said.

They rode on, swerving from side to side in the traffic. After he'd cut up a few buses, pedestrians, car drivers, cyclists, couriers and delivery vans, the cabbie half-turned towards her as they stopped at traffic lights. 'You got that Able Mabel on again today?' he asked.

'Yes,' she said. 'So they tell me.'

Able Mabel was about Adele's own age. An actress, Able Mabel had once been in a TV sitcom, where she had been cast as a chambermaid. She had become famous – worse still, earned that terrible epithet, *the nation's favourite* (which meant that she was shadowed everywhere she went, the press hoping that she would turn out to have a private life that included men in bondage chains, or a raving relative, or a habit) – and her role had included wearing a huge overall and surgical stockings. In real life, Able Mabel was actually Annabelle Heyho-Barnes, a trained thespian of some talent, quite glamorous, very shy and soft-voiced and rather cultured. But the nation didn't want to know that. They wanted roaring Mabel, who kept getting her words round the wrong way, and who was always unlucky in love, and whose spectacles looked like bottle-tops.

Needless to say, after the sitcom folded, Annabelle plummeted to earth. She did a couple of Mabel-like roles, but no-one wanted to know her. She couldn't get into the RSC, and she was too old to play the female lead in stage plays, and too young to play the character female in stage plays.

Unemployed and desperate, she had, three years ago, offered *Hey! Today!* a slot where she would be Mabel again, going round people's houses, looking in their waste bins. She was, in short, *Hey! Today!*'s resident garbologist. A comedy slot. A scrap, literally, of rubbish.

Poor Annabelle.

'It's all crap, that,' the cabbie said.

'Sorry?' Adele asked.

'That Mabel. Sell-by date gone, know what I mean? Got a lizard neck. You see that? Lizard.'

'Oh,' Adele said. 'Right.' She tightened her scarf.

The cab roared off again.

Adele tried to concentrate on the roads outside. After all, this is what she had dismissed her driver for. She didn't want to be cushioned against the outside world any more. She wanted to see and hear the streets. It was her intention, once they got a bit closer to Up-Line, to pay off the cabbie, and walk. Buy a paper. Have a coffee somewhere. Listen to what people were saying.

She wanted the world to give her a clue why her star was fading.

And where she would go when she fell to earth.

But, as it turned out, she didn't need to pay off the cab early, because she was getting the low-down right here.

'And that Fabian Walmsley,' the cabbie added, sheering round Hyde Park corner on two wheels. 'He makes me bleedin' throw up, he does.'

'Fabian?' Adele asked. 'Why?'

She actually thought that Fabian was one of her better people. He was their resident psychologist; a very pale, elderly, ascetic-looking Scot.

'Toffee-nosed git,' the cabbie said.

'He's very perceptive,' Adele said.

'My arse,' she was told. 'Ricki Lake, that's what I like.'

'Ricki Lake isn't a psychologist, though,' she said.

'All you get is a load of women ringing up crying,' he told her.

'But people like to hear other people crying,' Adele

protested. It was no use being coy, or saying that they were trying to help victims in crisis. The reason why anyone watched a psychologist on the telly was that they were hoping that whoever rang in to talk to him would be in a worse state than they were, so that they could sit back on their sofas and say, 'Well, at least I'm not as mad as that.'

It used to be different, Adele thought to herself. They really used to care. *She* used to care. Now, she realised, she sat in that studio every morning and did the mental equivalent of sighing and filing her nails, while the phone callers rambled on.

Maybe she *was* burned out.

Maybe Bugle was right.

She leaned forward in the cab. 'Excuse me,' she said, tapping the window between her and the cabbie. 'But do you like Jack?'

'Who's he?'

'He's done a couple of spots,' she explained. 'He did that thing about the weather.'

'Oh yeah. He's all right.'

'He is?'

'Not bleedin' queer, like the rest of them.'

Adele took a deep breath. 'So you like him?'

'Yeah.'

'What about Belinda Blanket?'

She shouldn't have asked, she knew. The cab was just reeling into the drive, brakes screeching. Oblivious to the road ahead of him, the cabbie suddenly turned round to her, a megawatt smile plastered over his face.

'OK,' she muttered. 'Fine. I get the message. A painting's worth a thousand words.'

Ten o'clock came all too quickly.

Adele sat in her armchair as the credits began to roll for the show, before her fake fire, in her fake sitting room, in front of a fake window. She was listening to the producer having a row with the floor manager through her earpiece.

Producer and director were an item.

'*And* you said it was carbonara *and* it wasn't carbonara *and* you said there was garlic in it.'

'I *never* said carbonara, I said fusilli.'

'*And* it wasn't fusilli.'

'It was penne. I *said* penne. I *admitted* penne.'

'Ten, nine . . .'

On the monitor, Adele watched her own face superimposed on a shot of London. The music roared over the pictures. Happy music, jolly bouncy music, to prove how happy and jolly *Hey! Today!* was. And here she was, Adele herself, La Suprema, on a dredger under Blackfriars Bridge. Here she was up the GPO tower. Here she was combing the goats on the city farm. Here she was sitting in a wine bar, surrounded by friends, actually actors, all smiling, nobody wittering about carbonara, all raising their glasses, and – so it appeared – laughing uproariously at her jokes. Here she was with the winning contestant from *Who Wants To Be A Billionaire*. Here she was rollerblading. And here she was, running over Clapham Common with a kite.

'Six . . . five . . .'

Bloody kite! She stared blankly at her own opening credits. What the hell had possessed her to agree to that? She looked ridiculous in combat pants. Bloody goats! They had eaten her Stella McCartney coat. Bloody dredger! Bloody Blackfriars! Bloody wine bar! Bloody friends who weren't bloody friends but bloody actors!

'Three . . . two . . .'

And here she was, final picture as the music died down,

'One . . .'

With a baby. Because market research – Bugle's market research – said that 24 per cent of the audience were in hospital or a long-stay institution, and needed cheering up with images of health and freedom, 32 per cent were of retirement age and couldn't be faffed to run anywhere with a kite, and were only too glad to see someone else doing it for them, 11 per cent were unemployed and were too depressed to comb their own hair, never mind a goat's, and so needed positive role models, and the remaining 32 per cent were mothers, stuck in the house with pre-school children and coming to the terrible realisation that it was the hardest job they would ever do, and that no-one had had the decency to tell them how devastating it would be, and they had already rung the Samaritans that morning, hit their husband with a steriliser unit as he went out of the house, and drunk a half-bottle of Baileys.

So here was Adele Buchanan, holding a baby, to show how easy it was.

'Big smile, Adele!' screamed the voice in her ear.

She smiled.

That final shot killed her every morning. Knife in the heart. Not to mention further down, in the parts that even a popular lager could never reach.

But how could she say so? How could she object?

Her ticking clock was a secret. She hoped.

Big, big smile.

'Good morning,' she said. 'And welcome to the show.'

'Barnaby, standby . . .' said the disembodied voice
from the control room, talking to the show's resident
gardener, who was on an outside broadcast fifty miles
away, at a stately home called Flattenall Hall.

'Now which of us,' Adele continued, 'hasn't seen
the news over the last few days and thought, How Can
He Do It?'

'Barnaby and Lord Cranberry,' the voice went on,
'in thirty . . .'

On TVs throughout the country, film rolled across
the screen. The ill, the incarcerated, the retired, and the
terminally maternal watched as Will Churchill-Twines
was shown, a tiny speck on a vast ice floe.

'How on earth can one man face the challenge, time
after time, of defying the elements?' Adele asked. The
picture switched back to her.

'Ponce,' said Lord Cranberry, through the earpiece.

Adele, professional that she was, paused for only a
millisecond. Lord Cranberry was the owner of
Flattenall Hall, and it was evident that they were
having trouble with him. But nothing in Adele's
expression to camera betrayed what she could hear in
her earpiece.

'Well, we're about to find out this morning,' she
said, smiling gamely, 'how he can do it, because
William Churchill-Twines himself is here at eleven, to
tell us just what it's like to take on one of the most
inhospitable landscapes on earth.'

'You bastard!' Barnaby screamed in Adele's ear.

She continued to struggle through the Morning
Menu. 'But here's what we have on offer today,' she
said brightly. 'Starting with Barnaby Sledge in Brand-
New Stately Pile, we continue our fabulous line-up,
including a super giblet supper in the kitchen, our

continuing series of Houses You Wish You Had, a brand-new item on Holiday Hells, and Fashion For a Few Pence.'

The screen flashed up the timings.

'Bash your face in!' yelled Barnaby, from Flattenall.

All hell seemed to have been let loose off camera. 'Bin Barnaby, he's gone mad,' someone called. 'Set up Fashion From Crap Shops.'

Adele ripped the piece from her ear, safe for a few moments until the TV audience had grasped what was going to be shown to them that day. She had maybe fifteen seconds to find out what the problem was.

'What the hell's going on at Flattenall Hall?' she demanded.

The floor manager, a woman of her own age, evidently thought the crisis funny. Like Adele, she had seen it all before. 'Lord Cranberry's taken exception to Barnaby's pyramid,' she sniggered.

In the control room, the outside broadcast camera had the two men on the screen, waiting for their cue.

Except they weren't on cue any longer.

They were trying to kill each other.

In the background, the well-known stately home of Flattenall Hall stretched into the distance, a charming vista of lawns and trees; in the foreground, *Hey! Today!*'s resident gardener and handyman Barnaby Sledge was supposed to be preparing to show Lord Cranberry how he had re-designed Lord Cranberry's front garden. Or the Royal Regency Terrace, as Lord Cranberry preferred to call it.

A year ago, *Hey! Today!* had negotiated a deal with Flattenall Hall to take over the grounds maintenance – which Lord Cranberry couldn't afford – in return for having a permanent gardening feature on the show. It was a case of you-scratch-my-back-and-I'll-scratch-yours. Lord Cranberry got his gardens looked after: *Hey! Today!* had a nice prestigious setting for their gardening slot.

When this arrangement had first been agreed, Lord Cranberry had been only too happy to let the TV cameras in. The benefits to him had appeared obvious. They weren't invading the house itself, they were relieving him of hefty expense, and he freely admitted to the crew that he despised greenery, flowers, roses, trees, and ponds, and could only just about tolerate hedges, providing they didn't have too many leaves. He had no feeling whatsoever for horticulture, but he knew that The Public (he would say this phrase with a twitch and a hiss, because he had to let them in, so that he could pay his electricity bills) loved a bit of garden.

So it was all all right. It was all fine, while the free Chianti was flowing and Lord Cranberry was happy firing his entire ground staff. The film crew had left him, the week before filming began, happily sauntering among the flowerbeds, drunk as a – well, as a Lord – shouting strange blasphemous curses at the evening sky and roaring with laughter by turns.

As the first project, Barnaby had reinstated the old Victorian walled vegetable garden. It was a perfect opportunity to show everyone how to be eco-friendly and grow your own greens, and Barnaby had a lovely time pouring horse manure from vast trucks on to what had, for years, been a thistly wasteland.

But Lord Cranberry had a Plan going of his own for the walled garden, which he hadn't told anyone about. Ever. Not surprisingly.

When his three daughters had left home a decade before, Cranberry had been left with a lot of guinea pigs, the girls' pets, in hutches in the old glasshouses. There was no way Lord Cranberry was going to feed them, so he had let the whole lot – all forty of them – go in the garden. Some had died, and some had multiplied, and Lord Cranberry had discovered that you could have endless amusement chasing guinea pigs through the undergrowth, and taking pot shots at them with a twelve-bore.

The place that the guinea pig population liked best, of course, was the old vegetable garden. And it was the place where Cranberry liked to chase them best, because it had rickety old benches where he could rest and have a fag, and re-load.

When the *Hey! Today!* trucks had started to arrive, Lord Cranberry had taken exception to them, and there had been three hours' negotiation until he would let them in. Once there, the crew had to film with the noble Lord eyeing them furiously from the glasshouses, waving a shotgun about and miming shooting them.

Once the greens were planted, Barnaby couldn't understand why something was eating them, and why his ranks of perfectly aligned cabbages were just stalks. He asked Lord Cranberry about rabbits, and all Lord Cranberry would do was laugh and say, 'Not rabbits,' and laugh again in a gurgling fashion.

So they had moved on to the Terrace.

Some weeks before, Barnaby had visited Athelhampton House in Dorset, and fallen in love with the yew pyramids. Realising that *Hey! Today!* was unlikely to give him the fifty or so years needed to grow something similar, Barnaby had hired a man in Chepstow to make him an Athelhampton. And so, that very morning, forty pyramids had arrived in juggernaut, forty pyramids which had all benefited from Barnaby's Vision. Which meant that they were painted pink and lime green, and violet.

'It's sixties chic, you know, that funky thing,' he'd explained as the doors to the lorry had swung open.

Lord Cranberry had taken five seconds to make his artistic views known. 'Funky thing?' he'd repeated, as if he were saying *Slurry pit?* 'You're not having that shit on my lawn,' he had decided.

At first, Barnaby had merely smiled. It was no more than he had expected, and he knew he could talk Lord Cranberry round. He was well known for the gift of the beguiling gab, and he had dealt with plenty of awkward clients before. People who asked for geraniums, and then got African Jumping Lilies, and people who wanted privet and got coconut palms. In Barnaby's experience, people really didn't know what they wanted until they saw it, and they could only see it when it was done, because most people couldn't Visualise.

He had been Visualising all his professional life, and he knew that green and violet would look lovely against the distant oak woods and the Corinthian columns of the Royal West Door.

'It's shit,' Cranberry had persisted, oblivious to Barnaby's talkative charms. He had his arms crossed, and his face had gone the colour of his name. 'Get them all off my property.'

'Imagine a pink one against the delphinium beds,' Barnaby suggested.

'Lord of Hosts on a tuning fork!' Cranberry had thundered. 'I don't want to imagine. Nancy pink! Gah!'

'Or the violet against the dahlia crescent.'

'Jesus H Christ up a flagpole!' Cranberry had bellowed.

The cameras had already been set up at this point. They had less than five minutes until they went on air. Barnaby had planned to have them film Lord Cranberry weeping with delight at Barnaby's creative skill.

But the man had vanished.

And come back with his gun.

'Ponce!' Cranberry had shouted.

Barnaby had paled. He had once had someone's husband come after him with a garden fork, but never a shotgun. He had held up his hands, and Cranberry had shoved the muzzle up his nostrils, at the same time shaking his lapel in his free fist. Barnaby had reeled backwards, clutching his face and crying, 'You bastard!'

Taking his hands down and seeing the blood, something had happened to the gardener. Thirty years of carefully nurtured upper-middle-class accent had peeled away. Barnaby had looked down at the long cuffs of his Ozymandias Shoo shirt, and the ripped collar of his Ozymandias Shoo jacket, and he had shouted, 'Bash your face in!'

Cranberry had swung at him with the gun.

Barnaby grabbed the muzzle. There was a deafening explosion, and both men fell to the ground.

Back in London, Adele, shocked, pressed her hand to her earpiece. 'Was that what I thought it was?' she asked.

'Just do the crap fashion, quick, quick,' she was instructed.

'Is he hurt?' she asked. 'Is he dead?'

'Only a little bit,' came the reply.

'A little bit hurt, or a little bit dead?' she asked.

The floor manager pointed at her, indicating that the viewers, once more, had her on screen.

She smiled helplessly. 'News from Flattenall Hall later on,' she said. 'But let's look at what spring is bringing us first, in the high street stores.'

'Shot!' screamed Barnaby, at Flattenall. 'Look, look! Oh my God, my God! The carnage!'

'What happened?' the control room at *Hey! Today!* asked the OB crew. Adele felt her world ripple a little; she felt strangely dizzy.

'Finished,' the crew confirmed. 'Feet pointing skywards. Sorry.'

'Not Cranberry!' London squawked.

'A guinea pig,' they were told. 'Just passing with a cabbage. Now passed completely.'

There was a pause just before eleven o'clock for the News.

Adele stood up, ripped off her microphone, and started to walk.

'Hey!' called the floor manager. 'Pee time not yet, OK?'

'I'm going,' she said.

She strode off set – it was surprising how small, how insignificant it looked once you had turned your back on it. She glanced over her shoulder just once, and saw the highly lit tableau where she had spent what seemed like most of her life. On screen, the set looked sumptuous and cosy: but only she knew how much that chair hurt. If you touched those heavy brick walls, they would keel over in a second, because they were made from MDF. If you opened the books, there would be no print inside them. If you lifted that coffeepot, there would be no smell but the tacky studio-smell of overheated egos and overcharged electricity.

Everyone, behind and beside the cameras, was looking at her.

'What's the matter?' the nearest cameraman asked.

She opened her mouth to say something. But nothing – nothing at all – came.

'Churchill-Twines on the back stairs,' someone called.

Poor man, Adele thought. Hauled in here, to this eighty-degree plastic box, so that a million people could stare at him over their cups of coffee and ginger biscuits. It wasn't worth it, she thought. It wasn't worth the biscuit, ginger or otherwise.

The whole plot was unravelling.

She had been holding this pattern for years, holding it tight, keeping all the mornings together. Now, it was running through her fingers. She had, quite literally, lost the thread. Suddenly, it all seemed so bloody pointless. She didn't want to sit at the hub of this manic merry-go-round any more. It was meaningless. It was trite. It was a sham, not entertainment, not educational, not the truth: just sham and pretend.

She put her hand to her forehead.

What was the name of that film with Katharine Hepburn, she asked herself, lost in a vague, confused cloud of thought. The one where Katharine's in Venice? She had watched it one wet Sunday afternoon not long ago.

In this film, Katharine was an American spinster, and she wants to fall in love, but daren't, and then she does. And she has a fling with a married man, and it all looks like it's going to be fine, and all the while you know she's headed into a corner, and you think she doesn't realise. And then, at the end, Katharine and her married Italian lover are sitting in St Mark's Square, watching the birds wheeling about over their heads, and Katharine says something like, 'I want to remember it all. I want to remember today. Because I never did know the right time to leave a party.'

And she leaves. She leaves him. She gets on a train, and her lover stands stranded and perplexed on the station platform, and Katharine's smiling and waving, smiling and waving, from the train window as it pulls away.

Because she's learned at last to go before the party finishes.

Adele looked at the cameraman.

Soon, this very same man would be looking at Belinda through this very same lens. There would be a different atmosphere here, and Adele was well aware what it was all in aid of. Friday had been given to Belinda and Jack as a dry run, a pilot, for the rest of the week. If they took off – and she was suddenly, completely, sure that they would – then she would be out. There would be no ceremony and no goodbyes; it would be a case of *thank you for the last few years, goodbye*. Almost Anne Robinson, but not quite. Because this time the final blow, the final ice-cold dismissive gleam in the eye, would be delivered by a dog, a little West Highland Terrier called Dido, curled smugly on her daddy's knee.

'Oh no,' Adele murmured, as the cameraman watched her.

This morning's fiasco had been happening too regularly, she knew. It was a symptom of decay. It was as if all of them, all her crew, all her team, all the

Mabels and Fabians, all the celebrity cooks, all the yoga gurus, all the weather girls, had caught the same deadly virus at the same time.

Suddenly, Failure Virus had swept through the station. They were carrying it. They were nursing it. For the time being, only she knew, via Lawrence, that her number had come up. That she was about to be yesterday's flavour. But soon, everyone would know it. The virus would develop, and come out: they would all have the mark on them. She, Adele Buchanan, would have transmitted her unpopularity, her infertility, to them all. Soon, they would all be behaving like Jack, turning away at the crucial moment. Not wanting to meet her eyes.

Soon, she would know that most terrible of put-downs, worse than a slamming door. She would know what it was like not to have her calls returned. Soon, Lawrence would be permanently in a meeting. Soon, he would be away, at lunch, on holiday, even – even when he was in the building. She would be told he was in Bora-Bora when he was actually at his desk. Soon she would feel the cold, the knife upon the neck. She would be sitting at the table in Venice watching the birds wheeling all on her own.

'Adele,' said the floor manager. 'Adele?'

She looked around the faces.

'Katharine Hepburn,' she murmured. 'Pigeons, St Mark's, Dido, chair facing west, beach in anorak. No.'

And, pausing only to kick off her shoes, she ran for the door.

13

Clementine Badger halted, her hands on the freshly ironed shirt, holding her breath, watching the clock.

All around her, Eric Cramm's house showed the results of her quiet industry that morning. There was not a single stray speck of dust, unfolded newspaper, dirty cup or plate, or unwashed piece of laundry. The taps, surfaces, sills and windows gleamed; the furniture in every room was set at precise angles, and at precise distances from each other, just as Eric liked. Even the books were arranged in alphabetical order and in subject category.

The same extraordinary neatness reigned through the whole house.

In Eric's room, the contents of each drawer were laid carefully in lines. Socks, starting with tennis white, and ending in funereal black, occupied separate compartments, curled in ironed balls. In Eric's wardrobe, the suits hung in lines, each in a plastic cover; in Eric's bathroom, the shampoo and shower gel were arranged with the names facing outwards, and the basin and shower cubicle had already been cleaned.

Eleven o'clock, Clementine thought anxiously to herself.

She closed her eyes and took a deep breath.

Far down in her subconscious, beneath all the layers

of labels, categories and cleanly folded clothes, beneath all the ironed newspapers, the charts and timetables and memorised instructions, a bell was ringing.

It always rang, every single day, at eleven o'clock.

She spread her hands flat on the ironing board, as if to support herself.

The bell belonged to a tower, in a grey little chapel. The chapel, built of slate, and set into a quadrangle, was high on a hillside. If anyone had managed to squeeze themselves into the belfry, they would have been able to look straight up and down the long narrow valley below. It sounded almost idyllic, to say it like that: a chapel on a hillside, with a view to the valley floor. But it was not idyllic at all. For the hillside was in South Wales in 1955, and the valley was filled with smoke, and the hillside was covered in coal slag, and all that could really be seen, down the grimy slope, was the wheelhead of the mine, and the village of stacked terrace houses, packed so tight against the mountain slopes that they looked as if they had been washed there by some catastrophic storm.

South Wales, in the time of coal and steel, was not a pretty place. It had been pretty once, and it would be pretty again, and it was inhabited by people with strong hearts, and even stronger voices. But all its beauty lay hidden under a sign, and the sign read *Coal Board Property*. It was not a place for the frail or the weak-willed; it was a place of industry and God, the kind of God who got up at six on a Sunday to listen to the roaring hymns from the churches, and who watched over the pit cages, and the coal faces, and whose very breath seemed to be contained in the rivers

of molten fire and the clouds of billowing smoke that
poured out of the steel mills.

God was not someone you argued with in Wales.
He had songs made for him like 'Guide Me, O Thou
Great Redeemer', and no-one who had heard that
hymn sung by a massed Welsh male-voice choir could
ever hear it again without emotion crowding their
breast and tears clouding the eye. God gave no quarter
and took none in these tough little towns. He was
obeyed with a passion.

Or so Clementine had been told from the day she
was born.

And she was born Gladys Vera Badger on 22nd
May, 1955.

No-one knew who her mother was. Gladys was
found in a shoebox packed with terry-towelling
nappies, with her date of birth pinned to her knitted
coat. The note said, *Please take care of my baby, she
was born on Saturday*. The three-day-old child was
taken to the local pastor's wife – Gladys – who, in
turn, passed her to the police, who passed her to the
hospital, who passed her to The Kingdom Foundling
Care Home.

She was not an attractive baby.

As she grew up, she had been told this often by Mrs
Cunningham, the Matron of the Home. She cried a
great deal, she was told. More than was natural. She
had a great shock of black hair. More than was
natural. She ate voraciously, more than was natural of
course, and certainly more than Mrs Cunningham
allowed.

It was a strictly run place, The Kingdom Foundling.

Mrs Cunningham, even if she had ever heard of
child psychology – which she hadn't – was of the

opinion that a child should be kept neat and clean and tidy, and silent. Her idea of health for the babies was to put them outside in their prams for hours on end, so that they could breathe the deeply polluted air. A nurse by training, she believed in floors of disinfectant-smelling lino, board-hard towels, and cold dormitory beds with hospital corners.

Gladys must have been three when she learned the hospital corner.

The sheet went over the mattress, and the part that hung down was grasped between thumb and forefinger, and the resulting triangle of cloth was looped back up on to the bed. The remainder was tucked in, and the triangular loop followed.

It looked easy when Mrs Cunningham did it. It took three seconds. Little Gladys would watch her, trying to see how it was done in those few deft flicks of the wrist; all the children would stand by their beds and copy the movements. The older girls had it conquered, but Gladys did not. She could still feel Mrs Cunningham's breath on her face. 'Not done it, Gladys?' she would ask, in a deceptively calm tone. 'Not done it?'

'No,' Gladys would whisper, knowing what was coming.

Mrs Cunningham had a stick called Henry.

Henry would get very angry if beds weren't cornered, just as he got very angry if shoelaces weren't tied properly, or plates not washed properly, or if colours escaped the lines in colouring books, or if someone sang off-key in chapel. There was no end to Henry's temper, and you could hear him coming down the dormitory, his lithe willow back lifting each counterpane and looking at the sheets. Henry was always furious when he got to Gladys's bed. 'We'll see what Henry has to say about it, Gladys,' Mrs Cunningham would tell her.

Mrs Cunningham wasn't especially cruel. She was just a product of her time. The cane was used in schools routinely, and children were slapped as a matter of course. There was no talk of human rights, or of abuse, then. It was just what you did. It was what children needed. Sticks like Henry, and the backs of hands, and, sometimes, fists. And sometimes hairbrushes.

Gladys's hair had been the bane of her young life.

Mrs Cunningham would brush all the girls' hair in the evening, and tie it in rags to make it curl. Outside the Home, this was one of the things that earned her such a good reputation. That she took the time, when she was undoubtedly tired, long after her working day ought to have finished, to make sure that the girls would look nice, with their hair in ringletted curls, the following day. Most children in care had pudding-basin cuts, but the Kingdom Girls had curls.

Such *dedication*, the public said.

Gladys's hair was wiry, and thick. It had a kink in it, so Mrs Cunningham decided. She would pull at the hair with the hairbrush, gritting her teeth, and saying, 'I don't know where an English child got such hair.' The brush would get stuck in the knots, and the hissing monologue would go up a notch. 'It's foreign hair, that's what it is,' Mrs Cunningham would grumble. 'Hair from a Dark Continent, that's what it is, you mark my words.' And, for good measure, as if it would miraculously untie the knots, Mrs Cunningham would give Gladys a smack on the skull with the brush.

The other children would look at Gladys, relieved

to the roots of their soul that their hair didn't come from a dark continent, and, at the same time, picking up the unspoken theme that Gladys had not sprung unsullied from good English stock, but from some *foreign* place, some nameless, unspeakable place that was not called England, and where everyone went about with hair sticking at right angles to their scalps, a mark of *foreign abandon*.

Mrs Cunningham would always leave Gladys till last, until her temper was all but extinguished. And so – because it was routine, and because this was what was done with awkward children – Mrs Cunningham would regularly lose her mind completely over Gladys Badger's hair, and lash out.

One night, the hairbrush broke.

It was a thick, blue, rigid plastic brush, and God only knew what repeated force it had taken to fracture it, but it suddenly broke clean down the middle. For a moment, Mrs Cunningham stared at it. Perhaps some other woman, in that moment, might have felt a twinge of guilt. She might have realised that, if the brush could break, then so could the fragile head underneath it. But nothing like that seemed to occur to Mrs Cunningham. There was silence for a few seconds, and then, amazingly, the Matron of Kingdom Foundling began to laugh. She laughed for some time, then sighed, and finally pushed Gladys away. 'Get off with you,' she said. 'You and your foreign hair.'

Gladys had eventually been turned out of the Home at fourteen, and placed in a convent in London. From here, she had got a job as a nanny for a Kensington family. They were distant, but polite with her, and paid her a pittance. The paucity of the wage never occurred to Gladys at all, because she had a room to herself, and plenty of food, and the children – deprived of parental affection themselves – adored her. She had effortlessly found her talent, in one fell swoop; and that was to relate to the very young. Parents loved her because, in contrast to the other teenagers of the Swinging Sixties around them, Gladys was old-fashioned, and quiet, and never went out, and never asked to use the car, and never made eyes or passes at the husbands, and never seemed to expect anything at all in the way of praise. Or pay rises.

And children did what she said. In a world of newly available drugs and sex, Gladys clung on to discipline and quiet determination. It was ingrained in her. Perhaps the children recognised her invisible badge of honour. She knew what they knew: loneliness in a bed at the top of the house, mothers that were about as approachable, and holdable, and tangible, as a dream. Fathers who were similarly absent. Like Eric Cramm ahead of them, the babies in her charge knew that Badger Understood.

She earned herself a reputation for reliability, and was never out of work. One summer when she was eighteen, the father of the family she worked for was posted to Boston. She went with them. In Boston, she was passed on to an American family, who offered her what seemed like a king's ransom to look after their four children. From Boston, she went to Denver, then New York, and, finally, California.

And all the time she worked, she saved.

Having lived for so long in households where money and finance were openly discussed, she picked up an ability to invest. And, by the time that she reached the house in Los Angeles where Eric Cramm found her, she had amassed a tidy sum in stocks and bonds.

She had no idea what she was saving for. Her old age, maybe.

She was already beginning to *feel* old.

She had never had a lover, let alone a husband. Once, in Kensington, she had joined a bridge club, and been pursued for six horrible weeks by a retired Colonel with one false eye. Once, in Boston, she had held hands with a man who was interested in prehistoric fish. In California, she had been rung up repeatedly by a strange evangelistic sect to whom she had foolishly given her name in a shopping mall, and who would insist on telling her that Satan lived in CD players.

But she didn't think that counted, as far as romances went.

She knew that she wasn't romantic material.

Her legs were too mountainously long, and too thick. Her figure was box-like, and square. She was very shortsighted, and years of squinting, before she got contact lenses, had lined her eyes. The only thing that she thought was possibly in her favour was her limitless patience.

And oh, she had plenty of that.

She could wait in line. She had learned that from Mrs Cunningham: to wait in line, at first fearful, and then, in later years, resigned, to whatever was about to happen to her. If waiting had been an Olympic event, she could have waited for England. She would have been right up there with the world's greatest Olympians, and the roll of honour for England would have gone, *Steve Redgrave, rowing . . . Gladys Badger, standing in line*.

And, while she had waited all those years, she had considered things, absorbed them, learned about them. She had become expert not only at biding her time, but also at accepting and interpreting the world. And one of the prime lessons she had learned, in the last forty-six years, was that what goes around comes around.

She wished . . . no-one in the world knew what she wished. It was private, so very private that it was almost like a secret shame.

She bit her lip, thinking that she *did* feel ashamed. Irrational, certainly. But true. She was ashamed of her own desires, her feelings. Feelings buried so deep that they might have been at the bottom of one of those coalmines. She opened her eyes and glanced at the clock.

Nearly over.

Nearly 11.05.

She walked slowly out of the room, and went up the stairs. The sunlight was filtering through the skylight here, casting ripples of light and shadow on to the steps. She climbed steadily.

Her bedroom – which Eric had never seen, and might well have been surprised if he had – was not like the other rooms in the house. Here, at the very top of the building, in a small ten-by-twelve space, Clementine allowed herself to surface for the few minutes of the day that were hers alone. She closed the door, and listened, irrationally anxious even now, that someone would suddenly come running up the stairs and see what the room contained.

Right under the window – a slanted pane of glass that gave a view of the distant Lincoln's Inn Fields and the frothy tops of the trees there – stood a rocking horse. It wasn't a very large one – you couldn't have got a large one up the attic stairs. But it was Victorian,

and had been restored, and it was what she had always
dreamed of when she had been Gladys Badger under
the eye of Mrs Cunningham – it had a lovely grey
mane that reached almost to the frame, and beautiful
large brown eyes, and a proper saddle and reins, and it
was, in short, the dream of every small girl. She put her
hand on it now, and smiled to herself. She had never
got on it. She was far too big. But she stroked it every
day.

Behind her, on a small bookcase, was a yet more
surprising collection.

Clementine Badger owned two hundred and four
first editions of Mills & Boon. They went right back to
1962, when she had saved up to buy the first. Old-
fashioned now, the cover bore a lurid illustration of a
nurse, standing next to a doctor, gazing up into his
eyes. *My Heart In Your Hands*, it was called. And it
was lovely. Clementine remembered the day that she
had bought it, at the grocery store at the bottom of the
hill. It had been nestling among the bags of flour, and
iced buns, and trays of nails, and rolls of lino. *My
Heart In Your Hands* was in a pile of other titles –
Lady Of The Manor, *Thunder At Willerby Hall*, *The
Dandy of Berkeley Square*. Oh, she'd been so pleased,
so thrilled to own it! She'd carried it back in a brown
wrapper, and hidden it under her bed, and read it at
night, by the light of a torch.

And she'd lived in those books, in those romantic
places. She'd kept her own heart alive with the
constant diet of fictional desire. She'd breathed the
same air as those heroines as they sat under blossom
trees and had men proposing to them on their knees.
She'd been a princess in France, and a flower girl in
Putney, and a wartime heroine, and a keeper of horses,

and an heiress. She'd lived a thousand lives, huddled under the blankets and the cheerless roof of Kingdom Foundling.

And she'd never quite cured herself of the addiction.

She smiled at her acquisitions, running her eye along the titles. They were like her family to her. Her children. She knew them all intimately, and she liked to re-visit them. Still smiling, she knelt down and drew a box from under the lower shelf. She opened the lid, turned back the metal grip, and took out the papers.

For some time she sat on the floor, with the pages in her lap.

Dreams.

Dreams for a future that she was determined to have.

Her dreams of Eric Cramm.

She remembered when she had first seen him. She had been standing at the hedge, scissors in hand, and he had materialised on the other side.

'Are you English?' he had asked.

'Yes,' she had told him.

'I guess the best nannies in the world are English,' he had observed. He had been looking at her very acutely.

'I have many talents,' she had told him, truthfully.

He had simply nodded, several times.

She had never seen anyone quite so centred, and silent, as he. In that, they were alike. And it was not the only way in which they might have been brother and sister. Curiously, their similarities went very deep indeed; they had even been born on the same day. Gladys had been astonished to see the date on Eric's birth certificate when she had been organising his papers prior to the move.

He had been born in New York, the son of parents who had died young. Left an enormous amount of money in trust, Eric had been brought up by a paid nurse from the age of eight, living in his dead parents' house. His life, like hers, had been a regime of military order.

She took a long, deep breath, and looked now at her bedside clock.

It was 11.06.

Thank God.

Relief rushed through her, a feeling that she had had ever since she could remember at this precise time of day. Relief, and freedom. Guilt mixed with joy. At 11.06, when she was a little girl, she would be running again; out of the grey slate chapel, down the long corridor. And every single morning, at this time, she would turn the corner in the one part of the Home where you could not be easily observed – the passage to the kitchen – and she would dance, all alone, for a few seconds. Unformed, graceless cantering, kicking up her heels. She didn't doubt that, at such moments, she had looked like a monkey hopping over coals. But she didn't care. It had been worth it, after Confession.

All those years at precisely eleven o'clock each morning, there had been an orchestrated moment of truth in the chapel pews. One by one, Mrs Cunningham had required the girls to step forward and confess what sin they had committed in the last twenty-four hours. Although Mrs Cunningham was not Roman Catholic, she did believe that this one element of Catholicism was good for the soul. Except there was no privacy to it at Kingdom. You had to step out, in front of everybody else, and announce, in the loudest voice you could muster, what horrible vice had recently possessed you.

Gladys could never think of anything.

Girls all around her would routinely pipe up that they had scribbled on someone's book, or that they had hated the supper they had been served, or that they hadn't brushed their teeth properly. All that was needed – and other girls could do this, it seemed, without a flicker of effort – was to think of something – anything – and rearrange your face to look humble, and sorry.

But Gladys never could. Even as they trooped into chapel just before eleven, her mind would start to go blank. Her heart would begin thudding; her breath would become shallow. The damp walls would press in like falling playing cards; the ground would ripple and buckle ahead of her. She would panic, and sometimes not be able to speak at all, and Mrs Cunningham took this as proof that she was possessed of an original sin.

Henry would come out and bite Gladys's legs.

She had been a sinner every day at eleven o'clock for forty-six years.

She ran a hand across her forehead now. Standing up, she put the papers back into the box, and returned it to the darkness under the shelves. She went out of the room, locking the door, and down the stairs. Going back into the sitting room, she folded the shirt that was still lying on the ironing board, and put it carefully on to the pile. She took down the board, and carried the iron into the utility area.

Then, picking up a pencil and pad, she walked back into the sitting room, sat down on the sofa, picked up the remote, and switched on the TV.

Every day, Eric liked her to watch Adele Buchanan. Sometimes he would ask her what she thought of the day's performance. Sometimes not.

The first time he had shown her a tape, when they were still in the USA, she had noticed a curious change in him. A light was switched on inside him; he would wear a vague, slack smile. 'What do you think of this woman?' he asked her.

She had watched for a while. 'What's her name?' she asked.

'Adele.'

'Dyed hair,' she had pronounced. 'Too many teeth.'

'Sparky,' he had said.

'Possibly on drugs,' she had replied.

'Nobody like that over here,' he had told her.

In that, she had to agree with him. American television, was, in her opinion, almost as bad as eleven o'clock at Kingdom. In fact, sometimes, it was like an endless procession of eleven o'clocks. They would show the same film over and over on some channels, until you got a horrible sensation of déjà vu, as if someone had wound back the day. Groundhog television, it was. The news filleted so much that it was as if the entire population was only capable of thinking in three-word headlines.

Brit Cows Mad.

Saddam Ass Kicked.

Beside this, she supposed that Adele Buchanan was class itself.

Yet Gladys could detect, far down in Adele's voice, a faint twinge of Liverpudlian accent, and this revelation made Gladys curl her lip. She was quite sure that, if you scratched the surface, you wouldn't find a goddess in Adele Buchanan, but a quite ordinary girl from a very ordinary home, who had just got lucky. Adele would have no reserves, no inner resources, she was sure; because Adele had had an education, and a life, and would probably have never known a stick called Henry.

And she probably wasn't even called Adele. She was probably called Sandra. Or Kimberley. Or Janet.

'Adele,' she had murmured. 'Sounds false.'

It was around this time – one day when Eric had asked her to watch another Adele tape, that he had suddenly turned to her and said, 'What's your name?'

She had been taken aback. 'You know my name,' she'd said.

'I only know your surname,' he'd told her.

She had blushed. For a split second, it rushed over her that there was some personal reason, some significant personal reason, why Eric wanted to know her Christian name. She felt the blood rush to her face; she had swallowed hard. She was about to say *Gladys* when she suddenly thought that *Gladys* was a perfectly revolting name, with all the resonance of a blunt object hitting an overripe watermelon. *Glad-ys. Glud-ys. Glug-hiss.*

She had known, in that moment, that she could never tell Eric that she had such a name; she was seized with a totally uncharacteristic desire to impress him, to make him see the girl still trapped inside her, the one who was capable of dancing down the kitchen corridor. The one that, secretly, very very secretly, she knew she could be.

The name sprang unbidden to her lips, out of nowhere.

'It's Clementine,' she had lied.

She had watched his face, waiting for his reaction.

She had clutched her own hands into a knot, and hidden them behind her back, in a sudden agony of anticipation. Maybe he would think, as she did, that it was a very sweet name. A rather feminine kind of name. Maybe he would be reminded of the song. 'Oh my darling Clementine'. Maybe he would even say that. It was possible he could say that. Wasn't it? Wasn't it possible? After all, they got on very well together. They were very alike. She had never done anything to let him down in any way. She had always done whatever he wanted. Maybe – just maybe, just this once – a man would look at her, and he might say – it was possible, it was possible, why couldn't it be possible? – and he might take hold of her hand as he said it, and she would suddenly realise that she would never have to stand like this again, twisting and turning her own lonely hands over and over behind her back, because someone – some man – a man called Eric Cramm, in fact – would be holding them for her. Like other people did. Like other couples did.

Like lovers.

And he would say, *Oh my darling Clementine*.

But Eric Cramm didn't say it. And he didn't hold her hand.

He didn't even look at her.

Instead, he flicked the volume switch on the remote, so that he could hear Adele Buchanan better. And he raised his eyebrow – just a fraction, just a twinge of mild, objective, unmoved surprise – and he said . . .

He said, 'Uh-huh.'

Badger shook her head at herself, to free herself of the memory.

And it was only then that the cacophony on the TV screen filtered through to her.

The eleven o'clock news summary had finished, and the cameras had switched back to *Hey! Today!*, as usual. But, to Badger's surprise, there was no Adele sitting on the sofa. All that was visible on the screen were the guests: a very tall man with a beard, and a much smaller girl of about twenty-five or so.

Off screen, Badger could hear someone talking. It sounded like a much older woman.

'You can't leave them sitting there,' she was saying.

There was a babble of voices. A figure flitted across the set, from left to right, a headset and microphone clamped to his head and a clipboard in his hand.

'She's running across the car park!' somebody shouted.

Badger leaned forward, trying to make sense of what she was seeing.

She recognised the girl sitting on the sofa. It was the one that Eric had been talking about the other night; the girlfriend of the Arctic explorer. And that must be him, Churchill-Twines. He looked a little more human than he had done on the outside broadcast of the other evening; his hair was much shorter, and his beard had been cut. Badger smiled a little as she watched him: he looked like a giant bear who had been stuffed into a shirt and a pair of trousers.

There was a crash to one side of the couple, off camera, and they both turned to look.

A dog was barking.

A man shouted, 'Gone? Gone?!! Where gone?'

The girl on the sofa whispered to the explorer. They smiled at each other.

'Get her back!' the man's voice cried. 'What fire escape?'

The dog began to howl.

The screen went blank.

Badger sat back in her chair, astounded. After a gap of a few seconds, an announcer came on the screen. It was a man in another studio, who looked as if he had just been pushed on with a stick. He kept glancing to one side, and his tie was askew.

'Well,' he said. He smiled vacantly. 'There seems to be a . . . slight technical hitch at *Hey! Today!* . . . we'll do our best to get you back there as soon as possible . . . and . . .' He looked wildly about him. 'And until then,' he added, with a burst of inspiration, 'here's a short film about otters.'

Like the rest of the TV-watching population that morning, Badger's expression was of total bemusement. She stared at the vision of a hairy mammal scampering through bulrushes. She frowned hard. What on earth was going on? What was all that shouting about fire escapes?

Something had happened to Adele Buchanan, that much was evident. But what? Adele was a legend in television: she had never missed a single show. Had she been taken ill? Badger wondered. With what? What were they saying about shoes? Had someone kidnapped her?

As if in answer to her prayers, the phone beside her began to ring.

She picked it up, and immediately heard Eric's voice.

'She's gone!' he cried.

Badger stared in disbelief at the receiver. She had never before heard Eric raise his voice. 'She's run off, she's run away,' he continued, sounding grief-stricken.

'I know,' Badger said. 'I'm watching it.'

'What have they done to her?' Eric asked.

'I don't know,' Badger said. 'Is she ill?'

'She's never been ill in her life.'

'Then it must be something else,' Badger decided.

'It must be something else,' Eric muttered. 'She wouldn't . . .' he stopped. Badger could almost hear the thought processes whirring. 'She wouldn't unless . . . unless . . .'

'Something had happened,' Badger said.

'Something had happened, like . . .'

'Someone had upset her,' Badger offered.

'Someone had upset her, and . . .'

'Something about the programme?' Badger wondered. 'Something about her personally?'

'Something personal,' Eric echoed. 'Something . . .' His voice trailed away.

There were several seconds of utter silence.

Then, 'Clementine,' he said.

The blood rushed suddenly to Badger's face. Joy thundered in her heart. 'Eric,' she whispered.

'Do something for me,' he said. 'Can you do something for me, Clementine?' His voice had dropped so low that she could hardly hear it. He may have even had his hand cupped over the receiver, so that no-one else could hear.

'Anything,' she breathed.

'Quickly. Today. Soon. This morning. Now.'

'Anything,' she repeated. 'You know that.'

'I can't do it,' he said. 'Someone might see me. Might realise. Give the game away. Keep secret. That's the key. Secret. Just you and me, Clementine.'

'Of course,' Badger replied. She was in a daze of delight. Angels were dancing round the room. The Hallelujah Chorus had sprung up in her head. Cherubs were sprinkling her with fairy dust. 'Just say the word. What is it?'

'Find her,' Eric breathed seductively. 'Today. Find Adele Buchanan.'

14

'No,' Lawrence Bugle was saying, in his sleep. 'No, no, no.'

He was having the strangest dream.

He had slumped to the floor in *Hey! Today!*, right there in front of all the crew. He had felt strangely disorientated after rushing down from his office to the studio, finding Adele gone, and having his screaming fit during the showing of the otter film. Strange, because it was as if everyone and everything were rapidly receding down an ever-narrowing tube.

He had had another dream like that once, when he was dieting. He had been crawling down an enormous pipe, the kind of pipe that was used to lay drainage; and when he had started out he had been able to stand up in it, and when he was halfway along he had only been able to kneel down in it; and then, towards the end, just when he was seeing the light at the end of the tunnel, he had found that he couldn't stand up or kneel down, but had to crawl on his stomach. And he had at last got to the other end and found, to his horror, that he couldn't do anything but stick his head out through a small hole, and then even his head became stuck, and he had woken up ravenous, and terribly, terribly, afraid.

Funny, that. He wasn't afraid now. He was drifting down another tunnel . . . drifting, it seemed, about four feet off the ground, and the ground, instead of being the shiny floor of the studio, was strangely green and grass-like – in fact, it *was* grass, he noticed.

And it was the loveliest grass in the world. It was like the grass that there had used to be in the field behind his house when he was a boy. The field wasn't there any more, because an enormous Matalan store had been built on it, but he remembered how it had been, all those centuries ago, when, as a kid of three or four, he had been able to run out of the back door and hurtle down towards a sea of dandelions.

God, it had been so wonderful.

When he was a little boy.

All he had cared about in those days was how far he could throw a hedgehog. There were loads of hedgehogs in the fields behind the house, and he and the other kids used to go out and hunt them down, and then have bets on how far they could catapult them. There was quite an art to it, on account of the prickles.

Not like frogs. You could go down to the stream – this was at the other end of the road – and you could just pick up any old frog there – there were hundreds of them – and a frog flew through the air fantastically, with all its legs splayed out, trying to find purchase in the summer sky. They sounded brilliant when they landed, too. Not the thump of hedgehogs but a sort of squelch.

In his deep sleep, Lawrence smiled.

And then there were cats, of course. Tying a can to a cat's tail was an old trick, too boring to contemplate. But cramming a cat into a biscuit box, and kicking it all the way down the street, that was amazing. Or climbing a tree with a cat and then tying it to one of the branches. Or tying a cat to a car bumper. Or tying

a cat to the guttering over your bedroom window. Or
tying a cat to a swing in the park, or a seesaw.
Anything, in fact, that involved a cat, a length of rope,
and a moving object.

And then there were the fieldmice.

Lawrence sighed.

He had always loved animals.

His mind seemed to fly back now, fly far away to
that complete paradise, that stream. That field. And
further still across the dandelions was another great
spot, a stagnant pond, with a willow tree hanging over
it.

As he dreamed and drifted, a boyish grin came to
Lawrence Bugle's face. The times – he had lost count
of them – that he had hung from that tree and dropped
into that water. The first time he had done it, it had
been by accident. And the water had come up to his
neck, and he'd been scared to death, because his feet
had slithered about in the mud underneath him. But
the second time he did it, he did it for a dare, and he
had got out pretty quickly, having swallowed only a
couple of pints of the water, and then he got a name
with the other lads, for being able to Get Out Of The
Pond. And the best thing about Getting Out Of The
Pond was that you came out covered in green gunk,
even in your hair, and your mum would wail when she
saw you, and scrub you with a scrubbing brush out in
the yard, but that was all right too, because you were
already a Hero.

His mother wasn't used to heroes. She had never
liked them. They were not part of her philosophy,
which had been not to draw too much attention to
yourself. And Suffer. She had been quite good at the
Suffering part, because his father spent all his spare

time at the Nag's Head with a large barmaid of uncertain age. Lawrence's mother had been a very small woman with a very small, tight-lipped mouth, and her hair was always set in a very small, tight-wrapped perm. It was the kind of hairstyle that women excelled in in the late forties, women who had risen a few precious points up the social scale and could afford to go and get their hair done once a week, invariably by men called Toni, in sidestreet salons with pink frilled curtains.

Lawrence's mother had certainly considered herself to have her head well over the Lower Classes Parapet. She had a separate dining room, after all. And two toilets, and a stainless-steel sink, and a fitted kitchen without a separate pantry. Such things were considered daring in his street.

In The Mead.

On the Limetree Development.

He could still hear his mother's voice when she gave their address to anyone. 'We live in The Mead,' she would say, with pride. Not even a Road, or an Avenue. But a Mead. When, as a young lad, he'd looked it up in the dictionary, he'd discovered that it was another word for a meadow, *a mede Al ful of fresshe floures, whyte and red*, as Chaucer had it. *Riuers sweete along the meedes*, according to someone called Tusser.

It had puzzled him a bit, then. For, although there was a *mede* full of dandelions and hedgehogs, and a *riuer* full of hapless frogs, there was also a stagnant pool and, beyond that, stretching over the empty land behind for several miles, were stacks of breezeblocks, and lengths of pipe, because The Mead was the first street – Mead – built in the enormous Limetree Estate; the biggest estate, then, in Western Europe. Soon, by the time that he went to the grammar school, The Mead was surrounded by vast, sprawling crescents and cul-de-sacs and all the lesser Roads and Streets of his mother's nightmares. The hedgehogs and the frogs would be gone in less than ten years, and, when he went back to look at the Limetree some thirty years later, he saw their old house looking painfully ordinary in a painfully ordinary, if not decaying, road.

His mother had died by then. She had so wanted him to be something quiet, like a Sub-Postmaster. She had wanted him to wear a quiet dark suit, and say very little, and have a quiet dark life.

Lawrence had probably been a disappointment to her.

He had been loud, verbose, insistent, domineering. Moving on from the masterful frog-throwing qualities of his youth, he had forced his way to the front at everything, and that was how he had got to where he was today. That was how he had scaled the heights of broadcasting, by not being afraid of squelchy, gunky things. He was a leader of men; it was in his genes. It was his destiny. He had climbed the highest mountain. He had sailed the stormiest seas. He had . . .

He looked down.

He wasn't on a mountain now. He was on a riverbank.

He looked up, frowning, and saw that the water was very still, and very full of life. In fact, it was full of frogs. And the frogs were all looking up at him in an accusing fashion.

'Eh?' he wondered.

Where on earth *was* he?

'Cross over,' said a voice.

He raised his eyes to the opposite bank. And there, swathed in a long black cloak, was a man with a scythe. The apparition was waving to him, very slowly, with one bony hand. 'Come over,' he repeated. And he ran his thumb over the blade.

'I can't,' Lawrence called back. 'I have a Christmas scheduling meeting at twelve.' And he looked around himself, in vain, for the familiar landscape of his own office.

'There are no more Christmases for you,' the man told him.

'And I have to see my pensions adviser at two,' Lawrence added, unsure now. There was a gnawing feeling in the pit of his stomach.

'You have nothing to provide for,' the voice echoed. 'Cross.'

Lawrence took two or three steps back, all in a rush. 'Who are you?' he demanded. He squinted hard. 'Did you use to be on *Crackerjack*?' he asked, his voice beginning to quaver. 'Where is Dido?' he asked. 'Where is Adele?'

'Not here,' the man said. 'Cross.'

'If you want to know about your ten per cent,' Lawrence stammered, 'it's nothing to do with me. I didn't ask the agents to give it to me. It was a mere corrigendum.'

'Cross over!'

'I never said the Nine O'Clock News should move,' Lawrence protested. 'That was some other pertinacious individual.'

'Cross over now!'

'I've got things to do,' Lawrence squeaked. 'VAT return.'

'Look,' said the apparition. 'You're supposed to

cross. That's what it's like. I say cross, and you just cross.'

'Well,' Lawrence said. 'I shan't. Who are you, anyway?'

'Look,' the man in black repeated, 'it's not a negotiation, right? I wave, you cross. That's how we do it. Never mind who I am.'

'Well, I won't do it.' Lawrence decided. 'And I still don't know where I am.'

'It's not a choice thing. It's wave, cross, OK? Wave, cross. There's no discussion here. And you're in Limbo.'

'Come and get me,' Lawrence told him. 'What limbo?'

The apparition put down the scythe and stood with one hand on his hip. 'I haven't got all morning,' he said. 'I've got five thousand others after you. I won't reach my quota, and then what? It's like . . . whish, scythe, the days of man are as grass. You see the connotation? You're thinking about grass, and I come along and scythe you down. Over here. Not there. Cross!'

'No,' Lawrence said, after a few seconds thought. 'Make me.'

The man appeared to look to one side. He began a conversation with some invisible entity. 'Well, you heard him, what can I do?' he said. 'He won't cross.' There was a pause. 'Throw?' he repeated. 'What, with my arm?' He sighed heavily.

Then, he reached down, picked up the scythe, and pointed it, for what seemed like interminable seconds, at Lawrence's chest. Finally, without any further warning, he launched it. The blade came hurtling towards Lawrence.

And it hit him squarely in the heart.

Lawrence gasped, screwed his eyes shut, and then, just as rapidly, opened them.

A woman was standing over him, a woman of his own age who was vaguely familiar. She had her fist raised in the air.

'I can get out of the pond!' Lawrence cried.

'Bully for you,' Abigail said. She started massaging his heart all the more furiously.

'Even if he walks across, he won't assail me,' Lawrence whispered. 'He won't drag me under. I can get out.'

'Good,' Abigail said.

He looked at her narrowly. 'Worms,' he said.

'Heart attack,' she told him. 'Not worms.'

Lawrence could hear the siren of an ambulance far away. He grabbed Abigail's arm. 'Not me, you,' he gasped. 'Lots of worms.'

A head appeared over Abigail's shoulder. Lawrence knew it was the floor manager of *Hey! Today!*, but he couldn't think of her name. 'Is he dead?' she asked, hopefully.

'Filarial lymphangitis!' Lawrence announced triumphantly. 'Tube! Laboratory! Travel show!'

The floor manager frowned. She moved away – swam hazily out of his line of vision – and he heard her say, 'Verbal diarrhoea, no change there then.'

He reminded himself to fire her as soon as he could stand up.

Abigail was frowning at him. He gripped her tighter. 'You had them in a tube,' he said.

'What tube?' Abigail asked.

He waved his hand in an effort to describe it to her. 'A tube,' he rambled. 'Mosquitoes bite, infect with worms, worms live in bloodstream for ever and ever. You had a tube with formaldehyde . . .' Suddenly, his eyes widened. 'Aren't you dead?' he demanded.

Abigail sat back on her heels. 'Neither of us are dead,' she told him.

'A travel programme, years and years and years ago,' he said.

Abigail began, very slowly, to smile. 'One slot, five minutes, in 1968,' she confirmed. 'You must have a brain like an encyclopedia.'

He grinned, and pointed at his right temple. 'Image goes in,' he said. 'Never goes out. Not TV image. Never.' And his eyes swam with tears. 'You were great,' he murmured. 'Great! Worms in tubes. Walking up walls in waders.'

Abigail stood up. She glanced behind her, to see the doors of the TV studio swing open and two paramedics running towards them. 'Walking the walls of the wadi,' she told Lawrence, thoughtfully. 'Slight difference. Dry riverbed. I was writing a piece about oil fields.'

'That's it,' Lawrence agreed hazily. 'Walking in waders, oil prices, grass in the fields.'

The first paramedic looked down at him, then at Abigail.

'He was gone for a few seconds,' she said, in a matter-of-fact tone, rolling down her sleeves. 'Came back with a thud.'

A hand fastened round her ankle. She looked down at Lawrence.

'Don't leave me,' he gabbled. 'Bring waders yourself.' He sat up suddenly, and shouted, 'I'm not dead yet! I'm not dead!'

They began to load him on to a stretcher. As they

carried him out, Lawrence finally saw what was happening on the sofa. 'Whossat?' he screeched. 'Where Adele?' He craned his neck. 'Cameras on! What?'

'Hush,' Abigail said, clamping her hand over his mouth.

'I can Get Out Of The Pond,' he said. 'Remember that!'

But no-one could hear him.

They were all too busily listening as Harry talked to Will.

Harry was leaning back, utterly relaxed, in a little carefree world of his own, oblivious to the fact that the cameras had begun filming him, his legs crossed, and one arm arranged across the back of the sofa. Opposite him sat Meg and Will.

'You see,' Harry was saying, 'it was snow. I always hated snow. Didn't I, Meg? It was when you came back inside. Thawing your fingers out in front of the fire. That happened to me twice. I had a numb thumb. I couldn't write or draw or anything.'

'You don't do that,' Will told him. 'You don't thaw in front of a fire. It's too quick.'

'And peeing,' Harry said. 'Is it in a bottle, or what?'

'No,' Will sighed. 'It's outside. Quickly.'

'But what if you want a long one?'

'A long what?'

'A long pee.'

'You get dehydrated when you walk twenty miles a day,' Will pointed out. 'There are no such things as long pees.'

Harry nodded, digesting this piece of information.

'The crucial thing here,' Will said, glancing at Meg,

'is the effect that global warming is having on the Arctic environment.'

'You see,' Harry mused, 'I never used to get up in the night, but now I do. My father was like that. It isn't prostate or anything, you know. It's our family. Small bladders or something.'

'The Arctic is a vast self-supporting area . . .'

'And when the Beavers used to go camping,' Harry continued, 'there were always half a dozen of us up in the night, and we were young boys, so we wouldn't have a prostate problem.' He grinned. 'We had a Brownies problem,' he announced cheerfully. 'Over the fence.'

He turned to camera, and smiled engagingly at it.

Several women in the UK scalded themselves at that moment, pouring hot tea into their laps as they became convinced that Hugh Grant had taken up morning television. Harry leaned forward and ran a hand through his hair. 'It's nice just chatting,' he said. 'He's about to be my brother-in-law and all he's ever talked to me about is nautical miles. What a deviant!'

'Harry,' Will said. 'You're an arse.'

'Harry, darling,' Meg interjected hastily. 'Mouth open. Shut it.'

The floor manager stepped in front of the sofa. She hesitated a moment, and then, apparently giving up the effort, she sat down between Meg and Will. She looked directly into camera.

'Thank you,' she said, 'Harry, and Meg and Will. Thank you for hanging on so manfully through the last few minutes while we . . . er . . . while we had a little re-scheduling of the morning shows.'

'No problem,' Harry said magnanimously, winking at her.

Meg mimed a zip across her lips, and balled her fist at her brother.

'*Hey! Today!* is now ending our transmission for today,' the manager went on. 'In the light of . . . of . . .'

'Sad about Adele,' Harry said. 'Tragic. And Mr Bugle.'

Meg sat back on the sofa and put her hand over her eyes.

'In the light of Adele *being temporarily indisposed*,' the manager continued loudly, 'we'll say goodbye today, until *Hey!* tomorrow. Thanks for watching. Goodbye.'

The music swelled. The red lights on the cameras went out. The floor manager slid to the carpet and wept softly.

'Goodbye,' Harry said, to no one in particular. 'That was all just such *amazing* fun.'

15

Clementine Badger was not a running kind of person.

Other people, given Eric's instructions, and given Clementine's love for Eric, might have been tempted to sprint from the house without a second thought. But not Clementine. Putting down the phone, she stood deep in thought for at least two or three minutes. Then, she walked to the office, opened her filing cabinet, and extracted a file. She sat down at the desk, perfectly composed, and began to read. Another five minutes later, she closed the file, tucked it under her arm, and went to her room, where she slowly put on her coat. She was out of the house, and hailing a taxi, less than fifteen minutes after Eric had rung her.

South of the river, as she had fully expected, was a heaving mass of traffic and humanity. She paid off the taxi and began to walk towards the TV studios, looking to left and right. She wasn't looking for Adele. She rightly guessed that Adele had made a damned quick get-away. But she knew what kind of trail Adele would have left.

She saw the charity shop almost at once, and went into it.

Two women were standing at the counter, one leaning on the till and the other re-arranging the shelf of ornaments. They were evidently in the middle of a conversation. The woman leaning on the till was in full indignant flow.

'I said to him,' she said, 'I said, I'm not having stippling. It's like pies. I'm not having pies, either.'

'Excuse me,' Clementine said.

'You don't want stippling,' the second woman observed mildly, buffing up a chipped shepherdess. 'It'll crack.'

'It would if he did it,' the first woman retorted. 'You should see his flexible sealant up the stairs! I said, those stairs aren't right. I told him they weren't right. I said, "It'll flake." And what did it do? It flaked. But oh no.'

'But he did the stippling,' the second said.

'He said he had the right tool,' her friend retorted. 'I said, you don't need a tool for rolling. You need a rag and a pot of Morning Promise, that's all.'

'Excuse me,' Clementine repeated.

The other woman sighed in agreement. 'They just do it to be difficult,' she murmured. 'And then it's, "Oh, I'm such a martyr, I did what you wanted." And then you have to say, "Oh, thank you for doing that."'

'When you could have done it better yourself.'

'When you could have done it better yourself, like everything,' her friend agreed.

'Excuse me!' Clementine said.

They turned to look at her.

'Morning,' said the first. 'Is it clothes you want?'

'No,' Clementine told her, slightly affronted, but not surprised. She was hardly a fashion icon. 'I wondered if you'd seen a woman.'

The two glanced at each other. 'We see all sorts,' the first told her. 'And men.' She sniffed.

'Today,' Clementine said. 'Within the last half hour.'

'Trousers,' the woman continued, as if she hadn't

heard. 'The state of them. The things in the pockets.'

'Thermal underwear,' said the second. 'With stains.'

'Stains!' her friend cried. 'Can you credit it! As if we're a laundry!'

'This would have been a well-dressed woman in her thirties,' Clementine said, a little louder. 'In a hurry.'

The two women shook their heads. 'Seventies,' they said, almost in unison. 'Mrs Tapestry, we call her. We don't know what her name is, but she buys the wools.'

'Not seventies,' Clementine said. 'Young. Rushing in, rushing out.'

'Tall or short?'

'Five seven.'

'Blonde?'

'Yes.'

'Nicely spoken?'

'Yes.'

'No.'

Clementine blinked. 'You *haven't* seen a five-feet-seven blonde nicely spoken woman in her thirties?'

'No,' the woman said. 'Not anyone ordinary.' She seemed to lose interest in Clementine suddenly. She turned the page of the magazine in front of her. 'Taurus,' she announced, reading from the horoscope. 'The beginning of a new cycle.'

'Is he Taurus?' the other enquired.

'Excuse me,' Clementine repeated.

'No,' said the first, ignoring her. 'He's Aries. And anyone less like a ram I have yet to meet.'

'I thought he was Gemini.'

'Gemini?' her friend said, laughing. 'They talk, don't they? They charm people.'

'Hello?' Clementine said. 'Hello . . .?'

'Mine's Sagittarius,' her friend said. 'They're very deep.'

'And here's me,' the till woman said. 'A Cancerian, and I can't stick water, and I don't like being at home, and I haven't got a shell. Have I got a shell? No.'

Clementine walked right up to the counter. 'Is there another charity shop on this stretch of road?' she asked.

'No,' the woman said. She turned the magazine page. 'New Ways With Fish. A Plaice In His Heart.' She hissed. 'I know what I'd place in his heart,' she muttered. 'A sharpened stake about ten feet long.'

'Any other clothes shop?' Clementine persisted.

The woman frowned. 'No.'

'Shoe shops?'

'Half a mile away.'

The ornaments-dusting woman patted Clementine's arm. 'You want to look on the rail,' she said kindly. 'A nice mac.'

'Thank you,' Clementine answered, still trying her best to be polite. 'But no.' She turned for the door.

'Adele Buchanan took a mac,' the till woman said.

Clementine stared back at her. 'What?'

'Adele Buchanan.'

'When?'

'Just now. Before you came in.'

'She was here?'

'Of course she was.'

'But I asked you!' Clementine protested. 'I asked if you'd seen a blonde woman in her thirties . . .'

'Adele Buchanan isn't a woman,' the till operator retorted. 'She's on TV. You never asked if it was Adele Buchanan. I could have told you it was Adele Buchanan. You should have said right out,' she told

Clementine reprovingly. 'And we could have told you, and there you'd be, and you wouldn't have wasted everyone's time.'

Clementine was glad to get back in the street.

She looked down at the note she had made, of what Adele had bought.

A mac, green. A T-shirt with primroses on it. A pair of black stretch ski pants. A pair of brown brogue shoes with a tasseled tongue. And a brown wig.

'Like Gloria Estefan,' the till woman told her. 'In her heyday. Curly.'

'Did she say where she was going?' Clementine had asked.

'She wasn't going anywhere,' the woman said. 'Except out.'

'Back to work?'

'She got in a car,' Clementine was told.

Clementine had retrieved the piece of paper and pen from her pocket. 'What colour car?' she asked.

'Blue,' said the first woman.

'Red,' said the second.

'And the make?'

'Ford,' said the first woman.

'Vauxhall,' said the second. 'You know, Irene,' she added, almost dreamily, 'I don't think it was really a car.'

Clementine fought down the urge to scream. 'Was it a taxi?' she prompted.

'No,' the woman told her. 'It was a bus.'

Clementine managed to smile. 'Thank you,' she said. 'Number?'

'Twenty-one.'

'Sixty-eight.'

'Which way did it go?'

And they pointed, like Tweedledee and Tweedledum, in opposite directions.

Clementine looked up and down the road now.

She frowned, working through the possibilities. Certainly Adele wouldn't go back to her flat, she thought. It would be surrounded by journalists by now. And would stay that way all weekend. Perhaps beyond. And Adele wouldn't book into an hotel for the same reason.

If I were her, Clementine considered, I'd go to a station. I'd go in the ladies' loo, and I'd put on the change of clothes, and the wig, and I'd catch a train. I wouldn't care which train it was. I wouldn't care where it was going. If I were in Adele's state of mind – the kind of state that made you run out of a live TV programme without your shoes, after being told that same week that you were about to be eclipsed by a blonde with a false chest and a sponge for a brain – or so the gossip column in the paper had said that morning – then I wouldn't care a jot where I went, as long as it was the end of some line. As far as I could go without actually dropping off into the sea.

Clementine nodded to herself, oblivious to the crowds trying to get past her, constantly nudging her this way and that. The train was the obvious solution, she thought. And the nearest mainline station to here was Waterloo.

At that very same moment, a small light of discovery came on in Clementine's face. She reached into her overnight bag and drew out the file again, ran her finger down the page of Adele's biographical details, and stopped at the place of Adele's birth. She had remembered rightly. Adele Buchanan, alias Janet

Tebbs, daughter of a Liverpudlian bus conductor who had retired to warmer climes because of his bronchitis, had spent her school years in a small town on the south coast.

And it was served by trains out of Waterloo.

Clementine smiled to herself, put the file back, zipped up the bag, and set off at a determined pace. With the traffic the way it was, she thought happily, she could beat any bus to the station gates.

16

Just as Clementine Badger was not a running kind of person, Lawrence Bugle would not have described himself as a human fly.

He had never been overly keen on heights, and he couldn't say that he was getting any keener on them by the minute. He had never liked ski lifts, or even ordinary lifts. And especially not this kind, the kind that had see-through walls and went up the outside of buildings.

There must have been some sort of emergency, he told himself irritatedly. This particular piece of unnecessary free-floating engineering must have broken down mid-flight. What other explanation could there be for the fact that he was hanging just above ceiling height, looking down into a side ward of the Royal Brancome-Wellbeloved Hospital?

He sighed distractedly. He was feeling foolish, a sensation that had been entirely foreign to him since a girl in his primary school asked him to pay for looking in her knickers, and he had only had sixpence on him, and a half-eaten sandwich – neither of which she had considered adequate currency. He started to grind his teeth.

It was very dusty up here near the ceiling. You wouldn't have believed it if you hadn't seen it with your own eyes, he thought. Four thousand pounds a year paid into the most expensive private healthcare scheme in the country, and here he was, suspended like a light bracket among a neat collection of spiders' webs.

He was really getting rather seriously fed up with it all. He had been given, he supposed, some sort of injection to calm him down, and now it must be wearing off. For a while back there, he had been very calm indeed, drifting between sleep and waking, with no pain at all, and what seemed like a very nice lady's hand to hold, all the way here in an ambulance. The same effortless drifting had brought him, it seemed, through the swing doors of the hospital, through a horribly brightly lit resuscitation unit, and out again, while he had taken forty winks, into this bloody lift.

What would they put a patient in a lift on their own for, he wondered. Why would they abandon him like this? He could understand it if he was in a National Health Hospital. You would expect it there. He'd still be lying in a corridor if he weren't a paid-up member of Brancome-Wellbeloved. He'd still be stranded helplessly in some Third World A&E, rigged up to an electric shock machine that looked like it had come off the set of *Frankenstein*. He'd be fighting for his life in some desperate inner-city war zone, and inhaling the smell of rice pudding with every breath.

Instead of which, he appeared to be suspended between floors.

He tried to look around himself at the lift.

Very high-tech it was, he considered. So see-through that you couldn't actually see any sides to it. Why didn't they just lower him to a bed, to a nice soft bed in a discreet corner, like that man over there, he asked himself. He tried hard to focus on the patient lying prone beneath him. It was hard to make out the details, but the man did have a startlingly porcine face. He was about his own age, Lawrence considered. And about his own weight. And he was about his own height and he . . .

Lawrence gasped.

He was about his own weight, height and age because he *was* him! The pig in the bed was *him*, that bloated apology in a white sheet was *he*, Lawrence Bugle, head of a dynamic corporation, famous gastronome and darling of every wine bar between here and the M4.

'My God!' he whispered. 'My God . . .'

'He's not available,' said a voice.

Aghast, Lawrence turned his head.

Or rather, he turned what he thought must be his head, if he still had a head, which might well be in dispute, he realised with horror, since his own head appeared to be lying ten feet below him on a hospital bed.

Sitting in the opposite corner of the ceiling was the man with a scythe.

He was lazily trimming his nails with the blade.

'You took a long time coming round,' he observed, without looking up.

Lawrence felt his heart lurch. If it *was* his own heart lurching, which might well be in dispute, since his own heart appeared to be lying ten feet below him. 'Who are you?' he demanded, his voice trembling. Even to his own ears – if they *were* his own ears, which might well be in dispute, since his own ears appeared to be attached, etc – he sounded desperate.

The man still didn't look up. 'I've made a detour

from Bangkok, so don't start hassling me,' he said. 'Just come along.'

'Come where?' Lawrence squeaked.

The man sighed. He laid the scythe across his knees, re-folded the black shroud across his thighs, and stared at Lawrence with ill-disguised contempt. 'Look,' he said, 'I've got you down as an 11.08 arrival. You're two hours late, and I haven't had my lunch.'

'11.08?' Lawrence repeated. 'What do you mean?'

'11.08,' the man said. 'Time of death.'

There was a silence. A silence like the grave.

If he were totally honest – and it wasn't a quality he had exactly nurtured over his lifetime – Lawrence had known that the man in black wasn't just a figment of his imagination. And he knew quite well what his task was. After all, he'd had a decent press for the last few thousand years, and a pretty good title. The Grim Reaper was one of those names you never forgot. Tried to forget, yes. Actually forgot, no.

'Look,' Lawrence began hesitantly. He was trying not to look down now. Not just because he didn't want to see himself stretched out on the mortuary gurney – for surely, that was what it was – but also because he knew for sure now that he wasn't in a lift at all, but suspended right up on the hospital ceiling, having what he had laughingly derided for years. An out-of-body experience.

'That's right,' the Reaper confirmed. 'Out of your body. And never going to get back in again.'

'I can,' Lawrence said, still trying to get his head round this surreal predicament. 'People do. You read about it all the time. They have these experiences, and then – wham! – they're back. They're back in a ward drinking tea and telling the *News Of The World* about it.'

'You won't be telling the *News Of The World*,' the Reaper said. 'And there won't be any whamming. Sorry. Come along.'

Lawrence felt with his fingertips for the wall behind him, as if he could hold on to it. If they *were* his fingertips, which might well be in dispute, since . . . hmmmm.

'I can get back in,' he said. 'I can. I Got Out Of The Pond, and I can get back in there.'

The Reaper smiled. Grimly, naturally. 'You were nine years old when you last Got Out Of The Pond,' he said. 'And you were fit. You could still breathe after climbing a flight of stairs.' He smiled a little more broadly. 'Do you know what it takes to get back in a body?' he asked conversationally. 'You've got to squeeze into it. Takes an enormous amount of squeezing. Not to mention spiritual ability, of which you've got none.'

'I *have*,' Lawrence protested. 'I have loads of spiritual stuff. Thing. What you said.' Now, it appeared even his immense vocabulary was deserting him.

'Oh?' the Reaper raised an eyebrow. 'What, exactly?'

'I commissioned *Songs Of Worship*.'

The Reaper sighed. 'It takes a bit more than commissioning some half-hearted TV programme to worm your way back into your own skin,' he said. 'You've got to have faith.'

'I've got that,' Lawrence said.

'Have you?'

'Yes,' Lawrence lied.

'I mean faith in a Greater Being,' the Reaper told him. 'Not your own bloody self.'

Lawrence glared at him. 'I'll show you,' he muttered.

The Reaper crossed his arms and settled back against the wall. 'Fine,' he said. 'Go ahead. I could do with a laugh. You don't get many in my line of work.'

Lawrence set his jaw. He wasn't used to being laughed at by anyone, particularly not someone in a shroud. He looked away, back to the body below him, and he concentrated hard. For a second, he thought he felt his body, if it *was* . . . and all that . . . move. Just a fraction. Just an inch. He thought he felt himself jolt downwards. And then stop. Hard.

'You see,' said the Reaper conversationally. 'It's the laws of the fifth dimension. Sixth, seventh, even. Ad infinitum. Got to jump this gap between Reality as you know it and a Subsequent Reality. If you've never used your sensitivity, your third eye, you can't do it.'

'I don't need a bloody third eye to wake up in my own flesh,' Lawrence said. 'I just need determination.'

And he strained as hard as he could. The floor under him seemed to ripple for a second, and then it halted. A horrible lethargy washed over Lawrence a sense of the last of his strength running out of him.

'That's right,' the Reaper confirmed. 'Last of your strength running out of you. Not nice.' He nodded to himself. 'Not surprisingly really, seeing as you never had any morals. You see, it's quite a simple equation if you think about it. No morals, no inner strength. Kaput. Pond or No Pond.'

Lawrence gaped at him. He was beginning to feel weird, like a piece of tissue paper floating about. 'You know about The Pond,' he whispered. 'How? How'd you know that?'

'I know everything about you,' the Reaper said. 'I know about the frogs.'

'Oh,' Lawrence quailed. Then automatically switched to Lying Mode, his second nature. 'But they liked it,' he said.

'I know about Elaine Tenterthwaite,' the Reaper remarked.

'It was only once! It was only a little stick!'

'I know you cheated at A-Level Art.'

'I only signed a name!'

'I know about lying at your interview.'

'I *was* the war correspondent in Korea! I *did* get wounded!'

'You were the Basketball Correspondent on the Blackpool Evening Courier, so don't give me that,' the Reaper told him, sighing. 'And getting athlete's foot is not a war injury. *And* I know about Mark Blake's wife.'

'I . . .'

'And Henry Marchant's wife.'

'She . . .'

'And Peter Clay's wife.'

'They . . .'

'And what's more,' the Reaper added, leaning forward and pointing upwards with his thumb, 'so does He.'

Lawrence felt tears welling up in his eyes. It was a peculiar sensation. He hadn't cried for years. The last time that he had wept – if you didn't count the self-indulgent sniffling over Dido – was when his first wife had left him. And that was only because she'd taken the TV remote with her, the vindictive bitch. Why had it always been his lot to marry unpleasant women, he asked himself. It wasn't as if he himself were unpleasant. He was the absolute embodiment of the perfect husband, never asking for more than the most perfunctory of accounts to show where they had spent his money, and never stressing too heavily how he had kept a roof over their heads and clothes on their backs.

Why, he once forgave one of his wives for sleeping with his best friend! How much more saintly could you get than that! He'd turned a blind eye to it, and how many men could put their hands on their hearts and admit to such wonderfulness? Even allowing for the fact that Chloe sleeping with Martin had given him a great opportunity to fire Martin – well, even so. Even if he himself had been sleeping with two other women at the time. Had he mentioned Chloe's betrayal? Had he berated her with it? No. Not a bit of it. He hadn't even complained when, afterwards, she had locked herself in the guest bedroom and cried for a week. Never mentioned it! Never even mentioned it when she came out! Totally ignored it! Ignored the fact she'd lost a stone in weight and looked like death! Never uttered a single word! He was a *joy* as a husband, and all anyone had ever done in all his life was take advantage of his good nature.

He started to cry now in earnest. 'I want to go home,' he whispered.

'No use crying for yourself,' the Reaper said, unimpressed.

'I'm not crying for myself, you bastard,' Lawrence retorted, wiping his non-existent eyes on a non-existent sleeve. 'Shut up.'

The Reaper shook his head. 'Tsssk, tsssk,' he murmured. 'That won't earn you any Brownie points at all, swearing at me. What happened to all your nice long words? And you were a bloody awful husband, if you must know.'

'I was ill-treated,' Lawrence sobbed. 'Misjudged.'

The Reaper smiled. 'Well, now you've got your opportunity,' he said. 'Someone's waiting for you who hasn't misjudged anyone. Ever. In fact, when it comes to Judgement, He's the best.'

Lawrence shrank as far back as he could against the ceiling. He pointed at the Reaper. 'You're just a figment of my imagination,' he protested. 'I'll wake up in a minute, and you'll be gone. I won't even remember you.' He tried to stop himself trembling. 'Anyway,' he added, incapable of letting a good argument go, 'there's no such thing as Judgement.'

'I am not a figment,' the Reaper said. 'And who told you that piffle about Judgement?' He was standing up now, ready to go.

'The Archbishop of Bournemouth!'

The Reaper raised one eyebrow. 'Did he?' he remarked, smirking. 'Probably joking. He's a bit of a lad, you know.'

'He was not joking!' Lawrence protested. 'He said that Judgement Day was an outmoded Victorian concept.'

'Out what? Ha!'

'He said that dying would be like going into a Starbucks. You'd sit down, you'd have a quick flick through your Book Of Life, then you'd faststream on to Eternal Duvets And Harps, and, if you'd really done wrong, you'd get counselling.'

'Counselling!' the Reaper chortled, delighted. 'What a joker!'

'Because it wasn't your fault,' Lawrence babbled. 'Because nothing is ever really your fault, because everything's a result of someone doing something to you.'

'Now you've lost me,' the Reaper said, wiping his eyes. 'Run that past me again, do.'

'Well . . . well, say you murdered your mother,' Lawrence said. 'It'd be because she'd bottle-fed you. Or shouted at you during *Blue Peter*. Or refused to let you keep hamsters. Or forced you to eat boiled eggs when you didn't like boiled eggs.'

'Pardon me?' The Reaper was puzzled. 'And that excuses you killing her?'

'Because she's destroyed your childhood psyche. See?'

'No. Not at all.'

'Or . . . or you hit a clamper,' Lawrence rambled, in panic. 'You've had a beast of a day, you can't get parked, you double-park for *just two seconds*, and they clamp you. Just two seconds while you run – you actually run! – into the off-licence for a case of Merlot! And they *clamp* you! They *clamp* your Mercedes! I mean! I mean! How can hitting a clamper be wrong, for Christ's sake!'

'Excusable sin,' the Reaper murmured. 'Interesting idea. But crap.'

'It is excusable,' Lawrence cried. 'It is, you see? Because nobody ever wants to be a sinner, do they? I mean, for a start, it sounds so medieval! Sinning. *Nobody* talks about sinning any more, do they? Even vicars don't mention it unless they're forced. I mean, no-one actually sins, do they? They have a psychological trauma, or they're stressed, or their Feng Shui's gone pear-shaped. It's nobody's fault, is it? It's no-one's responsibility. *Nothing's* anyone's responsibility any more. It's the Government's fault. It's allergies. It's capitalism, or communism, or political forces, or market forces, or Life, for God's sake! Life! It's what it does to you! It's not your fault!'

'So you've not sinned,' the Reaper said.

'Of course not!' Lawrence exploded. 'Never! Never! I've never wanted to sin, I've never taken any pleasure in it, it's never given me any satisfaction, I've abhorred it all my life, I wanted to be a monk when I was nine, I've loved going to church . . .'

'Watch it,' the Reaper said. 'You're pushing it now.'

'I have!' Lawrence protested. 'All those lovely psalms, and the prayers, and all those wet Wednesdays in Lent, I've never been anywhere else but on my knees, praying, I've worn my knees out, I love churches! Fabulous places! Lovely! Stunning!'

'You're lying again,' the Reaper remarked.

'I'm not!'

'You're lying. Just as you've done all your life.'

'Never!'

'You're lying.'

'Only a fraction.'

'You're lying.'

'Maybe not every Lent.'

'Lying.'

'Maybe not stunning.'

'Lying.'

'I prayed sometimes.'

The Reaper looked at him for a long time.

'All right,' Lawrence said, finally. 'OK. I'm lying.'

Silence.

Lawrence looked away.

Far down on the bed, the man with the pig-like face was slowly turning grey. His lips were going blue. 'Oh God,' Lawrence whimpered. 'Look at me.'

He stared and stared. And, as he did so, he saw his face begin to disintegrate. It turned into a mask, at first merely plastic, and then, increasing every second, into a squashed cowpat. Instead of resembling a porker that had been inflated with a bicycle pump, he now looked like a walnut, wrinkled, puckered and totally dried-out. And what was worse, the expression on the walnut was cruel; the mouth was turned down in a sneer; the eyes were narrow slits. Greed was etched in every line. Greed and selfishness.

'Stop it!' he cried. He dragged his gaze away and stared at the Reaper. 'Stop, stop!'

'It can't be happening to you, can it?' the Reaper asked him. 'Because you're not a sinner.'

'Stop!'

'It can't be your fault, can it, all the misery you've caused?'

'Please!'

'You couldn't possibly own this face, could you?' the Reaper demanded. 'The face that shows you what you really are.'

Lawrence screamed in terror. 'All right!' he admitted, at last. 'All right! I did it all, I've been a bastard of the first order, it was all my idea, I enjoyed it . . .'

'And this is just the start,' the Reaper said. 'So you think there isn't a hell?' His laugh seemed to permeate the very walls, and echo in Lawrence's heart. 'You'll feel the griefs of your victims for eternity,' he said. 'And . . .' He began to float towards Lawrence, scythe upheld. Its blade glittered in the waning light.

'And, Mr Bugle,' he added, 'there is no Starbucks at Heaven's Gate, believe me.'

'Oh God!' Lawrence wept.

And, for the first time in his life, he cried – not for

himself, but for the hearts he had broken. 'I'm sorry,' he whimpered. 'I'm sorry.'

And he began, slowly and inexorably, to fall.

17

'Hello!' rang a voice from the depths of the patisserie. 'Gorgeous lady! Come in, come in!'

Meg stood on the threshold of Little Luigi's, looking around to see who on earth the owner was talking to. It was midday, and, surprisingly for England in the spring, it was staring to get hot. After the dramas in the *Hey! Today!* studios, Meg felt that she was stifling, and she stood in the doorway of the shop, taking off her jacket, watching Michael and Harry pay off the taxi.

Meanwhile, a very dark and very handsome Italian was advancing upon her, his arms open.

'You come in!' he repeated. 'Come, come . . .'

Meg looked over her shoulder for Michael.

'You and handsome gentlemen, come, come . . .'

Meg grabbed Michael's arm. 'Let's go,' she hissed. 'This guy must be crazy. He's called you handsome.'

'Thanks,' Michael responded drily, nodding and smiling at their host. 'But they serve the best smoked chicken panini in London. So put up with the compliments.'

He took her elbow and guided her to the table that was being offered. Harry settled down at their side. Luigi bustled around them with menus, flicking imaginary dust from the chairs with a tea towel.

'And coffee, yes?' he was saying. 'Espresso,

cappuccino, latte, mocha, mochachino, maybe hot chocolate, double flake, double cream . . .'

'Three espresso,' Michael said. 'Three smoked chicken. Thanks, Luigi.'

'Er . . . not for me,' Meg interrupted. 'Just coffee.'

The man threw up his hands in horror. 'Not enough to feed a bird!' He reached over and stroked her shoulder, feeling for the fat. 'You look, bones!' he screeched. 'No bones! We not want bones! Chocolate muffin, yes? Carbohydrate, yes? Lovely sweeties! Energy!'

'No.' She smiled, bemused. 'Thanks.'

'A little pastry, a little . . . I have marzipan mouse! So cute! Little mouse, little whiskers, you like, I bring mouse, teddy bear, elephant.'

Meg gritted her teeth. 'I couldn't possibly manage a whole elephant,' she said. 'Maybe just a lightly boiled trunk.'

To her dismay, the man howled with delight. 'Trunk, yes!' he declared, hopping from one foot to the other. 'Aaah, you kid, I understand. But yes! Whatever you say. We boil trunk, we braise it, we fry, you say, we bake, yes? Side salad, sauté, yes? Gorgeous lady!'

'I'll have her smoked chicken,' said Harry, helpfully. 'Bring all three.'

Meg glared at the owner's retreating back, then back at Michael. 'What *is* he on?' she asked.

Michael shrugged. 'Luigi's always like that. Water off a duck's.'

'He called me gorgeous and bony in the same breath. I've never seen him before.'

'It's just Luigi,' Michael repeated, apparently dismissing the man with a wave of his hand. In the kitchen, they could hear their host mourning the appearance of a bony person whom he had to feed up before she expired. 'She die on her feet! Is horrible!'

Meg shook her head. 'So,' she said, eyeing Michael warily. 'Spill the beans. Tell me what's worth dragging us into here. I should have gone with Will for his hospital check-up.'

Michael smiled. 'You saw what happened back there in the studios?' he asked.

She shrugged. 'You could hardly miss it.'

'What a fiasco!' Harry said. 'Hey, what d'you think of my word? *Fiasco, fiasco*. They just kept on saying it.'

Meg unfolded her napkin. 'Do you think he's all right?' she asked.

'Who?' Michael asked.

'That man who had the heart attack, of course.'

'Bugle.' Michael stirred the coffee that had been brought to him. 'I doubt it,' he said equably. 'He's dead.'

'Is he?' Harry asked.

'You saw the electric paddles.'

'I know, but . . . I saw Mum talking to him. Doing her First Aid stuff.'

Michael nodded. 'Uh-huh. But he had another attack in the ambulance.'

'How do you know?' Meg asked, horrified.

Michael held up his pager. 'Text.'

'My God,' she murmured. 'How terrible. Poor Mr Bugle.'

Michael shrugged. 'Don't spare any tears for him,' he said. 'He's hated throughout the industry. He's caused more heart attacks than Pamela Anderson. Trifle ironic he's had one himself.'

The food arrived. Meg was given a plate with a chocolate éclair on it.

'You eat, you get strong,' Luigi told her.

As he walked away, Meg murmured, 'I eat, I get size eighteen.' Nevertheless, she began wading into it with a fork.

'Listen,' Michael said, through bites of bread and chicken, 'more important than that. Much more important –'

'I wonder if Will found the right department,' she muttered. 'I wrote it down for him.'

'Are you listening?' Michael asked.

'What? Oh, yes.'

'Properly listening?'

She eyed him critically.

'I had another call while the pair of you were sitting on that couch,' he said. 'From Eric Cramm.'

She chewed on the éclair, unimpressed.

'He's offering you a job.'

'Job?' she said. 'But he hates me.'

'Job?' Harry echoed. 'For both of us? What sort of job?'

'Eric Cramm doesn't hate you, Meg,' Michael said. 'What gives you that idea?'

'The way he looks at me under those beetled brows. I didn't even know what "beetled brows" meant, until I saw them on him.' She paused, suspicious. 'Anyway,' she added, 'as Harry said, what kind of job?'

'On television.'

'Television!' Brother and sister exclaimed, together.

'Hosting a morning TV show.'

Meg swallowed hard, then stared at Michael. 'Sorry,' she said, 'but you'll have to run that past me again. I must be going deaf. I thought you said that he wanted us to host a morning TV show.'

'He does,' Michael told her. 'Isn't it great?'

'No,' she cried. 'Are you *mad*? Is he mad? I've never been on TV. I'm not a journalist. I'm not anything.'

Michael pointed his fork at her. 'That sort of attitude is not PC,' he told her. 'Women haven't been allowed to say they're not anything since 1963.' He sucked mayonnaise from his thumb. 'Anyway,' he added, 'you're somebody, aren't you? You've been in the papers all week.'

'Will's been in the papers all week,' she pointed out. She rubbed a fingertip on the frownline between her eyes. 'And what morning TV show?'

'Up-Line Cable are starting one. Cramm's been looking for an anchorwoman. Word is, he's been pursuing Adele Buchanan.'

Meg frowned. 'What does he want us for then, if he's got her?'

'But he hasn't got her, has he?' he said. 'And, after this morning's demonstration, I don't think anyone's going to have her. She's imploded.'

Meg leaned forward. 'I don't understand what happened,' she said. 'We came up from make-up, and we were standing at those doors, and we saw her run out the other side of the room. What was going on?'

'Nothing,' Michael said. He finished the sandwich, and sat back, satisfied, smiling. 'I reckon the star burned out. It's what happens when they get too big for too long. They burn brighter and brighter, and then – *wham!* – they're gone. Nothing left but a few bits of tinsel and a black hole. Or, in her case, a pair of smoking shoes.'

'You mean she's had a breakdown?' Meg asked.

'Probably.'

'Poor woman!'

He pointed at her warningly. 'Don't start poorwomanning,' he said. 'You've just finished poor-manning. That's quite enough for one morning.'

'But where did she go?' Harry asked.

'I don't know and I don't care,' Michael said. 'And you can bet your last dollar that no-one else in that studio cares either, because they'll all be running round like headless chickens now, trying to see where this puts them on the sticky little ladder to success.'

Meg pulled a face. 'She could be killing herself right now,' she said. 'And no-one cares.'

'Oh, they care,' Michael said. 'Would make a fantastic story tomorrow morning.'

'I never had you figured for a cynic, Mike.'

He looked hard at her. 'I'm not a cynic,' he said, 'but this is a good opportunity, and there's no getting away from it. Eric Cramm is offering you a job.'

'I don't want his job,' Meg said.

'I do,' said Harry. 'Fantastic fun.'

'Come on, Meg,' Michael said. 'If nothing else you need the money.'

'That doesn't mean I'm willing to make a fool of myself,' she replied.

'I don't mind making a fool of myself,' Harry volunteered.

'How much have you got in the bank?' Michael asked Meg.

'That's none of your business.'

'It is my business,' he said, 'if I'm going to be your manager.'

'And *are* you going to be our manager? Who says?'

'I do.' He held out his hand. 'Hello,' he said, 'I'm your manager.'

'You're Will's manager.'

He held out his hand again, 'Hello,' he repeated. 'I'm Will's manager, and I'm your manager.'

She shook the hand. 'You idiot.'

'Not such an idiot,' he told her, 'if I can swing this for you. Now then. Truth time. How much have you got in the bank?'

'I haven't got anything,' Harry said. 'Except about four pence.'

Meg nodded sympathetically. 'It's more a case of what I haven't got in the bank.'

'There you go then.'

'It's ludicrous,' she said. 'Be like Adele Buchanan? Sit on a sofa and talk to film stars?' She started to laugh. 'They'd never take us seriously.'

'Why not?' Michael asked. 'Film stars won't be looking at you, they'd be looking at themselves in the monitor.'

'I wouldn't know what to say.'

'Scripts tell you what to say.'

'Great,' said Harry.

'I wouldn't know what to wear.'

'Wardrobe gives you things to wear.'

'Great,' Harry repeated. 'Lead me to it.'

'I'd feel a fraud,' Meg insisted.

'Why?' Michael demanded. 'Why would you be a fraud? Why shouldn't it be you as much as anyone else? Look at you,' he said, waving his coffee spoon in her direction. 'You don't know your own worth, that's your trouble.'

'What worth?'

He raised his eyes to heaven. 'For God's sake,' he muttered. 'Have I got to spell it out?'

'Yes.'

'Jesus!' He drained the coffee in one gulp. 'Look,

Meg,' he said, 'you're young, you're pretty, you're articulate.'

'And so am I,' Harry said, finishing his sandwich. 'Prettier, if anything.'

'I'm argumentative, you mean,' Meg said.

'OK,' Michael said. 'You're argumentative. How do you think that Adele Buchanan got her big break? She trashed some Cabinet Minister on air. She didn't give a shit. She laughed her way to the bank and back again.'

Meg looked down at the table top. 'I'd be scared to death,' she murmured. 'I can't believe Cramm's serious. Perhaps he's had a breakdown, too.'

'Never,' Michael retorted. 'Cramm will never break down. He's made of reinforced concrete. And he told me over the phone that he likes you. He liked the way you spoke to those sponsors the other night.'

Her eyes widened. 'He did? I thought he was furious.'

'Only because Will had fucked up his coverage. He says he likes strong women.'

She grinned. 'Stroppy women?'

'Strong. Bright. He said you reminded him of Zoe Ball.'

Meg digested this compliment for a moment. She quite liked the idea of being Zoe Ball. She wouldn't mind Zoe Ball's hair, for a start.

'Who do I remind him of?' Harry asked.

They ignored him.

'Worth,' Michael said.

Meg dragged herself back from an imagined vision of herself with Zoe Ball's hair. 'Sorry?'

'Worth,' Michael repeated, smiling. 'Money. You didn't ask about the money.'

'We'd get paid?' she asked.

'Don't be a fool, Meg.'

'I mean, a decent wage?' she asked. 'Could I trade in my car?'

'I should think so.'

'Pay off my overdraft?' Harry asked.

'Possibly.'

'Not possibly,' she said, 'as it's the size of the National Debt.'

Michael's face broke into the broadest grin she had ever seen. '*Quite* possibly,' he told her. 'As it's one hundred thousand a year. Each.'

Luigi came back to the table, scooping up their plates and cups. 'You want little dessert now,' he said, his tone breaching no objection. 'Little dessert for gentlemen, maybe another éclair for the lady.' He glanced at Meg, and his face blanched. He looked across at Michael. 'What's the matter?' he asked. 'She ill? Want doctor? Smelling salts? What? Cold compress?'

'Air,' Meg whispered. 'I need a little air.'

18

Meg was quite right when she guessed that Adele Buchanan was having a breakdown.

The great TV star was sitting now, in a secondhand wig, on a shingle beach, staring at the sea. Which was quite a lot of S sounds in a single sentence, and matched her mood exactly – a kind of slow sibilant hiss of deflation. Her world, that bright buoyant balloon of hype, was rapidly reducing itself to a flat and saggy piece of latex.

Abbotsbury Beach was just as she remembered it. She had come here with her family a hundred times. There was no sand – except right near the edge of the water at low tide – and, because of that, the holiday crowds rarely came here. The beach enclosed The Fleet, an inland waterway, and held in its curved arm of low-lying land the Abbotsbury Swannery.

There was something magical about this place. For as far as she could see to left and right, there was nothing but the massive bank of sea-smoothed pebbled; millions upon millions of them, in shades of faded ochre and terracotta. Thousands of years of pounding by the elements had reduced the shoreline to a geographical oddity of enormous beauty, and Adele sat now, her hands plunged in the little pebbles, letting them run through her fingers, remembering the past.

She had come here in all seasons; winter, when the

sea and sky were electric ice blue, and the snow was in the fields and the lanes behind; spring, when the thrift began to grow. Summer, when the fishermen lined the shore at night to catch mackerel, and sometimes to light fires and barbecues, to eat them right at the edge of the sea. The skies could be astonishing here; and, as a child, she had often stood in the waves, looking west, watching the Channel, thinking of it broadening away into the Atlantic, thinking of the planes flying out in that direction, to America.

She had fantasised of being on one of those planes one day, with Abbotsbury Beach long behind her, and Los Angeles in front. She had thought, when she was about eight or nine, that she was going to be a film star. Then, at eleven, she was going to Washington, to be a foreign correspondent. And, in reality, she had landed somewhere in between, a celebrity mouthpiece, a one-tune wonder.

She closed her fist on the pebbles and shook her head.

She looked out at the sea now. Six feet from the shoreline, the land shelved sharply away. Swimming was not allowed from here. Even the strongest swimmer could be caught by that rapid, fierce tide, and never be seen again, until perhaps they turned up down the coast a little, at West Bay, or Lyme Regis, or eastwards, in the silt channels of the river as it came into Weymouth.

She had covered a story like that once. A woman had been pulled out of West Bay harbour. She had been in the water for more than a month. Adele had been sent there by the local paper, and remembered being very detached, very objective, as the body was brought out of the sea. When you had been in that long, you weren't human any more. You were almost part of the sea, like a length of weed, or a piece of driftwood.

She shuddered as she gazed at the ocean.

That's what she was already, she told herself. A piece of driftwood. She had no use for anything that made up the framework of her life. She had no use for the flat, or the clothes and possessions in it. She had no use for the new Jaguar parked outside it. She was of no further use to her employer, and was of no use or interest to any man. Jack had expertly proved that point to her.

She had no real skills, other than being able to talk to people, a skill that she believed she was losing. She could write, she supposed, but couldn't see herself sustaining a book. What earthly good had it been, she asked herself morosely, perfecting the ability to speak for no more than three minutes on any given subject, and never, in those three minutes, raising any contentious issue?

That wasn't journalism, she told herself. That was nothing. Nothing at all. She stood up.

Suddenly, the thought of stepping into the waves was immensely appealing. You wouldn't have to swim, or struggle. The water was so fast and so deep that you would be carried quickly away after less than a minute. You wouldn't have to do anything, other than allow the sea to do its job. You'd become cold quickly. It would be like sleeping.

She had been in a position like this once before.

It had been long ago; she would have been about nineteen. It was just after the incident with Danny. Just after he had hit her in the hospital car park. She had been too embarrassed to go into college, because he had fractured a cheekbone, split her lip and blackened her eye, and her face had looked like a pepperoni pizza. Instead, she had stayed away from classes, and had taken the family dog for long walks, right up across the Ridgeway, towards Dorchester. On one particular morning, she had felt helplessly miserable. It was winter, and the wind was scything across the hills. She had sat down, hugging her knees to her chest, worn out with her own black mood. As she sat, a train came into sight, negotiating the cutting that ran parallel to Bincombe. She had stood up and watched its progress.

And then, an idea had occurred to her.

It had seemed wonderful.

She could, she realised, get over the fence, and get down to the line. It might take a bit of struggling with barbed wire, but once she was there, she would be invisible from the hill and the road. She calculated what speed the train was travelling at. It would be enough, she decided. She could just walk along, and lie down, and, by the time that the driver saw her, it would be too late.

As soon as she had thought of this, the horror of it overtook her. She had stepped back from the fence, a hand to her throat, appalled at what had been going through her mind. But it wasn't the idea of dying that had so deeply shocked her. It was that the opportunity had seemed so easy and attractive. She realised that it was all she wanted: to stop the world. To stop mourning and crying. To stop feeling sorry for herself. And to stop having to pretend to everyone around her that she was really all right, when she wasn't, and was saying so simply to make everyone else feel better.

The idea of death had been so quiet.

So quiet. So nice.

She took off her coat now, by the swiftly churning sea, and stepped forward.

'Miss Buchanan,' said a voice.

She almost jumped out of her skin. She had been so sunk in her own black thoughts that she hadn't heard anyone approaching across the pebbles. She stared at the owner of the voice: a tall, drab woman, clutching a large bag.

'Miss Buchanan,' the woman repeated. 'My name is Badger.'

Adele blinked. Her name was what? *Badger?* People weren't called Badger. The woman was holding out her hand, introducing herself.

'I followed you from London,' she said. 'I'm sorry to intrude.'

Adele drew back. 'I don't know who you are,' she said. 'And I don't know what you mean. My name's not Buchanan.'

The woman picked up her coat. 'You'd better put this on,' she said.

Adele grimaced. 'And you'd better not come any closer,' she warned, suddenly afraid. *Followed her from London.*

'I was sent to find you,' Clementine told her.

'Why?' Adele demanded. 'I'm not who you say, so you've followed the wrong person.'

'You are who I say,' Clementine observed quietly. 'And I want to help you.'

'I don't need help,' Adele told her.

'You look very miserable,' Clementine said. 'And I'm something of an expert in the subject.'

'Why?' Adele demanded. 'What are you, a

psychiatrist or something? Because if you are, you can bugger off.'

'I'm not a psychiatrist,' Clementine reassured her.

Light dawned in Adele's head. 'You're a private investigator,' she breathed. 'And *he* sent you.'

'Who?'

'Bloody black-hearted Bugle, the bastard.'

The two women stared at each other. And then, by some total miracle, Adele laughed. She had just realised what she had said. 'Bloody alliterative bastard,' she added, and put her hand to her mouth, because a sob seemed to want to come out, and she was damned if she was going to stand here, and sob and laugh in the same sentence to a complete stranger, because then the stranger would genuinely have every reason to think she was mad.

Which perhaps she was.

Just temporarily.

The woman was smiling, too. 'He didn't send me,' she said. 'Not him.'

'Who, then?'

'Eric Cramm.'

Adele did a double take. *Eric Cramm?* Eric Cramm was Lawrence Bugle's sworn enemy. They had never met, or spoken, as far as she knew, but it was well known that they hated each other simply by virtue of being career rivals. She had once heard Lawrence say that Cramm was an android, because he wasn't, and had never been, married, and he didn't drink, and he ate very sparingly, and he didn't do lunch, or dinner.

'He's plastic,' Lawrence had once said, over his second bottle of Burgundy. 'One day he'll grind to a halt, and you know why that'll be? Not because he's had a stroke or anything. Not because he's got cirrhosis, which is the disease of the sociable man. Not him!' He had leaned forward, grinning from ear to ear. 'You know why he'll die?' he demanded, guffawing. 'Because his points corroded! Because his alternator failed! Because he ran out of petrol!'

Adele stared at Clementine. 'Cramm,' she repeated. 'I've never met him.'

'I know,' Clementine said. 'But he's your greatest fan.'

Adele had a moment of deep unease. The way that Clementine had said it had echoes of Stephen King's *Misery*. 'You can't be a fan of someone you've never met,' she said.

'Of course you can,' Clementine replied. 'Millions of people all over the world are fans of people they've never met.'

'I meant . . .' Adele began. But she didn't know what she meant, other than that Cramm's vote of confidence was useless, too late, and too utterly misguided.

'He watches you every day,' Clementine went on. 'He tapes your shows. He insists that I watch them, too.'

'Why?' Adele said. 'What are you, his secretary?'

Clementine shook her head. 'No,' she said. 'I'm his housekeeper.'

Adele frowned. 'You're his housekeeper, and he makes you watch tapes of my shows?' she repeated. '*Every* day?'

'Every day.'

Adele, shivering hard now, took her coat and put it on. 'That is creepy,' she said.

'Yes,' Clementine responded drily. 'He's quite obsessed.'

'Well, he'll have to get un-obsessed, won't he,'

Adele retorted. 'Because I'm never going back on
television again.'

'I see,' Clementine said. She was quite unruffled.
'How are you going to spend the rest of your life?'

'It's none of your business,' Adele replied. 'Why
should I tell you? You'll only trot off back to Cramm
and spill the beans, and it's none of his business either.'

'That's right,' Clementine said.

'And I don't take kindly to being followed by you or
anyone else, especially anyone . . . what?'

'Pardon?'

'What did you say just now?' Adele asked.

'I said, "That's right."'

'That's right, it's none of your business, that's
right?'

'That's right.'

Adele put her hands on her hips. 'You are very
peculiar,' she said.

Clementine smiled. 'He wanted me to follow you, to
persuade you to see him. I think he would like you to
work for him.'

'Tough,' Adele said. 'I wouldn't work for someone
who's obsessed about me. It's not a good start.'

'No,' Clementine agreed. 'He's nourished this idea
about you for some time.'

'Not healthy.'

'No,' Clementine agreed.

'He's never approached me,' Adele said, suspiciously.

'No,' Clementine agreed. 'It's often the way, isn't it?
The thrill is to worship from afar. He thought of you
as unattainable.'

'And now I'm attainable?'

'Perhaps he saw a chance.' Clementine reached
down, picked up a stone, and weighed it, reflectively,

in her hand. 'Or perhaps he wanted you for something personal.'

'Personal?' Adele echoed. 'Like what?'

'Perhaps he wants to marry you.'

'What!' Adele cried. 'You're not serious.'

Clementine rolled the stone from side to side, then let it drop. She stood looking at where it had fallen for some time, then raised her face to Adele's. 'I know that he's admired you,' she said, slowly. 'And I know that he asked me to follow you. And I know that he's probably lonely. He doesn't know that I know, of course.'

'He doesn't know that you know he's lonely?'

'He doesn't know that he is lonely, and he doesn't know that I know he doesn't know he's lonely.'

'But if he doesn't know that he's lonely, how lonely is he?' Adele asked. 'Has he ever mentioned it?'

'No.'

'Then you don't know,' Adele said. 'He could be perfectly happy.'

'Oh no,' Clementine retorted. Her voice was much stronger. 'That I *do* know.'

Adele let out a gasp of frustration. 'Can we just get off this knowing business!' she said, exasperated.

Clementine took a step towards her. Her expression seemed to have altered. From being almost stony, it had suddenly become suffused with brightness. 'I know,' she said, 'because you can be alone, and it can go down into your heart, and it can live there, and you become so used to the feeling of the stone inside you that you forget there's anything else. You just mark time through the days, and fill them with things, even with obsessions. And all the time,' she said, with absolute conviction, 'there's a space inside you, and someone could fill that space, and you would only know then, really know then, when that person gets through to you, when they touch you, when you let them reach out . . . you would only know then of all the empty years. And all the time you had wasted.'

Adele stared at her. The silence became heavy, fraught. Clementine looked away finally, blushing.

'You love him,' Adele murmured.

Clementine said nothing.

'How terrible for you,' Adele said. 'Sent to follow some woman, when you love him. What on earth did you do it for?'

Clementine shrugged. 'I wanted to meet you,' she said.

Adele smiled grimly. 'What a thrill for you,' she replied. 'So that makes two of us thrilled. Just thrilled and glad to be alive,' she added cynically. 'Care to join me in a swim?'

Clementine looked up, looked at the sea, and seemed to pull herself together. The air of hope-lessness, which had briefly surrounded her as she talked of being lonely, dropped away. It was not like Clementine Badger to dwell on problems, no matter how much they weighed you down, lost you your appetite, or, alternatively, forced you to eat cheesecake in the middle of the night. It was, instead, her nature to come up with solutions.

'Are you ever going back?' she asked.

'No,' Adele said.

'Not even when they offer you more money?'

'They won't do that.'

'They might.'

It was Adele's turn to shrug. 'I'm sure that, even now, some young thing is being recruited to replace me,' she said. 'If not by Bugle, then by your Mr Cramm.' She glanced back at the sea. 'And good luck to them. That's fine. It's someone else's turn.'

'You seem very sure,' Clementine observed.

'I am,' Adele told her. 'I've been in this three-ring circus long enough to be absolutely sure.' She sighed heavily. 'I just don't know what to do now. I would like to sleep, I think. Sleep for a week.' She looked at Clementine. 'You can go back and tell him that you found me,' she said. 'Unless you've rung him already, and a bloody car's rushing down here right now, complete with straitjacket.'

'I haven't rung him,' Clementine said.

'You'll disappoint him,' Adele replied.

Clementine was looking at her acutely. 'I have an idea,' she said.

'Oh?' Adele responded. 'What is it? Hire a sub-machine-gun, and wait for them behind the dunes?'

'No,' Clementine said. 'But you have to agree, or it doesn't work. You have to trust me, and I have to trust you.'

Adele sighed. 'Look,' she said. 'You seem like a perfectly decent person, but, frankly, you must be half cracked to come chasing after me on Cramm's orders. It strikes me that you'd do anything for him. So why would I trust you? Cramm might decide that he could get a few thousand by selling the story of my flight to the *Sun*. In fact, *you* could get a few thousand. And why shouldn't you? *TV Celeb Goes Bonkers*. I can see it now.' She turned her back on Clementine. 'Go on,' she said dully, over her shoulder. 'Go and ring them, and make yourself a few quid.'

'I don't want a few quid,' Clementine said. 'I've already got a few quid.'

'Wonderful,' Adele sighed.

Clementine stepped forward, slipping a little on the pebbles, until she was level with Adele's shoulder. 'What is it you want?' she asked. 'What are you running *towards*?'

Adele looked at her. She hadn't thought of it in exactly those terms. She had thought only of running away. But, now that Clementine had framed the words, she began to think seriously. What was it that she was running towards? Really?

'Peace,' she decided finally, after a long moment of silence. 'Contentment.'

'Where?'

'I don't bloody know,' Adele snapped. 'It doesn't come labelled in bottles. I can't buy it in Waitrose, can I?'

'Quite,' Clementine responded. 'And contentment is something different to each person.'

Adele shook her head. 'A house,' she said. 'Privacy. No-one calling. No-one constantly nagging me.'

'A house where?'

'In the country.'

'Roses round the door?'

Adele turned to her angrily. 'Oh, so you think it's a pipe dream. A fantasy? Well, it isn't,' she retorted. 'I know what living in the country means. I know it's not always summer, and I know that it can stink, and I know that you can be isolated. I know you can't get hold of things you need as easily, and I know people can be nosy. I don't imagine it'll be a fairy story. But it's what I want.' She rubbed a hand over her eyes, cursing herself for the tears that had sprung up, and were now falling. 'I want a life,' she muttered. 'Real life, stink and all.'

Clementine took a laundered handkerchief out of

her bag and gave it to Adele. She watched the other woman dry her face. 'I suppose there's a man in all this,' she observed quietly.

'You suppose wrong,' Adele said.

'But . . .' Clementine stopped.

'What?' Adele asked.

'But you've had men.'

Adele laughed shortly. 'Some.'

'You would,' Clementine murmured. 'Because you look so nice.'

Adele stared at her, her eyes ranging over the older woman's face. 'Looks don't count in relationships,' she said. 'At least they shouldn't.'

'I know that,' Clementine responded. 'But they help make him notice in the first place.'

'You mean Cramm doesn't notice you?'

Clementine's blush was crimson. 'Not like that.'

'Well, make him,' Adele said.

'How?'

'Take off your clothes,' Adele advised wearily. She saw Clementine's expression. 'Sorry.'

'I do all the things he likes,' Clementine said. 'I run his bath, I make his meals, I have everything arranged just so. The house runs like clockwork. He never has to make an effort about anything.'

'Aha,' Adele said. 'No work to do. Nothing to struggle for. No hunt. If a man can't hunt, he's not interested. That's your problem.'

'I don't understand,' Clementine said, frowning.

'You can pretend we're living in the twenty-first century if you like,' Adele told her. 'But, as far as a penis is concerned, it's the Stone Age.'

'What do you mean?' Clementine said.

'You're a mammoth,' Adele explained. 'No . . .

don't look like that. Stay with me. You're a mammoth.
Every Stone Age man wants to have a mammoth, so he
can hang it on the wall and show what a great guy he
is. Other Stone Age men will think, hey, what a king,
got a mammoth. OK?'

Silence.

'OK. But catching a mammoth is a tough business,'
Adele continued. 'No mammoth stands still. No
mammoth wants to get caught. Mammoths have great
big tusks. They're off doing mammoth things all day,
they don't look twice at a piddling little man. But that
Stone Age man wants that mammoth, he needs that
mammoth, and the more the mammoth tries to get
away, the more Stone Age man will pursue her. See?'

'I don't know,' Clementine murmured.

'The prize is no good if it just falls over in front of
him,' Adele pointed out. 'How many mammoths
would be worth having if they trundled along in front
of Stone Age every day, picking up his clothes and
making him beans on toast? Not interesting mammoth
at all. Just big shaggy dull old mammoth, domesticated
mammoth, gets in the way, bores him to death. But,'
Adele said, warming to her subject, 'mammoth standing on hill top, looking like hugely cool mammoth,
looking completely unconquerable – wow! That's a
mammoth worth having.'

'I've got to be a mammoth?' Clementine said.

'You've got to be visible.'

'And unconquerable.'

'*Possibly* unconquerable. Just a little window of
conquerability, to whet his appetite.'

'Not make him beans on toast.'

'Have something delicious in the oven, but make
sure you didn't make it. That's what caterers are for.'

'But he loves his dinner.'

'Of course he does,' Adele said. 'But he doesn't want *you* smelling of his dinner.'

Clementine looked miserable. 'It's the only thing I know how to do, keep house.'

'Look,' Adele snapped, 'do you want this Cramm, or not?'

'I want him,' Clementine whispered, barely audible.

'Then pay someone else to keep house. You can cook a dinner occasionally. But not all the time.'

'But what will I do all day!' Clementine protested.

'Whatever you want,' Adele said. 'Take ski lessons. Learn the bongos. Run TV shows yourself. You're an organiser, why not? Get facials. Shop. Teach. Travel. Run a bank. Run a brothel. Run a marathon. *Whatever you want*. Just for God's sake, don't make another cup of cocoa.'

'And you think that'll make him notice?' Clementine asked.

'Notice? Oh yeah. He'll notice. I guarantee it. Visible mammoth.'

'But what if he doesn't like it?'

'All right, say he doesn't like it. What have you lost? It's a damn sight more entertaining than pairing up socks.'

'Yes,' Clementine murmured. 'That's true.'

Adele was suddenly very tired. Her head was hurting. Angrily, she tore off the wig and threw it to the ground. 'God, what a day,' she muttered. 'Pissawful day.' Then she looked up at Clementine. 'What was the idea?' she asked.

Clementine tore herself away from the inner vision of a thousand paired socks, all the socks she had ever paired up for Eric in the last few years. 'I'm sorry?'

'You said you had an idea.'

'Oh . . . oh yes,' Clementine agreed.

'Well, what is it?' Adele asked.

Clementine shuffled a little. 'Well,' she said, 'on the way down here – I was in the train carriage behind you . . . and I saw the way you looked, and I thought . . .'

'Please,' Adele said. 'Just say it.'

'I thought that you must be desperate.'

'Right,' Adele said. 'Righter than Margaret Thatcher on a particularly right-wing day.'

'And I thought that it wasn't fair,' Clementine continued. 'It was like setting hounds off after a fox. And I didn't like feeling like the hound that gets in at the kill. I wanted you to get away.'

'If you wanted that, why go on following me?' Adele demanded. 'You could have stayed on the train and gone back to London.'

'Because I thought we could help each other,' Clementine said.

'Oh really? How, exactly?'

'Well, a bit like the mammoth,' Clementine said. 'Reversed.'

'You've lost me,' Adele said.

'I thought, if Eric saw you as you really are, if he came face to face with you . . .'

'Then it might break his fantasy.'

'Yes.' Clementine fiddled with the strap of her handbag, embarrassedly.

'And you figured, if you engineered a meeting, and I turned up looking like this, he'd go right off me.'

'Well . . .'

'I'm sure he would.'

'And I know of a place,' Clementine said, 'near here. A house. I thought, if I brought him down to this house, and he saw me in this house . . . looking like a mammoth, maybe . . . and you . . .'

'Looking like shit,' Adele prompted.

'Looking . . . not so nice as before . . .'

'He'd leave me alone, and focus on you, and you'd live happily ever after.'

'I'm sorry,' Clementine said. 'It's selfish.'

Adele regarded her for some moments. 'Pretty selfish,' she agreed. 'What's in it for me?'

'Privacy,' Clementine said. 'Peace.'

Adele smiled grudgingly. 'In this house you know?'

'It's my house,' Clementine said. 'I bought it. Nobody knows I bought it. You could live there. Rent-free. Till you get your life together. Find out what you're going to do. It's miles from anywhere. And I could tell people that you got on a ferry in Poole, or something. That you went abroad.'

'And you'd do all that,' Adele said. 'To cure Eric Cramm of his fixation with me.'

'No,' Clementine said, looking her directly in the eye. 'I'd do that to make him have a fixation with *me*.'

'Providing I helped you be a mammoth.'

'Providing you helped me be a mammoth.'

Adele eyed her for some seconds. Then, she kicked the wig into the sea. 'Well, I'm not exactly weighed down with better offers,' she decided.

And it beats the hell out of being pulled out of West Bay harbour, she added silently, to herself.

19

It was late in the afternoon when Lawrence Bugle woke up.

He was sure that the Reaper had kept his word, and that he had arrived in hell. There seemed to be a grey mist in the room, and someone close by was whistling 'It's Raining Men'. What other proof did he need? This must be the theme song on the other side of the Styx: where it was indeed raining men, all kinds of evil ones. And he was among them, and about to become a toasted delicacy.

He blinked harder.

The room came into focus a little. It wasn't entirely grey, but it was in shadow. Blinds had been drawn across the windows.

'So I can't see the torturing,' he whispered to himself.

'Hello,' said a voice. 'He's surfaced.'

He looked around. Abigail Randall was sitting by his side.

'Is he still here?' Lawrence asked her fearfully.

She leaned towards him. 'Is who still here?'

'The Reaper.'

She frowned at him. 'The consultant's just gone, if that's what you mean.' She started to smile. 'Did look a bit cadaverish, now you mention it.'

Lawrence fumbled for Abigail's hand. 'Is it hot?' he asked.

'It's always hot in hospitals,' she said.

'What did they send you here for?'

'They didn't send me,' Abigail told him. 'I came of my own accord. I was worried about you.'

Lawrence's eyes widened. 'You came here *because you were worried about me*?' he repeated.

'Of course.'

'Here!'

'Well, it's not that bad,' Abigail said. 'Dinner's coming round in a minute. Are you hungry?'

'Dinner?' Lawrence squeaked. 'What is it, boiled heads?'

'Liver, I think.'

'Livers!' Lawrence groaned. 'Oh God, oh God.'

Abigail got to her feet. 'Listen,' she said. 'I'll just get the nurse.'

Lawrence watched her go, choked with emotion. That any woman, he thought, should follow him to the gates of hell . . . it was a miracle. It was more than a miracle. It was impossible. His last wife wouldn't follow him round a golf course, never mind to hell. She wouldn't walk a hundred yards down the road to get him a paracetamol, let alone face the horrors of eternal damnation.

Perhaps, he thought, Abigail wasn't really a woman at all. Perhaps he had been given one last mercy. Perhaps she was some sort of guardian angel, who had offered to act as an intermediary for him. After all, she didn't seem fazed by being in the underworld one bit. She seemed absolutely matter-of-fact. Relaxed, even. And you could only be relaxed if you felt impregnable, couldn't you? Protected.

That's what it was, he decided.

She was an angel.

She appeared back at the door, accompanied by a nurse with a syringe.

Chapter One of Everlasting Suffering, he thought. *What's in the syringe? Green monkey fever?*

'She's got something for you,' Abigail said, swimming into his line of vision.

'I know,' he mumbled, terrified. 'Will I grow a tail?'

The two women looked at each other.

'It's perfectly normal,' the nurse said. 'A little bit of disorientation. I'll call Mr Simpkins back.'

She administered the drug. Lawrence watched in dread. He lay waiting for the tail to start sprouting from his bottom, and the horns to begin growing from his head. But, to his surprise, he felt nothing at all, other than a little better.

'Would you like the light on?' Abigail asked.

'Is it allowed?' he said. 'I thought it had to be dark.'

'What nonsense,' Abigail retorted. And she pressed the switch.

He opened his eyes.

Daring to look, he saw that Abigail was right: he *was* wired up to what looked like an ECG. The thing on his foot *was* a temperature clamp.

He glanced back at her, puzzled.

'Did he put them on?' he asked.

'Who?'

'Him with the cloak.'

Abigail tut-tutted. 'You'd better pull yourself together,' she said. 'Or they'll discharge you from here and book you into the psychiatric ward.'

'Ward?' Lawrence stuttered. 'What-what ward-ward?'

'On the other side of the hospital.'

'Hospital?' he repeated. 'Here? Hospital? Hospital here?'

'Are you deaf?' Abigail asked, amused. 'Or just a parrot?'

He frowned at her. 'Why do they need hospitals?' he asked her. 'I'm dead.' A ghastly notion occurred to him. 'Is it for . . . experiments?'

'You aren't dead,' Abigail said. 'Or, at least, you *were* dead. Four times. But not now.'

'Not dead?' Lawrence echoed. 'Where am I, then?'

'In the Cardiac Care Unit.'

For a little while, Lawrence hardly dared look. He clamped his eyes shut. He became aware of something very odd round his chest, and something else very odd on his big toe. He imagined, wildly, that this was a punishment devised entirely for TV executives: the chest bands would be reels of videotape, of old programmes he had ditched, and whose stars had ended up working for MFI in Solihull, or – worse still – tapes of current successful programmes that he had commissioned. He was going to be tortured for all time with re-runs of *Michael Conley Entertains* or *Lottery Bananas* or *Stars in Their Shoes*. No doubt, any moment, the bands would become red-hot, and start scorching his skin.

'Take them off,' he pleaded.

'What?' Abigail asked.

'My chest,' he whimpered.

'They can't take those off,' Abigail told him. 'They're measuring your heartbeat.'

'My foot,' he gasped.

'Measuring your temperature,' she said.

'My . . .'

'It's a catheter,' she said. 'You've had a nasty time of it.'

'My . . . my heart?' he whispered. 'Cardiac here heart?'

'Conked out. Not surprising, by the look of you,' she said. 'Not enough walking. Not enough fish. Got to have oily fish to keep you alive and kicking, you know.'

But Lawrence had interrupted her lecture. '*Alive?*' he repeated. 'I'm alive?'

'Didn't I say so? You should take loads of cod liver oil. And no cigarettes and no cigars.'

Lawrence's bottom lip wobbled. 'Alive,' he breathed. 'Not on a ceiling?'

'No spirits, no shouting, no late hours . . .'

'He said I had to check out at 11.08,' Lawrence mumbled. 'But he spared me. He left me!'

Abigail leaned over him and looked him in the eye. 'Who?' she asked.

Lawrence stared at her. Suddenly, the full magnitude of what had happened washed over him. He had been dead, not once, but four times. He had seen the messenger of the Doomed. He had been sitting on the ceiling, and he had felt, as the Reaper had promised, the misery of those that he had stood on and used and stabbed in the back to get where he was today. He had experienced their rage and pain as he had slipped down into what he had believed was an everlasting dark. He had felt his own heart break ten thousand times as he had fallen that great distance into the afterlife. And, for some reason that escaped him, he had been spared.

'I don't deserve it,' he whispered.

'Nobody deserves cod liver oil,' Abigail observed. 'Unfortunately, it helps keep the arteries clear.'

'I've been forgiven,' Lawrence said. 'Spared! Released!'

Abigail smoothed his sheet, raising an eyebrow.

He clutched her wrist. 'You don't understand,' he cried, 'I've been given a second chance! He wanted to take me, he had a scythe, he told me it was over, and yet I've been forgiven!'

Abigail turned to look behind her. The consultant was hurrying back into the room.

'He's off again,' she told the man peremptorily. 'Rambling.'

'Oxygen deprivation,' the consultant opined.

'Saved!' Lawrence shouted. 'I've been saved!'

'We do our best,' the consultant said.

'Not by you!' Lawrence screeched. 'By God! He forgave me! He forgave me!'

'Just lie quietly,' the consultant said.

But Lawrence wasn't about to be quieted.

He didn't need the consultant to examine him. He didn't care what the test results said, or what message the machine beside him might be bleeping out. None of it mattered, for he was beyond the reach of mortal man now. He didn't need their opinions any more! He wouldn't be afraid when he looked at the scales any more! He needn't decide he had cancer whenever he saw a cancer programme, or that he had motor neurone disease when he saw a motor neurone disease programme. Because he didn't have cancer! He didn't have motor neurone disease! He didn't even have a damaged heart – not any kind of damage that mattered a jot – because he was invincible! God had stamped his ticket. God had put money in his meter! His parking hadn't expired; his season ticket hadn't run out. God had paid his bill in full, and extended his life span by whatever God thought was necessary. Which was fine, which was wonderful. Which was just as it bloody well should be.

All was right with the world. All was as shiny as a Surf advert. All was singing and dancing. He was on a mission. He was on a journey. He had things to do, lives to alter, wrongs to right.

'It's all lovely!' he yelled deliriously. 'I'm alive, and it's all fabulous!'

'Hush, hush,' said Abigail.

'Glorious! Glorious!' Lawrence sang.

'Give him a sedative,' Abigail said.

But Lawrence wasn't about to be placated. He sat upright, sending the ECG into a minor cardiac arrest of its own. He swung his legs off the bed and caught hold of the consultant's tie.

'Mr Bugle!' the man protested.

'Listen,' Lawrence hissed. 'Listen to me. I want my clothes. I want my shoes.'

'You can't have them,' Abigail said.

'Yes I can,' Lawrence told her. He began ripping off the plastic discs and tubing still attached to him. 'I've got things to do, I've got people to see. I've got worlds to change!'

'Nurse,' said the consultant, 'the screens.'

But Lawrence wasn't about to be stopped. He wrenched himself from their grasp and started dancing in the middle of the floor.

'Worlds to change!' he sang at the top of his voice. 'Oh joy! Oh joy! Worlds and worlds and worlds to change!'

20

Will did what he always did when he was faced with a problem.

He climbed a mountain.

It posed a slight problem, as there weren't that many Everests between Westminster and Dorset. In the end, he decided on a place where he and Meg had gone when they first knew each other; when Meg had first brought him down to meet her mother.

What a weekend that had been, just over a year ago.

He had seriously considered breaking it off with Meg after witnessing the Randalls' Sunday lunch, which wasn't so much a lunch as a state of armed siege, Abigail behind her rampart of roast potato, and Meg bristling behind her boiled swede. Abigail had told him quite freely, over the first sherry, that Meg was a quite hopeless girl who would never make much of herself, and who was now stuck in some dead-end job near Holborn.

'It is not a dead end,' Meg had retorted hotly. 'And I am not hopeless.'

'Well, it isn't what you set out to do, when you went to London, is it?' Abigail had commented calmly. 'You were going to be a somebody, you told me. High-powered whatnot.'

Meg had flushed crimson. 'I'm working my way towards it,' she'd countered. 'It's the devil's own task to get any kind of job.'

'You won't find a way towards fame and fortune by registering trademarks in Papua New Guinea,' Abigail said. 'Or posting patents for steam-driven hairdryers, in that poky little rabbit-warren of an office.'

'I have to pay my rent,' Meg replied. 'At least I'm not sponging off you, like some people.' And she had glowered at her brother, who had simply smiled back at her.

Afterwards, on the way home, Meg had driven via Glastonbury, and insisted that they climb the hill there. 'It always calms me down,' she had told him.

'Have you ever thought of not arguing with your mother?' Will had asked, as they had set out from the car towards the chapel above them. 'I mean, you could just turn a blind eye.'

Meg had only smiled rather mysteriously. 'I've already got a blind eye,' she'd told him. 'Whenever Mum's around.'

He had stopped her, holding on to her arm, turning her towards him. 'Why does she call you hopeless?' he had asked her. 'Why do you let her?'

She'd looked him in the eye. 'Because she always has,' she told him. 'Because if you screamed at her until you were blue in the face – and, believe me, I have – she would forget everything you'd said by the next time you saw her.' She shrugged, and gave him a smile of very mixed feelings. 'Do you know what my secret is?' she asked him.

'No,' he'd told her.

She'd taken a breath, held it, and expelled it heavily before replying. 'I'll never be myself,' she said, 'until I do something big. Until I get out of that shadow.'

And the phrase had stuck in the back of his mind, and come out occasionally, like a little thorn periodically sticking in his flesh. *Until I do something big.*

He had always been nagged by the feeling that Meg's *something big* was not just being the partner of a man who could pee downwind of a polar bear.

He arrived now in Glastonbury at half past six, just after the last teashop had closed. He yearned for a while over the relinquished prospect of scones, butter and jam, but heroically accepted his fate and trudged out of town. Each step made him wince.

'Don't do any walking,' the doctor had told him, at St Thomas's. 'Just an amble. Just a stroll.'

'Well, two miles *was* an amble to him, he thought to himself. Two miles, including a stretch up a very steep incline that had most other tourists gasping for breath halfway to the summit.

He got to the top of Glastonbury Tor just as the sky began to turn pink.

For a spring day, it had been beautifully warm, and the fields spread out below him in a checkerboard pattern as far as the eye could see. He went inside the ruined chapel and looked out to the west, where, in the hazy distance, the Bristol Channel made the grey distinction between England and Wales. He looked north, to the dark green line of hills, and the vineyards tucked directly underneath them; and east, back in the direction he had come, towards the distant and vast suburban sprawl of the capital.

His face unconsciously darkened. He didn't want to live in London any more. It was bad enough when he had to stay there whenever he was home with Meg. If he had to live there permanently, wake up every morning to the sound of sirens and traffic, he would go bananas. He craved peace, and silence. He wanted to hear the leaves of trees rustling near his bedroom window. He wanted to hear the sound of his own footsteps when he went outside his front door. He didn't want to lie in bed at night and listen to people coming home from the pub on the corner, or the rumble of the Tube trains in the cutting a quarter of a mile away.

He had never once heard Meg complain about any of that, he realised. She *liked* the city. Actually liked it! It was almost as if there was something seriously wrong with her, he thought. Some short-circuit. Some twist in the frequencies. She liked to go to the art galleries, and theatres, and fight her way through Leicester Square every night. She didn't seem to hear the noise, or taste the taint of the diesel in the air. As for him, if he had to see just one more splatter of paint that called itself artistic, or sit through just one more screeching of violins that Meg claimed was Schubert, he'd pass out in public.

'London's alive,' she always told him. 'Alive with people.'

'It isn't,' he'd always responded. 'It's alive with rats and stockbrokers.'

He just didn't want to be near people. If people came too close to him, he always had this incredible urge to punch them between the eyes.

'Nice view, yeah,' a voice said beside him.

He jolted with surprise.

Next to him, as if having materialised out of thin air, was a guy of about twenty. His head was shaved; he wore a cheesecloth shirt, torn jeans and battered sandals, one shoe held together with a band of sticky tape.

'Conjunction,' the lad said. 'Ley power, right?'

Will eyed him suspiciously. 'I don't know,' he said.

'Not know?' answered the vision. 'Great meeting point of ley lines, man. Place of forces, y'know?'

Will did not know. He didn't have any time for mystics.

'Hey,' said the lad, suddenly looking hard at him. 'You that guy, man? That guy?'

'No,' Will said.

The lad grinned. 'Yeah, man, the ice man, the snow man. You a snowman, yeah?' and he laughed.

'No,' Will insisted.

The lad persisted. 'You been everywhere,' he said, determined. 'About.'

'I've been about, yes,' Will conceded.

'You seen those bears that catch fish?' the lad demanded.

'Grizzly. Yes.'

'Things that moult. Big stuff with eyes. Faces. Bony shoulders.'

'Caribou. Yes.'

The lad nodded. 'Going to Thailand,' he said, as if confiding the world's greatest secret. 'Going to Borneo, Australia, Philippines, man.'

'You are?'

'The works.' He grinned. 'Keep on keeping on,' he said. 'Ain't that the power, though. Keep on keeping on. Right stuff. No ties, freedom. Yeah, nice.' He leaned towards Will and grabbed his elbow. 'Hey, guy,' he breathed in Will's ear, 'what's everywhere like?'

Ten minutes later, Will walked back to the car, carefully closing all the field gates after him. On the little lane where he was parked, he stood for a long moment staring at the front garden of one of the cottages by St Catherine's Well, where a fall of aubretia, an almost fluorescent magenta, tumbled over the garden wall.

Somewhere at the back of the house, he could hear a woman speaking. She was calling the name of someone who, evidently, was inside the cottage. He could hear the chink of plates, and cutlery, and the sound of a kettle whistling as it came to the boil.

He stood transfixed, with a lump in his throat.

He didn't want to know where everywhere was like, he thought.

He had been everywhere, and he was tired.

He didn't want freedom.

He had known freedom, and it was lonely.

He only wanted to know somewhere, one some-where, with a stone garden wall like this one, and a voice calling.

A voice he could love, calling his own name from the garden.

21

That afternoon, Eric Cramm was in a state of high excitement.

What a day he had had. What joy he had experienced. What complete and utter satisfaction. He had signed up Meg and Harry Randall; he had sent Clementine to find Adele Buchanan and was in no doubt that she would find her; and, to add delight upon delight, Lawrence Bugle was dead.

He spent a very happy half-hour pacing his office, composing his speech for Lawrence's memorial service. He would say how much he had admired the man; he would say that he had been his own inspiration for years – thereby emphasising the fact that Lawrence was in his dotage, and he, Eric, was in his prime – and he would say that Lawrence had created exciting television.

All of which were lies.

Naturally.

But in one crucial respect, Lawrence's influence would genuinely be missed. There was no-one who was bastard enough to fill his shoes, no-one tyrannical enough to want to. There would be an enormous gulf, a vacuum at the head of Entertainment Scheduling, and there would be no-one insane enough to fill it. Lawrence's network would be thrown into disarray, enough disarray for him – Eric Cramm – to walk straight in and pinch Lawrence's best programmes from under his nose.

It would be simple, he thought to himself in complete confidence. Artistes would be wondering if their contracts still stood, and there would be no-one man enough to reassure them, and, being creatives, they would all start to get the jitters – for every creative person was merely a massive flatulent bag of ego, with no substance at all – and then he would come along. He would come along, calm and persuasive, and he would tell them that, indeed, true to their wildest nightmares, the whole network was crumbling around their ears, and they were all for the chop, and then – masterstroke! – he would offer Lawrence's best people new contracts with Up-Line, and his triumph would be complete.

Marching into Poland would be nothing compared to the coup on that day. A day that was very soon to happen. And the first artiste to fall into his lap would be Adele Buchanan.

Eric managed to calm himself for long enough to sit down and gaze at the view of the river. He was so euphoric that the sight of St Paul's only slightly irritated him. His eyes glazed over as he planned Adele's future.

She would have to come off morning TV, of course. She had abdicated that particular role already. No, what he had in mind for her was more Anne Robinson, more Richard Whiteley. He imagined her at the head of some quiz show – something bleak and nasty. Something that would suit the 4.30 TV audience. A cross between *The Weakest Link* and *Countdown*, with a bit of *Dog Eat Dog* thrown in.

He had been mulling a programme like this for some time, knowing that those over sixty were coming

up on the rails, forming larger parts of the TV
audience. Larger parts of the population, in fact. Grey
Power was looming large. By 2010, his researchers
had told him, the cult of the young would have
dropped and the cult of the Sixty-Somethings would
have taken over.

And what better to project Grey Power, than to
show senior citizens hellbent on destroying each
other? He thought of calling it *Guillotine*. All the
contestants would be over seventy. They would be
encouraged to drop the Nice Old Lady disguises and
become Real Old Ladies, knocking each other off
Zimmer frames and poisoning each other's cats.
Whoever was the nastiest and most scheming would
win, and Adele Buchanan would be the leather-clad
dominatrix presiding over the decline of the nation's
elderly. Old people must be totally sick of behaving
themselves and being quiet, he had decided. So he was
going to give them their heads. He was going to set
them free, to be bastards like their sons and daughters,
and Adele would be driving them on.

Liberation! Disaster! Peak viewing figures!

God, he hadn't had such a wonderful day in years.

At last, he could stand his office confinement no
longer. Looking at his watch, he saw that it was almost
five o'clock. He simply couldn't stay in the building for
another second. He walked out, ignoring the executives who were waiting in the outer office to see him,
and he got in the lift. All the way down to the ground
floor, he sang 'When Two Tribes Go To War' to
himself, with a smirk on his face.

It frightened the living daylights out of the
receptionists downstairs as he passed them. They had
never seen him smile before.

*

He took the footbridge across the Thames to Charing Cross.

Normally, of course, he either had a driver take him home – if it was rush hour – or, he left his departure until late at night when the streets were quieter. Either way, he liked to be sealed off from humanity.

Today was different, however. Today he positively enjoyed the walk – against the tide of homeward-trailing commuters – on the blackened path slung underneath the railway line. He looked to left and right as he strolled. It struck him that, when he was growing up in the USA, this was the view he had always wanted to see: Westminster Bridge to his left, and the Houses of Parliament; Cleopatra's Needle to his right, and the great westward-turning curve of the river. Just two bridges down was Tate Modern, housed in Bankside. God, how he loved that place! It was so deathly, so stark: a huge unrepentant brick box, with massive spaces inside, and the artwork littered about in *installations*. He liked art like that. He liked the sort of work that bemused other visitors: waste bins that had people hovering near them unsure whether to applaud or put their ice-cream wrappers inside. Tables where the frazzled sometimes sat down, oblivious to the fact that the entire thing was made of milk cartons and held together with masking tape, as a statement to modern consumerism.

He *loved* the transparencies of tree stumps, the empty Kleenex boxes, the baskets of flowers made of buffalo dung, the elephants' heads made of car doors. The whole dazzling concept of it – the echoing black cavern that smacked visitors in the face as soon as they walked in, the feeling of being in prison, the exhibits that frightened the life out of you – especially the moaning girl one in a dark corner, and the blood one lit by neon – he *loved* all that. What he couldn't stand at all was the floors where they had Cézanne. All the pretty colours looked so utterly naff.

He tore his eyes away from the direction of the Tate, and ploughed on through the crowds. The smell of petrol assaulted him as he climbed the stairs to Villiers Street and the Strand. Buses and taxis were locked in battle with motorcycle couriers; the pavements were clogged with foreign-language students, pickpockets, mothers pushing baby buggies, grey-faced merchant bankers talking to the metal aerials attached directly to their brains and quietly frying them; vacant-looking office workers in dusty suits; newspaper sellers, and tourists with a map in one hand and a bottle of water in the other. Anonymous hordes swept down from Whitehall, Covent Garden and Holborn towards Waterloo; armies of the exhausted; battalions of the depressed; regiments of the bored. Eric Cramm smiled at them all benevolently. After all, they were His People, His Public. They would all go home and switch on two things. The kettle, and the TV.

Maybe he could buy into kitchen equipment, he thought dreamily, as he turned into Sardinia Street. If he took out enough shares, he would then own the nation's psyche between the hours of six and seven in the evening. They would switch on his kettle, and switch on his TV. He managed a grin to himself as he got out his door key. It was the nearest Eric Cramm ever came to telling himself a joke.

'I've signed up Meg Randall and her brother,' he shouted, shrugging off his coat. He waited for

Clementine to appear, and looked up the stairs, frowning a little. The house was silent. No-one was coming to greet him. No-one had responded when he spoke. He was alone at the foot of the stairs, rebuffed. He stuck out his lip in petulant dismay, like a three-year-old who has just seen his ice-cream thrown out of the car window.

'I'm here!' he called. 'Tell Adele I've trounced her boss!'

Nothing.

He ground his teeth, then stopped himself. He didn't want to have to pay for another set of crowns. They would be the third in the past year.

'I wish I could see Bugle's face,' he said. Then thought a minute. Lawrence Bugle was dead. Had been dead for about seven hours now. 'On second thoughts, cancel that thought,' he muttered.

He climbed the stairs and emerged into the living room. He couldn't hear a thing. He couldn't smell a thing. The expression on his face darkened from petulance to anger.

No meal was cooking; no Horlicks was being stirred. And, worst of all, there was no scent of pudding, that wonderful English delicacy that Clementine had introduced him to. Every night, she would cook something different. Jam roly-poly. Apple dumplings. Treacle tart. He looked forward to those smells, he now realised. They gave him a warm feeling right down to his toes. And warm feelings were very hard to come by in his life.

'I'm thirsty,' he announced.

And then – better late than never – he realised.

He understood what the silence meant: that Clementine was not at home. He swayed for a second, a small sapling suddenly robbed of its support; then he took a deep breath. Why wasn't she here? he asked himself. How long would it take to track down Adele Buchanan? The woman could only have got so far in her bare feet; she would have been a sitting duck.

When nothing had appeared on the news reports about Adele Buchanan being found, or filmed getting back to her house, he had assumed – why wouldn't he assume? – that Clementine had found her, and brought her back.

His good mood had been entirely based on this simple assumption. Set Clementine a task: the task was completed. Tell her to do something: the thing was done. There were never any other calls, the kind of calls you might expect from any other mortal, like, *What shall I do now?* or *I've lost her, sorry.* No, the very fact that there had been nothing from Clementine since eleven o'clock this morning had simply settled into his subconscious as proof that she had located her prey and overcome her and that Adele Buchanan would be sitting in his own house, trussed, metaphorically speaking, and waiting for the oven. Or, if not in his own house, then somewhere equally safe and secure.

But she wasn't here. Neither Adele, nor Clementine.

What on earth did it mean?

He sat down heavily on the couch.

Now that he thought of it, this had happened once before. Just once. It had been soon after they had arrived in the UK. He had arrived home early, at six, like today. And Clementine had not been waiting for him. Mind you, he had only got as far as the top of the stairs when she had arrived, slightly out of breath, and slightly red around the gills. 'I'm so sorry,' she had said as she had come into the room. 'I needed to go out. Please sit down. The dinner is already on. I shan't be a moment.'

Breaking the habit of a lifetime, he had shown curiosity about another living human being, and asked her where she had been.

She had blushed, and lowered her head. 'I had to see a dentist,' she had murmured.

'Can't he have routine appointments at a reasonable time of day?' Eric had asked her peevishly.

She had blushed even deeper. 'It wasn't routine,' she had almost whispered. 'I had to have my wisdom teeth out.'

He shook his head a little now. Wisdom teeth – all four of them – had only delayed her by three minutes. She should have sorted Adele Buchanan in an hour, maybe less.

He got up and strode into the office.

No light was winking on the answerphone.

He turned on the laptop.

No emails were waiting.

He pulled off his jacket, felt in the pocket, and checked his mobile.

No messages.

He glared about him.

No written note.

Damn it! He thought, furious.

Where in hell was she?

By half past six, he had managed to fix himself a little supper, and his black mood had abated slightly.

In fact, the blackness had been replaced by something else: something very strange and very foreign to him, and immensely disturbing.

He sat looking at the congealed piece of cheese on toast, a feast that had tasted entirely of rubber and not, as it did when Clementine made it, of succulence and delight. He fiddled with the knife and fork, trying to locate the source of the uneasy sensation settling over his heart.

The feeling took him back a long way, more years than he cared to remember. It took him back across the Atlantic, and up another flight of stairs, a flight of stairs in an immense brownstone in New York, and into the dreary expanse of plush and gilt that had been the drawing room of his parents' home. When his parents had died in the road accident, he had already been away at school, and so their real loss had not struck him until the first time that he had come home during the vacation. A loner at school, he had already been used to solitariness, but nothing had prepared him for that extreme, acute sense of being alone as he had sat in that house, the servants downstairs, and his own small nine-year-old self inhabiting the echoing floors above. He had had no aunts or uncles; his parents had both been only children. His grandparents were all dead, and he knew no-one well enough at school to invite them to stay. He had known then how truly alone he was, sitting on the hard Louis XIV seat, staring at the heavy-framed landscapes on the walls. Perhaps this alone-ness ran in his family. Perhaps it was actually in his blood. Looking around the room, there were few human touches: only a couple of photographs, but no books or magazines, and no pictures with people in them.

But he had accepted his lot. He grew to like the spaces. The severely arranged furniture. The hard lines and edges. They had invaded him, and become part of him, and they had never restricted or chafed him.

Until now.

Until tonight.

He got up, struggling with the feeling creeping over him.

He wanted someone else with him.

He wanted Clementine.

He almost ran out of the room, inadvertently knocking the cheese-on-toast plate to the floor, but not hearing it fall. He ran up the second flight of stairs, that led to Clementine's quarters. At her door he hesitated, guilty that he should even think of invading her room; but, as he had come up the steps, a fear had washed through him, a fear so terrible that he had trouble catching his breath. He had suddenly wondered if Clementine had left him. If she had finally had enough, and, wordlessly and without explanation, departed. She had done almost that when she left California: a bare couple of sentences of explanation had been all that his wailing neighbour had been given. Perhaps she had done the same thing now: made an instant decision, angered, maybe, by the orders he had given her that morning. Perhaps it had been one instruction, one trespass on her good nature, too many. People did break. They broke and ran, like Adele Buchanan. They broke and died, like Lawrence Bugle.

She couldn't have died, he thought.

She couldn't have died?

The insane thought made him push open her door. In her trust of him, she had not locked it.

His eyes ranged around the room. He had never been in here before. It was more feminine than he might have imagined. Almost more childlike. He looked at the rocking horse, perplexed. He looked at the books. Dozens and dozens of . . . well, what were they? He picked one up and looked at the title. *Lady Pamela's Desires*. He stared, and then lifted another. *Nurse Welkin's New Job*. He had had no idea that she even read books. And she came up here, at night, and she read . . . *The Dashing Swordsman of Bute. The Devil in Mr Dashwood. The Last Chance of Happiness.*

He was transfixed to the spot, trying to put two and two together. Half of him disapproved of this show of apparent weakness on her part; but the other half of him – the half that seemed now, after years of sitting in the background, to be pushing forward and demanding a better view – was drawn to her. All this time, he thought, she had been sitting up here reading about manly heroes, and all this time, he had been sitting a floor below her thinking that he was one.

She couldn't have thought so.

Could she?

Would she need to read the books, if she lived with one?

He tossed the paperback on to the bed. It was a very tidy bed, with a very small Steiff teddy bear sitting on the starched pillow. He stared at the bear, and his heart, which had been sitting shrivelled in his chest for decades, suddenly beat hard. He stared at the poor little bear, obviously a survivor of many years standing, with its tufted ears almost bare of fur.

Then he turned on his heel, pushed open the door, and ran downstairs. He went into his own room, threw open the door of his wardrobe, and knelt down. Right at the back was a holdall, and he pulled it out now, and unzipped it.

There was an immediate smell of school locker room. Of stale socks and staler boys, and old books, and forgotten sandwiches. He pulled out the contents: a rugby kit, worn only two or three times until he had been allowed to sit on the sidelines, because he was such a liability to the team. A copy of *Bleak House*. A desk calendar, stuck at 4 January, the day that his parents had died. A dozen school exercise books, all with their matching stars and ticks and class awards, that had given him five minutes of pleasure, and five years of bullying in the showers; a piece of toffee, wrapped in tin foil, that he had kept because a boy had once given it to him, and no-one else ever had.

And right at the back was his most treasured possession of all.

No-one had ever seen it, not even at school. He had managed to keep it hidden all his life, and no-one on earth knew that it travelled with him in his hand luggage whenever he went abroad, and slept with him every night, and that it was kept in here, in the dark at the back of the wardrobe every day, so that not even Clementine would see it as she made his bed each morning.

He took it out, and held it to his chest.

His teddy bear.

Exactly the same Steiff bear as Clementine's.

22

Evening was coming to Halfpenny Acre.

Down the hill, the water meadows in the valley were doing their utmost to out-do a Constable painting, with cattle knee-deep in the slow-flowing streams. The horse chestnut trees were just coming into flower, and stood in the centre of the nearest meadow like huge green umbrellas tiered with white candles.

Penny Arthur stood on the threshold of the house, staring down at the view, tears in her eyes.

She knew what she should have done, of course. She should have scraped together the money to buy Halfpenny Acre herself, years ago. It was she who had found the advert in the estate agent's window, and pointed Abigail and Ernest towards the sale. Not ever believing that they would buy it – she had always thought that Abigail liked to be nearer London – but more out of interest for herself, so that she could go with them when they viewed it, and see inside the cottage that she herself had coveted ever since she had come to live in the valley.

The plan had backfired when they had actually put their money down, much to her surprise. God! How envious she had been! Still, she had always thought she owned Halfpenny at one remove; she knew every inch of the grounds, every gnarled twist on the apple trees, every patch of bluebells, every grey-lichened tile on the roof.

'Damn it,' she muttered, for the twentieth time that day, and walked back into the hall.

She had spent all day packing boxes.

She looked at them now, neatly parcelled and taped and labelled. She had made a start in the sitting room, and had almost finished wrapping the ornaments in tissue paper and stacking them between leaves of newspaper.

'You'd think it was your own stuff,' she'd told herself in a reprimanding fashion, at lunchtime, dust in her hair, her fingers blackened by newsprint. She hadn't even had time to switch on the television and see Will and Meg's interview: she would do so, she told herself, when she got home. She had put the videotape in before she left.

One more favour for Abigail. One more day in the house. Abigail had said that the buyer wanted to move in as soon as possible. Soon, Penny had been telling herself all day, she wouldn't even have Halfpenny once removed. She'd be out, just as Abigail would be out, and whoever this person in TV was who had bought it would steam in, and, metaphorically or actually, lock the gates against her.

'Ridiculous,' she'd muttered, more than once. 'Ridiculous to get attached to someone else's bloody house.'

What on earth was she going to do when she couldn't come here any more? she asked herself. She was so fond of the place that never seeing it again would be like wrenching out her own heart. She'd have to figure out a different way to drive up to Shaftesbury and Sherborne, for a start. The long way round, avoiding this valley. She'd have to take jobs well away from this village. She'd have to be strict with herself, make a point of it.

And there was more than that, of course. Much more.

She wouldn't see much of Abigail, either. And she would see less of Meg. And God only knew what Harry was going to do. Perhaps he would want to come and live with her, she thought. She wondered wryly to herself if she could stand him for more than eight hours a day. Charm had a shelf life, particularly poor Harry's witless, sunny variety. It would be like living with an Old English Sheepdog. If nothing else, she would have to get him to cut that floppy hair.

Sighing heavily to herself now, she taped up the last box she'd finished, wrote *Sitting Room* across it in black marker pen, and straightened up, rubbing the small of her back.

And then she heard the car coming.

She walked out swiftly again to the front, and saw Will, driving Meg's beaten-up Peugeot. She shaded her eyes, and squinted at what could be seen of him through the windscreen. He was driving slowly, which was not the Will she knew. Perhaps he was tired, she told herself. It must have been a long day. A long couple of days, even.

As he stopped the car, she walked out to him. 'You look shattered,' she told him, kissing his cheek. 'What are you doing here? Where's Meg?'

'London,' he said. 'Isn't she here yet?'

'No . . .'

'I thought she might have got back here by now,' he said. 'She rang to say she was coming down here with Michael and Harry.' He glanced sideways at her, raising his eyebrows. 'Something important to tell us,' he said.

'Really?' Penny replied. 'I wonder what. She didn't ring here.'

'Probably busy,' Will said. 'Did you see the telly?'

'No. Why?'

He shook his head. 'They're all mad up there, you know, in London. Completely barmy.'

'I know,' she agreed. 'Did you go for your check-up?'

'Yes,' he said. 'Apart from walking like a duck, I appear to be all right.'

'But Meg went with you, to the hospital?'

'No.'

'No?' She frowned. 'Not like her.'

'There's a lot that's not like her,' he grumbled, slamming the car door, and wincing as he rubbed the base of his spine. 'You have no idea, Pen.'

She looked at him narrowly. 'I see,' she said. 'You'd better fill me in. Tea?'

'Yes. Thanks.'

'Go and sit in the shade,' she told him. 'I'll bring it through in a minute.'

She brought the tray out to him as he sat in the knot garden. The little fountain she had installed – a small trickle from a green-man head into a half-circle by a wall – made a comforting, relaxing sound in the evening air. Except that Will didn't seem to be relaxed at all, sitting hunched over, twisting a grass stalk between his fingers. As she got near him, he eventually tore it in two, and threw it to one side.

'Well,' she said, setting down the tray and pouring tea into the cups. 'Give.'

'What?' he asked.

'Whatever's making you look like a wet weekend.'

'I'm fine,' he said, taking the china cup from her.

'This is me you're talking to,' she reminded him. 'Not a doctor in London.'

He grinned at her, sipped the tea, then set the cup back on the tray.

'Meg won't marry me,' he told her.

'Oh, Will! You asked her?'

'Half a dozen times.'

She looked at him closely. 'Did she give a reason?'

'Too young. Doesn't want children.'

Penny nodded. She let the silence unfold for a while before she replied. 'She's never been a babies sort of person,' she said.

'But I do,' he said. 'I am.'

'I see. But not totally insurmountable, surely?'

He looked at her. 'What do you mean?'

'Well, you might find, when she's in her thirties . . .'

'But that's years away!'

'If she's the right person . . .'

He rubbed one fist against his eyes, then sank back against the seat as if defeated. 'I'm no good at all this,' he muttered.

'Of course you are. Give her time.'

'I'm not,' he retorted. 'And I don't want to wait. I don't want to discuss it. I just want to do it. I don't want to talk about it, on and on.'

Penny frowned. 'That's rather inflexible, Will,' she said.

'OK,' he told her. 'So I'm inflexible. I just don't think it should be complicated. We ought to think the same.'

'Meg isn't a facsimile of you, Will,' she chided gently. 'You can't expect her to think as you do.'

'But I *do* expect that,' he replied. 'That's the whole point, isn't it? You're supposed to think the same, want the same things.'

Penny bit her lip for a while. Beside her, Will looked about himself. 'God, I can't stand cities,' he murmured.

'No,' Penny agreed. 'Dreadful noisy holes.'

He glanced at her. 'Perhaps *you'd* better marry me, Penny.'

'OK,' she agreed. They smiled at each other.

'I just want to settle down,' he said. 'Is that so terrible?'

She put her hand on his knee. 'No,' she said. 'It isn't terrible.'

'She's pulling one way, and me another,' he said. He looked utterly baffled, and she thought for a second – a second she would not have shared with him – that he was totally unlike Meg, who was all fire and action, like a scalded cat, or some sort of sprite. Meg had always been the one to get into scrapes, always the one to argue with her mother, always wildly up in the air or down in the dumps, and always full of ideas. Penny didn't think she had ever seen Meg sit still for more than two seconds together. Whereas Will . . .

She tried to imagine him as a child. She thought of the biggest boy in the class, the perseverer, the anchorman on the tug-of-war; the slower one, and the stronger one. The outsider, probably. She was overwhelmed with affection for him, because the picture she had just painted was almost identical to that of her own son Robbie, who was now in Edinburgh. The taciturn loyalist, the archetypal man of few words.

She could see Meg's attraction to his stoicism,

especially after the stormy influence of Abigail. But as for whether it was a match made in heaven, she wasn't sure. Her own boy's wife was just like him, quiet and placid, slow to burn, quick to cool. They matched perfectly.

But Meg and Will didn't match. They contrasted.

Meg was many wonderful things, but she was not slow, and she was not taciturn, and, when she wanted something – something, for instance, like not wanting to get married – she would quite likely dig in her heels so far that they would appear in Australia.

Oh dear, she thought to herself. *And I so like Will. And if he and Meg break up, I won't see him any more. And that'll be another bloody horrible loss, on top of all the others.*

And she had to look down, and look away, and pretend to be abruptly extremely interested in the flowering hebes, because a great wave of self-pity had overtaken her, and threatened to make her cry.

They were both suddenly interrupted in their thoughts by the sound of another car pulling into the driveway.

Will stood up. 'That must be Meg now,' he said.

They walked out on to the driveway.

But it wasn't Meg.

It was two police cars, their lights flashing, with a huge white Mercedes between them. The Mercedes was kangarooing along, lurching from side to side. It was like watching two collie dogs harassing an expensive sheep.

'Who's that?' Penny wondered.

'Abigail,' Will said.

'Abigail? But that's not Abigail's car.'

'It's Abigail driving it.'

They hurried over. The police cars came to a stop, the Mercedes stalled, and a uniformed constable got out of the lead vehicle, putting on his hat with an extremely weary expression. 'Is this Halfpenny Acre?' he asked.

'Yes,' Penny said. 'What on earth's happening?'

At that moment, the driver's door of the Mercedes was flung open, and Abigail got out. She was rapidly followed by a small, fat West Highland Terrier which waddled to the edge of the drive, stared in disbelief at the sweep of lawn, and then ran helter-skelter across it, barking its head off.

'What a machine,' Abigail complained, brushing herself down. 'Calls itself automatic! It isn't automatic. It can't even cope with a slight misapprehension with its handbrake.'

Penny went forward to her. 'Abigail,' she said. 'What are you doing in that car? Whose dog is that?'

'Revising my opinion of German engineering,' Abigail retorted. 'And that was Dido.'

The passenger door of the Mercedes opened. A man got out.

Penny stared at him. He was extremely odd-looking, not just because of the lilac suit, yellow shirt and white-and-brown shoes, but because he wore a face of such beatification, such joy, that you had to look twice at him to make sure he was actually human, and not an animated cartoon.

'This is Lawrence Bugle,' Abigail said.

'I know him,' Will murmured. 'He's dead.'

Lawrence came towards them, smiling hugely. 'How do you do?' he called. 'How does anyone do? Isn't it marvellous? What a world! Spring! Spring in England! Oh, to be in England now that April's there!'

And he wheeled around, and flung his arms out, as if encompassing the entire valley. 'What a view!' he trilled, transported. 'Cows! Lovely cows!'

Down the lawn, Dido was doing something she had never done before. She was chasing her tail, in celebration of meeting the biggest piece of open grass she had ever seen.

Penny pinched Abigail's arm. 'Is this man all right?' she whispered.

'Quite harmless,' Abigail said.

'Not *quite*,' the policeman corrected. He was opening a small notebook.

'Oh, don't take any notice of him,' Abigail said. 'We had a few mishaps.'

The policeman raised an eyebrow at her. 'Obstructing the highway,' he read out slowly. 'Careless and dangerous driving. Endangering the life of . . .' he paused, counting, 'seven pedestrians, two cats, a woman on a bicycle, a Scout, a minibus on a Townswomen's Guild outing, four boys on skateboards, a miniature Schnauzer . . .'

'That was Dido, not us,' Abigail said. 'Anyway, don't go on. You've said all that four times already.'

'Mounting the pavement, going the wrong way down a one-way street, traversing a pedestrian-only walkway across the A37 . . .'

'Abigail!' Penny said, aghast. 'You're such a good driver!'

'I wasn't driving,' Abigail retorted. 'Lawrence was driving. I've only been driving since we left the police station in Yeovil.'

'Cows and blackbirds and horseflies!' Lawrence continued happily to himself. 'God's wonderful creation! Praise him!'

'Police station?' Will said. 'I can't believe they let you out.'

'Is he drunk?' Penny asked, glancing at Lawrence, who was capering about on the gravel like a superannuated Ariel.

'No,' the policeman said. 'Sadly. Could have thrown the rest of the library at him if he was, and not just the book.'

'He's a little euphoric,' Abigail said. 'So would you be if you'd come back from the dead.'

Lawrence had begun to sing a hymn. 'Oh Lord my God, when I in awesome WONDER, consider ALL the WORKS Thy hand hath MADE . . .!'

'They said at the TV station he'd kicked the bucket,' Will said.

'He was at the TV station?' Penny asked, her head turning from Will, to Lawrence, to Abigail, and back again.

'He owns the TV station,' Will replied. 'As good as.'

'Owns it! Who is he? Should I know him?'

'I see the SKY! I hear the MIGHTY THUNDER . . .'

'He's Lawrence Bugle,' Abigail said. 'He had a heart attack when Meg and Harry were on, and the woman running the show ran out barefoot and was never seen again.'

'What?' Penny echoed. She put her hand to her forehead. 'Who? Not Adele Buchanan?'

'The very one.'

'Thy power THROUGHOUT the universe displayed!' yelled Lawrence. He suddenly dropped to his knees and clutched at the ground. 'Oh, the ants!' he said. 'Whole cities, you know! Never credit it, so little. Amazing! And strong! Carry a house. Right under our feet! Bless them! Bless their little feet.'

Penny grabbed Abigail's arm and tried to pull her away. 'I think your friend needs help,' she whispered.

Abigail considered the grovelling Lawrence with interest. 'They said he's a bastard,' she observed mildly. 'I can't say I've seen any evidence of it. When he ran over the old lady's foot in Henstridge just now, he jumped out and gave her five hundred pounds.'

'But,' Penny murmured, still trying to get her head round what she'd been told, 'if he's had a heart attack today, he should be in hospital.'

'He discharged himself,' Abigail said. 'And I thought, well, he can't be left alone, I had better keep an eye on him.'

'You must be mad,' Will said. 'As mad as he is.'

'He is *not* mad,' Abigail said. 'Actually, he's a very interesting person.'

'I can see how interesting he'd be to a psychiatrist,' Will replied.

'He is perfectly sane,' Abigail said. 'Just very pleased to be alive. He had a kind of revelation while he was unconscious, I think.'

'What kind of revelation?' Will asked suspiciously.

'He saw the Grim Reaper, who evidently looks a bit like Eddie Izzard – you know, when he does that comedy routine about death – and the Reaper let him off with a caution,' Abigail said.

Will rolled his eyes at Penny, and tapped his index finger significantly on his temple.

'Abigail,' Penny said quietly, 'have you taken any sort of . . . pill, or anything like that?'

Lawrence, with some difficulty, had now got up. He approached the first policeman, grabbed his hand, and started pumping it for all he was worth. 'Can't thank you enough for escorting us, so kind, so very kind,' he said.

The policeman disengaged himself. In the car behind, his two colleagues were trying hard not to laugh. The first man made an unpolicemanlike gesture at them. 'Not a question of kindness, sir,' he told Lawrence severely. 'More a question of public safety.' He turned to Abigail. 'You can guarantee he's going to stay here?' he asked her.

'Naturally.'

'Abigail . . .' Penny began.

'My little light of mine!' Lawrence warbled. 'I'm gonna let it shine!'

'You can't really have guests,' Penny told Abigail. 'I've packed, like you asked.'

'There's beds, isn't there?'

'Well . . .'

'And food?'

'A bit.'

'Fine,' Abigail said. 'We shan't be here more than a night or two, anyway.'

'Why?' Penny asked. 'Where are you going?'

'You should let your light shine,' Lawrence told the police. 'This little light of mine, let it shine, let it shine. Let it . . .'

A car horn blew on the drive behind them.

They all turned.

Michael was driving, and Meg was hanging out of the window, waving.

'Thank God,' Penny muttered. 'Sanity at last.'

Before the car had ground to a halt, Meg had jumped out and was running towards them. 'Wait till you hear!' she said. 'Just wait!'

Harry had leapt out behind her, and was wreathed

in smiles. 'Hey, Ma,' he said, picking Abigail up in a bear hug, so that her toes only just brushed the floor. 'Your boy done good!'

Michael was walking up behind them, swinging his car keys on one finger. 'I might change my name to Svengali,' he said. 'Or what's the name of the guy in the Lavender Hill Mob, who organised it all?'

'Meg,' Penny said. 'Your mother has a problem.'

'A new one?' Meg asked.

Penny caught her by the shoulders and turned her round to face Lawrence Bugle, who was picking daisies on the only bit of sloping lawn that the mower wouldn't reach. 'Look,' she said. 'What is that?'

'I'd say it was Lawrence Bugle,' Meg guessed. 'Except he's dead.'

'I *wish* you wouldn't all keep saying that,' Abigail interrupted.

'His body's alive. His brain's dead,' Will told them.

Meg had kissed him, rather fleetingly, on the cheek. 'What are the police doing?' she asked. In her walking-on-air oblivion, she had only just noticed them.

'Taking your mother to a funny farm,' Penny said.

'Oh good,' Meg replied.

Will was gripping her hand. 'Wait till we hear what?' he asked.

'Praise to the LORD, the ALMIGHTY, the KING OF CREATION . . .'

'Oh Jesus,' Will groaned. 'More fucking hymns.'

'I see Lawrence Bugle singing hymns while picking daisies,' Michael said, mesmerised. 'I see it, but I don't believe it. Pinch me.'

'Perhaps we could shoot him with a tranquilliser dart,' Penny decided.

'He's dead though, isn't he?' asked Michael.

Abigail gave a little scream. 'If anyone says that again, I shall scream!' she protested.

'You are screaming,' Meg pointed out. 'But listen, listen . . . guess what's happened!'

'I was on TV,' Harry said.

'Did you see us?' Meg asked Penny.

'No, darling. Not yet.'

'There was this . . . crisis . . .'

'Adele Buchanan threw a wobbly,' Michael interjected.

'And she ran off, and there was no-one left to host the programme,' Meg added.

'I interviewed Will,' Harry said.

Penny turned to Will. 'How did it go?' she asked. 'Did they show the pictures of your rescue?'

'They did,' Will said. 'With a voiceover by Harry, talking about ice-cream and whales.'

Penny started to laugh. 'Oh Harry,' she said. 'You twit.'

'That's what I said,' Meg added. 'I kept telling him to shut up.'

'That was one of the things Eric Cramm liked,' Michael said. 'The relationship between Meg and Harry. Tension. Sparks. Contrast. All that.'

'You were telling Harry to shut up?' Abigail suddenly demanded of Meg.

'Mum,' she said, 'Will couldn't get a word in edgeways.'

'But you were telling him to shut up, in front of millions of people?' Abigail insisted. 'How could you!'

'Because he's an idiot!' Meg retorted.

'Your brother is not an idiot!'

'I'm not a real idiot,' Harry complained. 'Not a gold-plated one.'

'When I rule the world . . .' Lawrence began singing.

'You are,' Will said.

Meg turned to him. 'Don't say that to Harry,' she objected.

'But you just said it.'

'Well, I'm allowed to say it.'

'Why?'

'Every man will have a new song to la-dee-la la la la . . .'

'Children, children,' Michael interrupted, soothingly.

'Let's all sit down,' Penny suggested. 'And start, very slowly, very clearly, from the beginning.'

'As soon as my back is turned, you start insulting your own brother, who works so hard,' Abigail told Meg.

'He doesn't work hard,' Meg objected. 'He just plays. Penny told me.'

'Penny!' Abigail cried, outraged, staring accusingly at her friend.

'And now he's going to play all day in front of millions, and talk a load of wittering tosh, and get paid a packet for it,' Meg added.

'So no change there then,' Michael said, grinning.

'La la la la la la la la . . .'

Down the lawn, Dido began ripping up clods of turf and throwing them into the air.

Penny clapped her hands to her head. 'Will everyone please stop talking at once,' she begged. 'And singing!' she bawled, at Lawrence, who was just struggling up the last foot of daisy-strewn slope, looking like a Teletubby on speed.

'Please,' Penny said, turning back to face them all. 'What on earth are you all talking about?'

And it was at that very moment that Clementine Badger's hire car pulled into the drive.

23

Because the light was beginning to fade, it was hard to make out the occupants of Clementine's car.

As she got out, the assembled company in the driveway stared at her. It was hard to credit how such a very tall woman had managed to fold herself into a Cinquechianticento.

'Someone's got lost on the top road again,' Penny muttered. 'They come here asking if this is the Little Chef.'

'This is Halfpenny Acre?' Clementine called.

'Yes,' said the nearest policeman.

'Is it somebody else you ran over?' Penny asked Abigail sweetly.

Clementine was making her way down the drive, glancing curiously at the Mercedes and police cars.

'Can I help you?' Penny asked.

'I'm Miss Badger,' Clementine said.

'It's Miss Badger,' Abigail announced.

'Yes?' Penny said.

To Penny's surprise, Clementine stuck her hand out to Abigail. 'We meet again,' she said.

'I thought you were in London,' Abigail answered.

Clementine smiled. 'I could say the same of you.'

There was a silence. Meg coughed. 'Mum,' she murmured, 'would you like to introduce us?'

'Miss Badger!' Lawrence shouted.

They turned towards him. He was advancing on Clementine with a maniacal grin, his arms outstretched. Clementine took a step back.

'Before you say anything,' Abigail said, 'he's not dead.'

Lawrence grabbed Clementine's hand. 'BAFTA awards, 1999,' he said. 'A slight altercation.'

Clementine looked at him severely. 'You broke Eric's secretary's nose,' she said.

'Yes,' he agreed enthusiastically. 'Dreadful! Dreadful! I was aiming for Eric.'

'I know that,' Clementine said, withdrawing her hand distastefully.

'How *is* he?' Lawrence enquired.

'Quite well.'

'Darling man,' Lawrence said.

Clementine blinked.

'Excuse me,' Will interrupted, 'but who are you, exactly?'

Clementine looked at him. 'I own this house,' she said. 'And you're William Churchill-Twines.'

'Yes, but, I . . .'

'You are a remarkable man,' Clementine said. 'Quite magnificent.'

Will blushed. The words froze in his mouth.

'You own this house?' Meg echoed. 'What, you mean *this* one? This one here?'

'If this is Halfpenny Acre,' Clementine replied calmly, 'I own it as of midday on Friday, I believe. To be exact.'

'What!' Penny gasped. She pulled on Abigail's arm. 'But you said three weeks!'

'We exchanged contracts early,' Clementine said. 'We met in London two days ago. There was no need for delay. I did the conveyancing myself.'

'You . . .' Penny stared at her. 'You're not in television,' she said.

'Connected to television,' Clementine answered politely, 'if that's of any bearing on the matter in hand.'

'The matter in hand?' Meg said. 'Which is?'

'Well,' Clementine replied, 'I had rather hoped the house would be empty. I had rather hoped to stay.'

'Before you own it?' Meg said. 'That wouldn't be right.'

'Perhaps not to the letter of the law,' Clementine conceded. 'But Mrs Randall gave me to understand that the house would be empty.'

'You did?' Penny demanded of Abigail.

'You did?' Meg said.

Abigail shrugged.

'You really are the limit,' Penny told her.

'It's my house,' Abigail said.

'I sometimes think you have no feelings at all,' Penny observed.

'What have feelings got to do with it?' Abigail asked her.

'Oh Mum,' Meg snapped. 'Poor Penny.'

'Poor Penny? It's my house!'

'It's your family home,' Penny said.

'It used to be,' Abigail said. 'But I hardly see my family in it these days.'

Penny threw down the duster which, up to now, unconsciously, she had been gripping. 'I must be completely mad,' she said. 'To support you in anything, God help me.'

'You're not supporting me,' Abigail said. 'You just want my garden.'

'Mum!' Meg gasped. 'That is an awful thing to say!'

'It isn't awful,' Abigail pointed out. 'It's true, that's all. Penny hasn't let me pull up a weed or plant a geranium for twenty years. If I walk on the lawn, I feel like a trespasser. But it's all right. I don't mind. I hate gardening.'

'You're the gardener?' Clementine asked.

'No,' Penny said. 'Well, yes. No.'

'Did you lay out the knot garden?'

'Yes.'

'It's wonderful,' Clementine said. 'Quite perfect. I bought it on the basis of that alone. That and the thatch.'

Penny looked narrowly at her. 'Well,' she finally said, grudgingly, 'thanks.'

Meg had grabbed her mother's elbow. 'When are you going to learn to be nice to people?' she demanded.

'I am nice to people,' Abigail objected.

'Oh yes,' Meg said. 'You're a saint, that's true.'

'Meg,' Harry said. 'Be gentle with Mother.'

'Why should I?' Meg said. 'She's never gentle with me.'

'You don't need me to be gentle with you,' Abigail retorted. 'You always fought me like a cat.'

'A *what*?' Meg cried. 'I did not!'

'Arguing black was white.'

'I do not!'

'You're doing it now.'

'I am bloody well not!'

'I've never liked arguments myself,' Abigail said.

'You do!'

'I don't!'

'Neither do I,' Harry said. 'Hello, Mr Bugle,' he

added, grinning at Lawrence. 'I'm going to be on television. Opposite channel.'

'Shut up, Harry,' Meg snapped.

'Are you?' Lawrence replied. 'How thrillingly terrible for you.'

'Pardon?' Harry said.

'For myself,' Lawrence announced, 'I shall never pass over that particular threshold again. I shall wring my soul on the altar of deceit nevermore.'

'Mother,' Meg said, after having taken several deep breaths. 'I come and see you often. How you can say that I don't?'

Abigail sighed. She paused a moment, looking at her feet. 'I shall tell you how often you've come,' she said evenly. 'Twice in the past week. Once in the month before that, and at Christmas.'

Meg opened her mouth, and then closed it again. Because it was true. She *felt* like she was always at her mother's beck and call, and she was, but only in her head, where Abigail occupied centre stage, holding a mixing spoon like an offensive weapon. She looked hard at her mother, who seemed diminished now in the rapidly growing twilight, and she saw a spark in her mother's eye that was neither awkwardness nor belligerence, but something else . . . something else she had never seen before.

'I don't mind,' Abigail said calmly. 'Just like I don't mind Penny lording it over me in the garden. But . . .' And her gaze brooked no discussion, 'I'm tired of looking at four walls and wishing you would come and see me, and feeling my life has come to a dead halt.'

Meg bit her lip.

'And,' Abigail added, 'if you've had some wonderful news, and if it's anything to do with what Harry just said, then I wish you well, darling. But I shan't be here, knitting bedsocks. That's all.'

Meg suddenly found that she had no reply.

'But where will you live?' Will asked.

The strange expression in Abigail's eye suddenly became very marked indeed. 'Oh, I think I shall go where the wind blows me,' she said. 'Like I used to.'

'She's coming with me,' Lawrence said. 'Into the wild blue yonder, to seek our spiritual paradise.'

Will lunged forward, in an attempt to clamp his hand over Meg's mouth, but he needn't have bothered. Meg's automatic objection to her mother wandering wherever the wind blew Lawrence Bugle dried in her throat as a shout went up from the more distant of the two police cars.

'Hey'yup!' they heard a man say. 'It's you!'

One of the constables was leaning down, looking in the window of Clementine's car.

'Are you all right?' the policeman yelled.

They couldn't hear the reply.

'She's not kidnapped you?'

More muffled words.

'Half the country looking for you,' the policeman bellowed through the shut window. 'Missing person report and everything.'

Clementine gave a small groan. She set off up the drive. 'Stay in the car!' she shouted.

'Who is it?' Michael asked. 'Who got kidnapped?'

'It's not Shergar, is it?' Harry said.

Meg stared at him. 'Sometimes you take my breath away,' she remarked.

'I know,' Harry said, and smiled modestly.

'I haven't kidnapped anyone,' Clementine was saying. 'Please don't crowd the car.'

'She's missing, she is,' the policeman repeated.

'She isn't missing, she's all right,' Clementine told him.

'Who is missing?' Abigail said.

'It's a woman,' Harry said.

'Shut up, Harry,' Meg said.

'Please don't come any closer,' Clementine was saying. She opened her car door. 'She just wants to be left alone,' she added. 'I'll come back tomorrow.'

'Just a minute,' the policeman objected. 'What's your hurry?'

'It's Adele Buchanan,' Michael said. 'Good God.' And he set off up the drive like a hare, with Meg and Harry and Will in quick pursuit.

Just before Meg reached the car, however, Will caught her up, and spun her round. 'Now tell me,' he said. 'Tell me in words of one syllable what's gone on with you today.'

'Not just now,' Meg said.

'Now.'

'Somewhere quiet. In a minute.'

'Now.'

'Let her go!' Clementine shouted. Adele had got out of the car on the other side, and had tried to run away down the drive. The policeman had tackled her, and was holding her in a half-nelson. 'You have absolutely no right!' Clementine screamed.

'No,' Adele was begging, 'I haven't done anything, I haven't done anything.'

'She isn't feeling well,' Clementine insisted. She tried to get between Adele and the policeman.

'Adele!' Lawrence screamed. 'Adele, Adele!' And he launched himself up the drive, looking for all the world like a jellyfish that had been stranded on the

beach when the tide went out, and was trying to flop
back into the waves.

'Your heart!' Abigail shouted to him.

'My conscience!' he shouted back. 'Adele, my love!'

It must have been the sight and sound of Lawrence
that finally propelled Adele out of the policeman's
grasp. With an almighty wrench, and a leap like a
startled gazelle, she broke free of the strong arm of the
law and scrambled back up the drive, out of the gate,
and disappeared into the wooded lane.

'Adele!' Clementine called. 'Adele, it's all right!
Adele, please!'

Will dropped Meg's hand and strode up to
Clementine. 'What's the matter with her?' he asked.

'She's just . . . she's not well,' Clementine said.
'She's a little frightened . . . all this fuss . . . she just
wants peace . . .'

Will glanced over his shoulder at Lawrence, who
was coming up on the rails, blowing heavily and giving
off a wreath of steam. Will took one disparaging look
at him, then stuck out his foot. Lawrence made a rather
graceful flying fall in the circumstances, and landed
spread-eagled at Will's feet, face down in the gravel.

'Lawrence!' Abigail cried.

'I'll get her,' Will told Clementine.

'Please be careful.'

'I shall.'

Clementine stared after him as Meg drew level with
her.

'What a man,' Clementine breathed. 'What a hero.'

'I could write a book,' Meg murmured, sounding a
little choked.

'Could you?' Clementine asked. 'So could I. I
should love to write one about *him*.'

'Would you?' Meg asked, astonished.

'Oh, I've heard the stories a hundred times,' Clementine murmured, somewhat obtusely. 'But never in real life.'

'Was it her?' Michael demanded. He had been stopped in his tracks by the prone whale that was Lawrence, and was now occupied in helping the older man to his feet. 'Was it really her?'

'Leave her alone,' Meg said. 'Two deals in one day is enough.'

'I could make it a hat trick,' Michael said. 'I bet Eric would like her.'

'You beast,' Meg retorted. 'I positively refuse to let you hire any opposition to me.'

He smiled at her.

'I only wanted her to forgive me,' Lawrence heaved.

'I don't think she wants your forgiveness,' Abigail told him, brushing bits of leaf from his suit.

'She wants to live on a farm,' Clementine said, sadly. 'About as far as she can get from a TV studio. That's all she wants.'

Meg stared at her. She looked back to the gate, where Will had just disappeared in pursuit of Adele. Then she looked at her feet, and put her hand to her mouth.

'I have so many people I need to see,' Lawrence was saying. He fumbled in his pocket for a handkerchief. 'So many who need to absolve me of my transgressions.'

'Oh, tosh,' Abigail reassured him. 'It was just a few pedestrians and a dog.'

'I don't mean this afternoon,' Lawrence sniffled, two large tears rolling down his face. 'I have been a sinner for so long.'

'Rubbish,' Abigail said. 'Let's go inside. I'm sure these nice policemen would like a cup of tea.'

'I have been a traveller in the wasteland,' Lawrence burbled, sobbing. 'From the day I was born.'

The crowd began to drift away, Penny shooing them towards the house.

'I have forsaken my own blood,' Lawrence whimpered. 'I must retrace my steps.'

'We'll retrace them tomorrow,' Abigail assured him. 'Mind that honeysuckle now. It's curled round your trouser leg.'

'To Abertyssgoch,' Lawrence hiccuped.

The night was almost upon them now.

Down in the valley, the cows were wending their way through the mist from the river, vague grey shadows against the darkening green. Lights were coming on in the valley, and, in the hedgerow along the lane, a blackbird broke into his heartbreaking liquid song.

Out of the twilight came Clementine's voice.

'Where?' she asked softly. 'Where did you say?'

Lawrence was sorrowfully folding the handkerchief. 'Abertyssgoch,' he bleated. 'I fathered a child there when I was sixteen, and forced her mother to abandon her. She ended up in the Kingdom Foundling Home, may God forgive me.' He shook his head in grief.

It was some seconds before a very strange, strangled little whisper came out of the gloom from the other side of the car.

'When was this?' Clementine breathed. 'Exactly?'

'My only daughter,' Lawrence replied, without looking up, 'was born on 22nd May, 1955.'

And those were the last words that Clementine Badger heard before she fainted.

two years later

postscript

Meg lay on the floor of the car, waiting for the man with the ladder.

She even had time to consider what fun it would be.

What headlines.

Just too bloody marvellous.

Royal totty MARRIAGE!!! the tabloids would say. Getting it totally wrong, of course. As usual. It wasn't *her* marriage – God forbid. It wasn't even a marriage, it was a christening. And she had only spoken to the Prince twice in her life. But she had no doubt whatsoever, with the past two years experience behind her, that none of that would matter to a journalist.

'Can you see anything, Duncan?' she asked her driver.

Duncan, a dour Scot in his fifties, was used to this scenario, as he had been driving celebrities around for twenty-five years. He peered out through the windows at the sublimely pretty church of Alton Pancras, arranged in its frame of trees. All around it, the low hills kept a green guard of such extraordinary peace that it seemed crass even to breathe.

It was spring, and all the hawthorns were in blossom, swamping the hedgerows, so that they looked as if they had been blanketed by waves of white foam. There was the heavy green scent of countless leaves breaking out of bud. It was loveliness itself, and the church – set back from the narrow country road in a tunnel of beech and horse chestnut – as the loveliest of all.

Duncan was paying particular attention to the trees.

'No ladders, portable steps or telephotos that I can see,' he told her. 'Reckon you're safe.'

Meg raised herself to a sitting position, and grinned at him in the driver's mirror, cramming her hat on her head. 'What d'you think?' she asked. 'Will I do?'

'If you like pink,' he said.

She got out.

She *did* like pink. It was fun, and she had never had so much fun in her life as she had had these past two years. She smoothed down her skirt, and grinned at the sight of her feet in the silk shoes, two strips of lime green and pink that qualified as instruments of torture. She didn't really give a damn. She hadn't bought them. She never bought any clothes any more. They materialised on her doorstep and in her dressing rooms like magic.

She took the enormous parcel from the passenger seat, with the helium balloons attached to it that had driven Duncan mad all the way down here.

'Meg!' called a voice, from the porch of the church. 'Meg!'

It was Penny.

She came charging down the path, and hugged Meg hard. 'You look wonderful,' she said.

'So do you,' Meg answered. 'Wow! What an outfit! Where did you get it?'

Penny did a little pirouette. 'Clementine took me shopping,' she said.

For the last two years, Penny had been housekeeper at Halfpenny Acre. For all practical purposes, this meant that she lived in the house as if it were her own. Occasionally, Clementine and Eric came down for weekends, or short holidays, but on the whole they were too busy running Up-Line together to get away very much.

For some time after the scene in the Halfpenny driveway two years ago, Clementine and Adele had kept out of circulation. Adele – so Clementine had hinted to Penny – spent six weeks at a very exclusive retreat, emerging afterwards heavier, happier, calmer, and with a very definite glint in her eye that had nothing at all to do with the retreat and rather more to do with the new man in her life.

Clementine was also in retreat.

For the same six weeks, she did not contact Eric. She lived at Halfpenny Acre, and came to a most satisfactory agreement with Penny about her and the house's future, and she metamorphosed, in that time, into a version of Adele's mammoth that she could live with.

She had her hair styled; she bought new clothes. She considered the kind of cosmetic surgery that Adele had had, and dismissed it as ludicrous. But she paid attention to herself in a way she never had before, and, one evening, she and Penny had ceremonially burned every item of grey clothing that she owned.

She spent a long time out of each day walking the water meadows below the house, with a deliriously happy Dido for company. It was here that she finally managed to adjust to the fact that she was someone's daughter, even if it did take slightly longer to adjust to Lawrence Bugle being her father. And it was here, one day after a month or so, that she finally realised that she had not had a panic attack at 11 am for ages.

She also spent a great deal of time watching Up-Line, with a small notebook alongside her.

And all the time she kept an eye on Eric from afar, and kept in touch with a few willing spies within the station. He was miserable, they told her. He wasn't his old self. He didn't keep the Silent Quarter any more, and he didn't yell, and he had even been seen holding a small teddy bear to his chest, when he thought his secretaries weren't looking.

Clementine had made friends with the women in his outer office, and they reported to her that he was obviously sickening for something. They even hinted darkly that he was losing his grip.

One day, when she judged the time was right, Clementine had gone up to London on the morning train, Penny driving her to the station and giving her a good-luck thumbs-up as she walked away from the car. She arrived at Up-Line at eleven o'clock with a sheaf of documents under her arm, and a small smile on her face.

The secretaries watched her go into Eric's office, and close the door behind her. For a while, there had been silence. Then, they heard raised voices. Then, one of them swore ever afterwards, they were sure that they had heard Eric Cramm weeping.

Half an hour later, he came out, holding Clementine's hand.

He insisted on making her a cup of tea himself.

He called a meeting of executives that very afternoon, and Clementine was appointed Creative Director.

And they had been married last year, in a very private ceremony at this very same church.

'Who's here?' Meg asked Penny now, as they

walked to the door.

'Michael got here five minutes ago,' Penny said. 'Eric and Clementine arrived last night. That nice producer and his wife are here – and we had a card today from Harry and Belinda in Barbados. And Abigail and Lawrence, in Jaipur.'

Meg transferred the parcel to her other arm. 'What did they say?' she asked.

'Well,' Penny told her, 'Harry and Belinda said, *Have a so cool christening*, and Lawrence said, *Blessings and prayers are with you*, and Abigail said, *Cannot find a decent lavatory in the entire subcontinent.*'

Meg raised her eyebrows. 'Good old Mum,' she sighed. 'She doesn't change.'

'Oh! – and you'll never guess who else is here,' Penny added. 'The man from Bulldog Sausages.'

Meg started to laugh. 'Don't tell me, he's slapped a logo on the nearest nappy.'

Penny nodded. 'He lives in hope, you know,' she said. 'Of Will setting out again on his travels.'

'Not much hope of that,' Meg observed, 'while there's three hundred pigs to feed.'

They entered the church.

It looked wonderful, decked with meadow flowers tied in displays at each pew end. The scent of the first hothouse roses, brought from Halfpenny Acre, filled the air. And, as Meg and Penny sat down, four people in the first row turned round to smile back at them.

Two were very small people indeed.

Their names – as the rest of the congregation were soon to hear – were Ranulph William Churchill-Twines, and Sophie Adele Churchill-Twines, and they were very intent on decorating each other's christening gowns with gummed rusk. Meg smiled at the twins now, pressing her fingers to her lips, and blowing them a fervent kiss.

Over the heads of her children, Adele looked back affectionately at the woman with whom she had changed places in more ways than one.

'Didn't you bring that nice man with you?' Penny whispered, as the congregation stood up. The service was beginning.

'What nice man?' Meg whispered back, opening her hymnbook.

'That weather man on your show,' Penny answered. 'The one that the paper said was madly in love with you.'

Meg raised her eyebrows. 'Jack?' she replied off-handedly. 'Oh, that never really got started.'

'What a shame,' Penny murmured.

'Not really,' Meg replied. She glanced towards Adele, suppressing a smile. 'I invited him round to dinner,' she confided in Penny's ear. 'And told him I was seeing someone else.'